"The clergyman lifted the baby from his mother's arms and turned to face the altar, where a small white cloud floated in midair. The choir's voices swelled again, sending goose bumps through the assembly.

As baby Bradley was carried toward the altar, Adam grimaced in pain. Chapel Vision distorted before his open eyes.

The golden-lit cathedral disappeared. Only a dark and dreary, crumbling shell remained. The choir still sang, but they sounded discordant, eerily off key. The organ sounded lifeless and uninspiring, its melody punctuated by the missing notes of cracked pipes. Even the brilliant windows were dull and dirty. Many were broken.

Adam looked toward the clergyman and was shocked to see that the cloud awaiting baby Bradley masked an infant-sized operating chair equipped with body and head restraints."

Nightmare images haunt Adam Porter's every waking moment. Did his recent head injury cause these hallucinations or is he seeing things he's not supposed to see? And will he live long enough to find out?

Lou Grantt and Cyd Ropp

REALITY CRASH

Copyright © 2008 by Lou Grantt and Cyd Ropp
Contact the authors at
PO Box 1797
Lucerne Valley CA 92356

Excerpt from "Tarzan of the Apes" by Edgar Rice Burroughs
Haiku from "Driftwood; Afloat On An Ocean Of Eclectica" by Lou Grantt
Cover concept and illustration by Cyd Ropp

To buy more books by these authors:
http://www.lulu.com/lougrantt or
http://www.lulu.com/bluebirdbooks

ISBN: 978-0-615-26326-7

Dedications

Lou Grantt dedicates this book to Aunt Vilma, who helped make her dreams come true.

Cyd Ropp dedicates this book to her husband and best friend, Gary--always a good sport.

Acknowledgments

We would like to give our heartfelt thanks to the following readers whose observations and notes helped bring this world to life. To Bill Martell, who read the earliest version of this story way back when; to Phil Reynolds, whose close reading helped improve many a small detail; to Bill Puett, whose ideas and comments have been a part of this story's genesis from day one; to David Puett, whose suggestions spurred many small improvements; to Lew Yee Berkheimer, whose inside knowledge of law enforcement helped us refine our cops and methods; and to Barb Puett, a true fan who really enjoyed the story without reservation. Thank you all.

MONDAY

A sound startled him awake. Or maybe it was the big gray mutt trying to crawl into his lap. Wary, he looked around, alert to anything out of the ordinary. An ancient leather davenport and his equally worn easy chair still occupied the center of the room, looking as though they had spent decades drying in the prairie sun. A black, cast iron wood stove crouched in one corner.

The cabin's split log walls were hung with paintings of golden prairies and undulating hills; galloping wild horses, manes flying behind them like wings; and an elderly Indian Chief whose stern expression seemed to disapprove of napping in the morning.

Everything looked just as it had when he'd closed his eyes and drifted off to sleep a short time earlier. He listened more closely, but all he could hear was Bo's eager panting.

"Okay, okay, I'm awake!" Adam Porter pushed the shaggy dog off his chest and wiped the warm slobber from his face. Bo jumped down and did a galumphing doggie dance as the big cowboy shoved his lanky six foot frame forward in the chair. Adam reached for the dented tin mug on the table beside him and took a big swig.

"Damn! Coffee's cold. Hey Bo, how long did you let me sleep? Shit, I'm gonna be late for work." His scuffed mahogany boots clunked on the flat timber floor as he crossed to the open window and tossed the stale coffee out. It made a soft splatting sound on the sun-baked earth and just as quickly disappeared, sucked into the dry soil like a sponge.

The morning sun felt good and warmed his skin through his thick flannel shirt and faded jeans. He shifted the intricately carved holster draped on his bony hips and patted the Colt .45 Peacemaker that was nestled at his right thigh. Of all the guns available to him, this was his favorite. When he held it in his hand, it just felt right—a part of him, like his fingers, like his skin.

Bo joined him, paws on the window sill, eyes turned up adoringly to his master's face. Adam gulped the fresh mountain air and squinted into the early daylight. He searched the nearby scrub brush for the source of the sound that had jolted him out of his unscheduled nap but again, there was nothing. It must have been the dog after all.

Adam gazed out across a wide valley. The cerulean sky overhead was a work of art, a masterpiece dappled with pearlized pinks and yellows. In the distance, trees huddled together in pockets of dark green, as though trying to ward off the dry, barren plains that threatened to someday overwhelm them. The outlying mountains stood guard over a herd of bison grazing peacefully in a meadow to the south. Bo's tail waggled at the sight of them, accompanied by his deep, melodious whine.

"Not today, Bo. You can play with them tomorrow. Let's see if there's any hot coffee left, what do you say?"

The mutt's big, dark eyes gazed up at Adam. He gladly followed as the man turned and headed for the table in the corner of the room. The rough-hewn table was laid out with simple Western fare: a chipped crockery pot of coffee, a basket of biscuits, and a particular pleasure for the cowboy—a bowl of plump red strawberries. Adam popped one of the crimson fruits in his mouth and poured the steaming coffee. He tossed Bo a biscuit and was just about to bite into one himself when...

Suddenly, bullets hit everything at once, exploding the coffee pot, splintering the table, shattering pictures, and disintegrating the biscuits and the basket they came in. Adam quickly dropped to the floor and scurried behind the leather chair. He whipped the Colt .45 out of its holster and cocked the hammer.

The door flew open and in strutted a shotgun-toting desperado so ugly his face would make a freight train take a dirt road. More bandits, no prettier than the first, crowded the open windows. Guns blazing, they elbowed each other for first rights into the room. But Adam's Colt was smoking. He popped off round after round until the big guy in the doorway dropped with a thud, his shotgun skidding across the floor.

Yelp! A bullet pierced Bo's shoulder and he went down. Abandoning the safety of the chair, Adam belly crawled to Bo's side, still shooting.

Another nasty looking outlaw took one in the chest but like some kind of weird zombie, he just kept coming. Adam stood up and landed a right cross to the guy's grizzled jaw. His garbled scream as he hit the floor added to the din of Bo crying and bullets smacking into everything breakable in the room.

Beep-beep! Beep-beep! Beep-beep! An electronic beep. Insistent. Adam ignored it and raised his gun to fire again.

The terminal beep-beeped again.

"Pause!" Adam shouted impatiently.

The desperadoes froze in place; their bullets hanging in mid-air.

Adam spun the Colt around his finger and deftly slid it back into its holster. He walked over to the framed print of the sour-faced Indian Chief and poked its nose with his finger. The Chief morphed into a vidphone image of Brad Jameson, a gee whiz, life-is-swell kind of guy, and Adam's best friend. Brad's red and white checkered Western shirt clashed with his orangey-red hair and freckles, but the effect was comical and made Adam smile.

"Hey, buddy! What's cookin'?" Brad said.

"Nothing much. Just some target practice before I head in," Adam replied.

"I should have known," Brad said, turning to find his bubbly young wife, Suzanne, at his shoulder.

"Howdy, Sheriff!" Her girlish voice practically gurgled cuteness as she spoke. "Glad to see you're still on the job protecting us poor defenseless citizens from them ornery desperadoes."

"That's right, ma'am. Ever vigilant." By way of a salute, Adam reached up to touch the brim of his cowboy hat and was disappointed to find it not on his head but hanging on a hook by the front door.

Suzanne smiled and blew him a kiss.

"See you later," she said as she left the room.

"You won't forget about this afternoon, will you?" Brad asked when she had gone. "It's the beginning of the christening celebration for the baby."

Adam frowned. "Brad... I don't know... That place..." He hated these kinds of functions anyway, especially now, and especially there, at that cathedral.

"Hey, no one else can be our baby's godfather but my best bud. And, well..." he hesitated, "three years is long enough, don't you think? Please?"

Adam reluctantly nodded his acquiescence and reached out to touch the screen.

"See ya at work," Brad squeezed in, just before the call ended. The Chief's somber face reappeared, no happier than before. Adam touched the screen again.

"Off line," he said.

The Chief nodded. "Entered and accepted," he intoned. His somber visage vanished, replaced by a flat screen monitor hung on the wall. The monitor flashed the Virtual Vision Network's garish logo, its three red initials swirling against a pulsating silvery background, and then continually displayed advertising scenes of VVN's premium channels.

The rustic interior of the log cabin immediately dissolved into a drab, contemporary living room. The desperadoes vanished, as did Bo, a hologram like the rest, but no less a buddy to his human friend.

"So long, big fella," Adam spoke to the vacant spot where Bo had lain bleeding moments before. Fortunately, the blood was gone, too. In fact, all evidence of the gun fight disappeared. It was as though it had never happened at all.

He looked around at the boring beige and brown sofa and chairs that now stood where his leather davenport and chairs had been. He much preferred the cabin to this. The tables were still old and scratched, but they lacked warmth and character. The place was barren and plain except for the ductwork and wiring conduits rimming the walls, a necessity to facilitate frequent repairs. These walls were badly in need of paint, and the exposed ducts and wiring did nothing to improve the décor. In actuality, it made it so much uglier. Adam turned away from the drabness and went back to the window to find a different view this time.

Outside it was a bright sunny day, with a pale blue sky the color of a robin's egg. The chaparral was gone, as were the hills, the trees, and the bison. From his second floor vantage point he could see a small, modern city. There were no concrete skyscrapers. The tallest of the simple gray high rises stood a mere dozen stories above the empty streets. In the distance, a train slowly made its way toward the center of their small metropolis.

Adam's modest apartment building dominated a block otherwise comprised of faded pastel cottages and a dull yellow apartment building on the next corner.

Across town he could see his place of employment, the Virtual Vision Network office tower. Even if it hadn't been the tallest building in the city, the VVN tower would have still looked imposing—forty stories of black glass and gleaming steel. A thirty foot spire sat atop the roof, holding aloft a rotating marquee flashing the bright red Virtual Vision Network logo, large enough for all the city to see.

"And hello real world." He scowled at the tower, dreading the workday ahead.

From the monitor, a peppy pitchman endlessly promoted VVN's premium channels.

"Give the kiddies Cartoon Vision for their birthdays, holidays, and just because you love them so darn much! Turn your home into a cartoon wonderland today!"

Adam, dressed now in everyone's "uniform of the day"—a loose-fitting, unisex tunic over elastic-waist pants—crossed the room to the long table set against the wall. On it was a framed photo of a young woman. No longer sepia-toned, her sparkling blue eyes smiled out at him. Adam stared at his face in the large mirror above the table. In happier days he always had a grin and a twinkle in his bright hazel eyes. Now, the all too familiar sadness dulled his eyes and added ten years to his looks.

"Somebody shoot him and put him out of his misery," he said to the wretched looking guy in the mirror.

"UltraModern Vision brings you the finest life has to offer. Enjoy the elegance of the future, right now!" the announcer carried on, as he would all day and night.

Adam ran his fingers through his thick blond hair trying to tame it, without much success. He tried again. His eyes dropped from the mirror to the woman in the photo.

"Morning, Trisha," he said out loud.

He hesitated. Should he do this to himself again? Every morning it was the same. Always painful, and yet he couldn't help himself. He had to see her. He knew that obsessing over Trisha was not healthy, and yet here he was again.

He tapped the small button on the corner of the frame. A holographic image of a very pretty, very pregnant woman coalesced and projected itself, life-sized, into the room. He turned from the mirror to face her. She flashed a loving smile, and cupped her huge belly.

"Happy Anniversary, darling!" her ghostly image said. "For five years you've been a wonderful husband and I know you're going to be a wonderful father! You're the greatest! I love you, Adam! I love you so much."

Trisha's hologram blew Adam a kiss and then winked out. A wave of grief washed over him.

"I love you, too, baby," he said. He picked up the picture frame and stroked it. "Three years and it doesn't get any easier." He set the frame back down and trudged over to the chair next to the front door. His hands were shaking as he picked up the old leather briefcase. He knew he was pathetic, but he didn't care anymore. He hurried back to Trisha's photo with the intention of slipping it into the briefcase and taking her with him to work. It wouldn't be the first time. His hands hesitated a few inches from the frame. He looked at himself in the mirror again.

"Give it a rest, asshole," he said with disgust. He set the picture down quickly and headed for the front door.

Behind him on the monitor, unmindful of its lack of audience, the announcer continued: "And for the pioneer in you, the cowboy, the hunter, make today a Frontier Vision day."

Adam left his building and walked out into the center of the tree-lined street. Birds flitted overhead, chirping at him as he made his way south toward the tower. A pair of squirrels chased each other, jumping from branch to branch and tree to tree. The neighbors were also on foot, well-dressed, smiling.

Parents walked their little ones to the school and waved good-bye at the gate. There weren't many children anymore. Adam noticed, but he couldn't bring himself to dwell on it—not yet; maybe not ever. Everyone seemed happy enough, except him. The morning exodus from home to work and school had begun.

Over seventy thousand people had once lived in the small city of Appleton. Its population now hovered just under twenty thousand and continued to dwindle every year.

The town was less than five miles across and ringed by an unused freeway system. It had been a hundred years since cars, trucks, and buses had regularly driven the roads of this or any other city. People either walked or rode the two trains that criss-crossed the town. No one thought this was strange, because no one remembered any other way. The world they knew had shrunk to the size of Appleton, and they didn't know and didn't particularly care that the world outside was nothing but a loose collection of isolated towns just like their own, each living their own, isolated lives. The regional governors and their immediate staff were the only ones who knew the truth of their situation and how it came to be that way.

It had taken decades for scientists to convince governmental authorities that global warming was an ever increasing threat to the planet's survival. By the time global warming was obvious to even the most thick-headed heads of state, it had heated up a chemical stew so potent that it had eaten away the ozone layer, allowing harmful radiation to flood the earth, bringing with it a killer epidemic of skin cancers among humans, severe weakening of the planet's flora, and a devastating global kill-off of plankton that wreaked havoc on the ecosystems of the seas.

The radiation-weakened vegetation had fueled unstoppable firestorms that stripped the land of its greenery and filled the air with choking smoke on and off for decades. Temperatures had climbed dramatically as the planet's fiery heat was reflected back to the surface by the smoky atmosphere, turning large areas of the earth into dry, lifeless wasteland and wind-whipped dust bowls.

There hadn't been nearly enough food to go around. Mass starvation soon decimated most of the planet's population. Vector-borne and zoonotic diseases like Lyme disease and West Nile virus flourished and attacked weakened immune systems, killing hundreds of thousands more.

The remnants of the rain forests were the next to go, cut down in an attempt to grow crops to feed the people and livestock that remained. But the spindly new crops failed to quell the starvation. The people died; the animals died. Long dead skeletons still littered the sun-scorched plains, not that anyone ever saw them. Like Appleton, most of the surviving cities and towns were walled or fenced, keeping the small populations insulated and under control. GovCorp didn't want them to see what lay outside.

What Adam did see was Virtual Vision Network headquarters, its cold steel and glass looming larger with each approaching step. He joined the river of employees entering the huge smoke-mirrored doors etched with the ubiquitous VVN logo. The throng shuffled across the polished marble floors toward the elevators. The old guard at the front desk didn't even look them over as they came in. He had long ago stopped scrutinizing every face that passed by his station in the huge lobby.

The group waited impatiently outside the elevator doors. Like Pavlov's dogs, at the sound of the *ding* all eyes raised in unison to the lights above the elevator doors, hoping theirs would be the next to open. When the doors nearest Adam finally parted, he squeezed inside the box with the rest of them, and turned to face the closed brass doors. He hated being the last one on the elevator because that made him the designated button-pusher, and he didn't want to be bothered. "Seven, fourteen, eleven, twenty-three. . ." they called out. He didn't want to be a schmuck, so he did his best and pushed the buttons in order. But his duties didn't come with a smile.

A grumble came from the nearest riders when he accidentally pushed the Emergency Stop button after being jostled. No alarm sounded; it had shorted out long ago and never been repaired. He corrected the mistake and the car began its ascent. He remained stone-faced until he exited on his own level, the fourth floor. Let someone else do the honors from now on, he thought.

Adam threw his briefcase down on a chair by the door as he entered his office. The room was thirteen feet by sixteen feet. Not too big, not too small, but spacious enough for a programmer. He even had a window, which was a pretty good deal for a lowly cog like him. Computer renderings of period buildings, gardens, and sets from various network channels were tacked to the walls of the office.

The paperwork that overflowed his desktop and hung on the walls was actually paperless, printed on thin plastic sheets called poly-view. There hadn't been any real paper for a very long time because wood pulp was so difficult to come by. Some paper had been scavenged from abandoned cities and was trucked in along with other supplies that could no longer be manufactured. The paper could be recycled by soaking it and drying it on screens, but it was seldom suitable for the programmers' drawings. Hence, the poly-view. Without fresh industry, civilization hung on tenuously only by using and reusing what had been produced before.

Other than the pictures on the walls, the office looked the way offices usually do, down to the dull gray steel desk you see in institutions everywhere. The rolling office chair had slightly worn upholstery in a muddy brown, with grooves in the arm rests that fit him just right. Like any other office, it had a row of four-drawer filing cabinets with a couple of drawers half open. The tile floor had an indistinct abstract pattern that, if you stared at it long enough, created a swirling Rorschach effect in which bizarre animals and strange faces started popping out at you, like three-eared rabbits, kissing whales, and clowns with big noses. Adam had been staring at it a lot lately.

At one end of the room, a five-foot wide ribbon of silver ran along the floor, up the wall, across the ceiling and back down the other wall. This was the Simu-Strip and it was the real business end of the office.

Adam flopped into his chair and turned to the computer. Despite the older furniture, the computer was modern and new. He tapped the corner of the screen and it sprang into life, displaying the red VVN logo. Another tap and he pulled up the graphics of an elaborate and colorful formal garden.

He traced a finger across the image to enclose a portion of the garden in a blinking red box. Then he put his finger on the corner of the box and pulled it out and up, enlarging the container until its border stopped blinking and held a steady blue. An evergreen shrub with double white flowers filled his screen.

"Simulate the Shangrila garden preview centered on these coordinates," he said.

The silver strip behind him buzzed with static, then coalesced into a life-sized, five foot cross section of the garden pictured on the screen, with the white-flowered shrub in the center. It was breathtakingly beautiful. Not only was it more lush than any garden since Eden, but the colors were super-saturated: intense yellow calendulas, vibrant scarlet lobelias, and an incredibly varied pallet of green foliage. The only thing lacking was any sign of death or decay—no brown-tipped plants beginning to wither, no insect-chewed laceworks of leaves, no petals curled lifeless on the ground beneath drooping, bare stalks. It was all quite perfect and quite surreal.

Adam left his desk and entered the Simu-Strip. He stood beside the white-flowered shrub he had called up from the computer and waved his hand through it.

"Identify selected plant."

The label "Gardenia Jasminoides" appeared on the monitor screen, along with the plant's coordinates: "324-WI-SHANGRILA."

"Gardenia Jasminoides," the computer reported out loud. The image had been reproduced in three dimensions based on decades-old scans of gardenias that resided in the deepest bowels of the VVN computer hard drives. All of the flowers, trees, and shrubs were based on similarly stored images. Adam compared the current plant that stood so beautifully in front of him to the ones in his own photographic memory and was satisfied.

"Good. Now produce a sample of the Gardenia Jasminoides fragrance," he told the computer.

He leaned into the ghostly shrub's flowers and inhaled deeply then stood back up and shook his head. It wasn't quite there. Maybe a little more sweetness might do the trick.

"Now mix in a little clover honey scent with that." Adam sniffed the flowers again. "More," he said. This time he nodded his head with satisfaction. The scent was good; now the visual just needed a tweak.

"Add a touch of golden sparkle to these flowers," he commanded.

The Gardenias were suddenly ablaze with gold ruffles.

"Too much! Too much! Dial back the intensity of the gold," he told the computer.

The flowers immediately reflected his preference with a soft dusting of pale gold. "Much better," he said.

The computer beeped to announce an incoming call.

Adam went back to his desk. "Answer," he instructed the machine.

The screen filled with the image of Governor Jonathan Copley. He might have been ruggedly handsome in his youth, but now his sandy brown hair was shot with silver gray. The creases on his face reflected the habitual scowls with which he wielded his power, with no smile lines to balance them out. His tunic was expensive and well-cut, obviously tailor made. His body looked in decent shape for a man in his fifties, and his authoritative bearing more than made up for any physical weakness brought on by aging.

In short, Copley's appearance befitted the top man at Virtual Vision Network, which is to say, the top man of the corporation-based government of Appleton. Politics and elections no longer played a part in society. Regional governors like Copley were often network executives appointed by the vestigial Big Brother government in Washington. They ruled their isolated domains with dictatorial power.

"Porter, I'm still not happy with the Shangrila colors and scents." There was no love lost between these two. "They aren't vivid enough. I want them stronger, brighter. I want the subscribers to drown in this shit."

Brad Jameson entered Adam's office while Copley was talking and sat on the edge of the desk out of the vidphone's view.

"I've already pumped them up 53 percent over yesterday's levels," Adam replied. He tried unsuccessfully to mask the irritation in his voice. They'd had run-ins like this before.

"Then pump them a hundred and fifty-three! I want the users to crave this stuff like a kid craves candy. Do you understand what I'm saying? Or do I have to put someone else on this?" Copley didn't try in the least to disguise his annoyance with his underling.

Adam sighed. No use fighting with the boss; it was a never-win proposition. "I'll make the changes, Governor Copley."

Copley scowled and ended the transmission. The garden read-out returned full screen.

Adam cocked his finger at the display like a gun. "Bang, asshole." He resented Copley's intrusion into his horticultural designs. Not only had Adam been trained in his field, he loved horticulture, and took great pride in his contribution to making virtual vision flowers, trees, bushes, and fruits as vivid and lush as possible. Adam had never visited a garden like the ones he created; such an abundance of life had perished in the great climatic cataclysm. He gained his great knowledge from his own extra-curricular research, which grew out of his devotion to earth's past ecology.

"Candy? Did he say candy?" Brad rooted around on Adam's desk, hoping for a lemon drop or mint to magically appear. He glanced at the Simu-Strip. "Ahhh... the heavenly land of Shangrila. How's it coming?"

"Just about ready to send it upstairs to the geeks for incorporation," Adam replied. He waved his hand in the direction of the Simu-Strip. "Check out that bush in the middle, the one with the white flowers."

Brad's rooting had dislodged a pile of sketches, sending a particularly large sheet of poly-view wafting off the desk. He abandoned his fruitless candy search and walked over to the Simu-Strip. He poked his head inside and sniffed.

Brad turned back to Adam with a big smile on his face. "Nice! What's this one called?"

15

Adam picked up the piece of poly from the floor and turned it over. It was the printout of the garden he'd been working on. He reached into a desk drawer, looking for a tack. He had three, and two of them were rusty. Not much was new anymore, mostly scavenged and recycled from the abandoned parts of the city. He picked up the third tack and shoved the drawer closed.

He looked around for a blank space on the cluttered wall and spotted one high up near the ceiling.

"Golden Gardenia. And old man Copley wants me to make it stronger!"

"You've got to be joking!" Brad said. "It's perfect!" Brad entered the Simu-Strip and stood in the middle of the Gardenia bush, looking for all the world like a half-man/half-flower monster. He turned his head and sniffed the air, a big grin on his face. Adam, meanwhile, had rolled his swivel chair over to the wall and stepped up on it, picture and tack in hand.

From the middle of the Gardenia bush Brad said, "I've just found Shangrila's first perfume campaign. Two months from now you won't be able to walk down the hall without smelling my Golden Gardenia on every gal you meet. Thanks, old buddy!"

"Don't mention it," Adam laughed. "Whenever you feel like stealing my work, just help yourself." Adam positioned the drawing high on the wall and started to push in the tack. The chair wobbled and Adam grabbed the wall to steady himself.

"Whoa there!" he gasped. He slowly reached overhead and again tried to push in the tack. Suddenly the chair took off, shooting out from under his feet, sending him crashing to the floor. He smacked his head hard on the corner of the desk on the way down. It sounded like a batter connecting for a home run.

Brad rushed to Adam's side and knelt beside him. "Damn, Adam! You alright?"

Adam sat on the floor and tried out various parts of his body. "Yeah, I'm okay. Lucky my head broke the fall."

He winced as he pushed himself to his feet with Brad's assistance.

"You sure you're okay?" Brad asked. "Maybe you should sit down."

Adam rolled his neck carefully to make sure it wasn't broken. He gently rubbed the right side of his head. "I'm fine. It's only my skull. It'll mend."

Brad righted the chair and rolled it back to the desk. "It's a good thing you're so hard-headed," he told Adam as he patted the seat of the chair.

Adam suddenly grabbed his head with both hands, gripped with pain. He doubled over. When he straightened back up, he looked around, confused.

"You sure you're alright?" Brad asked.

Adam nodded, still rubbing his head.

His vision flickered. Adam caught vague, shimmering glimpses of his office in shambles. Everything remained in the same locations, but the furniture and objects alternately flashed into worn, faded versions of themselves. Even Brad looked faded and gray. Beneath the computer renderings the walls buckled with stains and mold. The clean air alternately thickened with dust. Rust and corrosion enshrouded bare, leaking pipes.

"Okay," Brad said, taking his word for it. "I have to go. You're going to make it to the christening later, right?"

"I'll be there." The pain was still intense but his back was to Brad so his friend didn't notice. Brad was again focused on the garden and distracted by his family's plans for the christening that evening. He had no idea of the severity of his friend's injury.

"Thanks, Adam. This really means a lot to me and Suzanne." Brad grinned and ducked out the door.

Adam held tight to the side of his head and took deep breaths. He squeezed his eyes shut and shook his head. Slowly, he reopened his eyes, afraid of what he'd see.

His office appeared normal again. Adam rubbed his eyes and then the side of his head. He was confused and a little scared but the strange images seemed to have gone away. He didn't know what else to do so he turned back to his work, a little shaky.

Brad paced up and down outside the entrance of a majestic gothic cathedral. He half expected Adam not to show. He felt bad about practically forcing his friend to come here, knowing how incredibly difficult it would be for him, yet his own joy was so profound it was all he could do to keep from dancing up and down the cathedral steps. He had a son! There weren't very many babies being born anymore, and he had been blessed with a son! A healthy, beautiful son. And today's christening would be a momentous occasion for the whole city, if his baby's godfather would just hurry up and get there. He was relieved when he finally saw Adam trudging up the street behind a cluster of people who were also arriving for the ceremony.

"Cutting it kinda fine there," Brad said. "Thought maybe you'd changed your mind."

"I said I'd be here. I'm here," Adam replied.

"I know this is hard for you. This place has loads of good and bad memories, for all of us. If we could have held the ceremony anywhere else, we would have, but you know it's the only game in town."

"I know, I know. Don't worry about it. I'll be fine. Better get in there. I'll join you in a minute."

"Thanks, buddy." Brad patted Adam on the shoulder. His face broke into a wide grin as he bounded up the steps past the queue of late arrivals who were filing through the open doors.

Adam took a deep breath. He turned his back on the cathedral and stuck his hands in his tunic pants pockets. His gaze turned to a passing train that ran parallel to the road in front of him. Silhouetted in the windows, dozens of anonymous faces passed quickly before his eyes, on their way to their everyday lives, perhaps coming home from work or meeting friends for dinner. He wondered if they were happy, but he couldn't know. They were as oblivious to his pain as he was to theirs.

He lingered for a moment longer, even after the train had passed. He really didn't want to go back into this cathedral where his own joy had begun with such promise and had just as abruptly ended with such unexpected sorrow. But he had made a promise to his friend, so he turned and slowly mounted the steps.

A smiling usher greeted each arriving guest with a vigorous handshake as they entered the red-carpeted foyer. Adam was one of the last to enter, hanging back until the young man approached him. He stuck a friendly hand out to Adam and gently pulled him across the threshold.

"A fine day, isn't it, sir?" the usher asked rhetorically as he pumped Adam's hand up and down.

"Just swell," he replied dryly.

The torture had already begun. He hated this place and he hated this usher, even though he'd never met the man before. The gloom that had hung over his mood since Trish's passing descended with full force upon him. He'd rather be anywhere else but here.

Memories of the funeral hit him like a hammer—the angels, the polished silver casket, the tear-stained faces of the rented choir, and Trish, even more beautiful in death than in life. There was another memory, too, so painful that it rarely crossed the threshold of his recollections, yet today he found it inescapable. There, beside Trish, a tiny pink and silver casket holding the baby that had taken Trish's life in its desperate struggle to be born.

Those memories overshadowed the more joyous memories of their wedding here eight years ago. That day had been the happiest of his life. He knew he would never feel that way again. To see her radiant smile; to smell her hair; to feel her hand in his...

He had to stop this; stop the memories, all the memories. It ripped his heart out to remember.

"This way please, sir." The usher's voice brought him back to the present as he guided Adam to a glowing CRT screen set just inside the door. He ceremoniously took Adam's hand and placed it on the screen. In the blink of an eye, the foyer shifted to Chapel Vision. Chapel Vision was VVN's ceremonial channel—the one reserved for watershed occasions such as weddings, funerals, and today's event: baby dedications. Adam and the usher both appeared clothed in full-length, impossibly white robes.

The cathedral looked even more impressive than before, with ornately carved beams that vaulted overhead. Shining golden angels held globes of light aloft in exquisite chandeliers and adorned every post and pillar. Huge stained glass windows portrayed images of sentimental family themes and threw rainbows of light on the burnished wood pews. At the front, on a raised platform behind the altar, a magnificent pipe organ thrust its golden tubes upward toward heaven. There were no overtly "religious" scenes anywhere in the decor, as this cathedral represented people of all faiths, with arms outstretched to all and no possible offense to any.

"You're the godfather, aren't you?" the usher asked.

Adam dumbly nodded.

"Follow me, please," the usher said over his shoulder as he strode out of the vestibule and into the great vaulted nave.

They moved up the aisle, through the roomful of white-robed guests, toward the massive altar covered in flowing white linen and resplendent with flowers and flickering candles, their holders shimmering gold.

Adam spoke to the usher's back as they walked what seemed to be a full mile to the front of the great church. "Uh, what does a godfather do? What, uh, what am I supposed to do?"

"Try to look dignified, sir. And don't drop the baby."

"What!? I have to hold it?" Adam's despondent mood was suddenly stabbed through with a dagger of genuine terror.

The usher rolled his eyes and sighed. Why some men feared babies was a mystery to him. He took Adam to Brad's side near the altar, where the two shook hands and gave each other a quick buddy hug. The usher hurried back up the aisle to the foyer.

A distinguished clergyman cloaked in red and gold satin posed pompously before the congregation. By his side, a beaming Brad and Suzanne cradled their cherubic one-year-old crowned with a glowing halo. The baby's dovelike wings fluttered behind him as he fretted in his mother's arms. His mother fretted a little, too. She tried to soothe him, comfort him.

In the back of the cathedral, a choir loft hovered high above the entryway. The organ started playing an inspirational overture, filling the space with its magnificent sound. From the loft, the choir joined the beautiful hymn. Their voices blended in rich, heavenly harmonies. After a stirring verse or two, they hummed softly in the background.

The clergyman smiled out on the congregation. "We wish to thank you all for coming today to witness this rare and blessed event." He turned to face Brad's family and held his arm out toward them, and then led the congregation in a round of applause. "A new baby in our fair city! Welcome the child!" The applause grew as their voices raised in greeting.

"Welcome the child!" They chanted as one over the applause. "Welcome the child! Welcome the child! Welcome the child!"

The clergyman lifted the baby from his mother's arms and turned to face the altar, where a small white cloud floated in midair. The choir's voices swelled again, sending goose bumps through the assembly.

As baby Bradley was carried toward the altar, Adam grimaced in pain. Chapel Vision distorted before his open eyes. Flickering bands of black rolled across his vision as shapes twisted and wavered.

The golden-lit cathedral disappeared. Only a dark and dreary, crumbling shell remained. The choir still sang, but they sounded discordant, eerily off key. The organ sounded lifeless and uninspiring, its melody punctuated by the missing notes of cracked pipes. Even the brilliant windows were dull and dirty. Many were broken.

Adam held his breath, trying not to cry out. The pain and queasiness had returned, but the last thing he wanted to do was disrupt the ceremony. He looked toward the clergyman and was shocked to see that the cloud awaiting baby Bradley masked an infant-sized operating chair equipped with body and head restraints.

Robotic arms attached to the chair held a drill and a small electronic chip. It was like something from a Frankenstein movie or a mad scientist's lab.

The baby screamed and struggled as the clergyman strapped him into the chair. Suzanne wanted desperately to go to her child's side but knew she couldn't. The ceremony had to continue.

Adam saw that the clergyman's ornate robe had vanished, revealing a threadbare brown tunic. He instinctively stepped back, horrified. The image flickered and... he once again looked on in Chapel Vision, as the clergyman nestled the baby deep into the cloud, his cherubic wings beating the air. The congregation oohed and aahed at the inspiring sight. The choir sang beautifully again, and then hummed quietly.

The clergyman stood ceremoniously beside the hovering cherub.

"Bradley Jameson Junior, may you always be cradled and protected in the loving arms of your family, as this cloud cradles you today. May you carry yourself proudly, esteemed by your peers, crowned with the blessings of society. And may your spirit be free to carry your soul to great heights, even as these wings lift you up today." He laid a gentle hand across the baby's brow.

Baby Bradley cried very hard, as if in pain. Suzanne's motherly instincts kicked into high gear. It was all she could do to keep herself from rushing up there to grab her child and cradle him in her arms to quiet his crying.

Once again, Adam cringed as his vision distorted and the beauty of Chapel Vision slipped away. He felt sick to his stomach. The choir's discordant singing nauseated him. On the altar, the machine's arm swung out and away from the crying baby's head.

Suddenly, the baby stopped crying and began to gurgle and coo. Suzanne relaxed a little as the baby settled down.

A panic attack washed over Adam. He couldn't catch his breath. He tried hard to act natural, but he saw Brad looking in his direction, worried. Oh my God. Brad! Brad was dressed in a faded gray tunic, and he looked gaunt and unhealthy. Even his trademark orange hair was dull and sparse. Adam glanced at the congregation—they all looked the same as Brad, like a room full of zombies. Again, Adam's vision rippled and distorted, and returned to Chapel Vision.

The ornately-robed clergyman bent down to pluck the baby from the cloud. He handed him to his father, who joyfully reached out for him. The clergyman gave Brad an "attaboy" clap on the shoulder. He shook Suzanne's hand, then turned to face the congregation.

"From this day forward we welcome Baby Bradley into the loving and sheltering arms of society," he declared. His arms opened wide, as if he were the sheltering arms of society incarnate. "Welcome the child!" he called out.

The smiling congregation stood and chanted, "Welcome the child" over and over, applauding as the proud father held the laughing baby aloft, his happy cherub wings gently swiping the air, halo glowing brightly. The choir's song swelled to a soul-touching climax.

Adam stepped back into the shadows and gripped his head in pain as his vision shifted away from Chapel

Vision again. Now in the dim, dirty cathedral that once again filled Adam's vision, his best friend held his baby boy in the air. Baby Bradley's wings and halo were gone. An ugly smear of blood dripped down his scalp and neck. The choir ended their hymn with a crescendo of ear splitting dissonance.

Terrified, Adam found a side door behind him and bolted from the cathedral, out into the late afternoon sunshine. He felt like throwing up. He gasped for breath and leaned on the railing of the steps, his legs weak and rubbery. He couldn't understand how he could be drenched with sweat even though he felt freezing cold. And then, as suddenly as it had left him, normal vision returned. It wasn't Chapel Vision anymore since he was outside the cathedral; just normal, everyday vision and he was relieved to see it. He heard the door open behind him. It was Brad, looking clean and normal again. And worried.

"Geez, Adam. I'm really sorry. I didn't think it would be this hard for you."

Still gasping, Adam nodded his head. "Yeah, I didn't think so either." Adam had known it would be tough coming back, but he hadn't imagined it would hit him this hard. He faked a smile and patted Brad on the shoulder, reassuringly. "Look, I'll be fine. You better get back inside."

"You sure?"

"There's nothing wrong with me that a month in Frontier Vision wouldn't fix. Go on. Get back in there."

Brad nodded, frowning, then turned and went back inside.

Adam walked home through the quiet streets, wary, tired. He stopped briefly at the corner market to pick up a few credits worth of groceries—bread, sliced meat for sandwiches, and his favorite dessert: strawberries. He had other choices but this was his usual fare and he wasn't feeling experimental. On the next corner, he stopped in at the Laundromat to pick up next week's tunics. He was glad the place was almost empty and he didn't have to wait in line. Usually, it was packed with people dropping off and picking up their weekly allotment of clothes.

On the wall above the counter, the ubiquitous vidvision monitor ran a silly graphic of a man in a tub with a huge brush bobbing up and down on his back and chest to the incessant accompaniment of an irritating jingle. "Don't forget or you'll regret! Saturday, Saturday, bathe and shave on Saturday! Don't forget or you'll regret! Saturday, Saturday, bathe and shave on Saturday!" Over and over and over. Adam figured the man behind the counter must be deaf or he'd go insane listening to that jingle all day, every day. He couldn't wait to get out of there.

"What color you want?" the guy behind the counter asked. "Gray, brown, or black?"

"Gray," Adam answered. It matched his mood. It always did. He hadn't worn anything but gray since Trisha's death.

A block from his building, a neighbor nodded at him. He forced a smile and nodded back. It was late afternoon, still daylight. He was grateful that the masses had already found their way home from work and had left the empty streets to him.

He reflected on what had just happened at the cathedral. This was the second time that his eyes and mind had deceived him, and each time it had been painful and nauseating. Illness was uncommon among the citizens of Appleton, so he didn't think he had contracted a cold or the flu. His mind bounced between the confusion of those events and the heartbreak of being in the cathedral again, flooded with memories of Trisha. He continued to brood all the way up the stairs of his building to the door of his apartment.

Adam placed his palm on the identity verification pad to the right of his front door. "Adam Porter," he said to the pad. The door unlocked with a click. He pushed it open and stepped inside. He could hear the ever-present VVN ads on his vidvision monitor.

He put the groceries away and headed for the bedroom where he tossed the clean tunics on the unmade bed. Then, returning to the living room, he trudged over to the couch and plopped down. He was bone tired. He closed his eyes and put his head back.

"Vidvision channel change," he said to the house computer.

He peeked at the screen as the announcer was silenced and a film came on. It was a very old black and white movie from 1934; a young John Wayne in "Randy Rides Alone." Nah; not in the mood.

"Change."

The vidvision index randomly selected Buster Crabbe's "Flash Gordon" movie from 1936, with smoke-sputtering rocket ships and bad dialogue.

"Change," he said again. He just didn't care. Nothing grabbed him. Adam closed his eyes and put his head back again.

A documentary came on the vid, narrated by the same narrator who's done every nature documentary since time began.

"... with growing concern scientists feverishly worked to slow down the ever increasing hole in the atmosphere above the polar regions." The screen showed enhanced satellite photos of the hole in the ozone layer above the North Pole growing larger and larger.

Beep. Beep, beep.

"Answer, 'pip'," Adam said.

A 'picture-in-picture' box appeared on the screen. The announcer's audio faded under Brad's voice, though Brad's picture was the smaller one in the corner.

"Hey, Buddy. Just checking up on you."

"I'm touched."

Brad finally got annoyed at Adam's sarcasm. "Cut it out! I'm worried about you."

The narrator's voice droned on in the background.

"I know you are, Brad. I'm sorry. Nothing's wrong. I'm okay, really."

Brad wasn't quite buying it, but he couldn't force the guy to confide in him.

"Say 'hi' to Suzie for me," he said, hoping Brad would take the hint and hang up.

"Wellll, okay. See you tomorrow." Brad nodded as he ended the transmission. The screen went full on the documentary, where a time-lapse CGI showed the planet being restored. The hole in the atmosphere shrank and disappeared, the sky changed from brown to blue, and the barren landscape greened with new growth.

The announcer's audio volume faded in. "Things looked very bleak. But then, near the end of the last century, our brilliant scientists discovered a way to mend the hole in the atmosphere and to clean the air and water of toxins. The planet was able to heal herself, and the land and sea were once again full of life."

An image of Governor Jonathan Copley appeared on screen, smiling and nodding. Behind him, in the traditional "vice president" spot, Maxine Markles. To her left, Joseph Branton.

At forty-five Markles still retained some of her youthful attractiveness. Her brunette hair was a little shorter than shoulder length and well-coiffed. She wore the female version of an executive tunic, in a tasteful shade of blue. Branton stood a full head taller than Markles. His hawkish nose was the most prominent feature on his long, thin face. Whereas Copley's expression reflected unbridled authority and artificial benevolence, Branton just looked grim, even when he smiled.

"And thanks to the tireless efforts of our benevolent Governor, Jonathan Copley, and the visionary members of the Executive Committee, we citizens of Appleton continue to enjoy the beauties of a healthy ecology."

Adam got up and crossed to the terminal screen. He jabbed it hard.

"Bull shit. Shut that off. Frontier Vision. Day."

He laid his palm across the monitor.

"Entered and accepted," the computer replied, once again in the guise of the melancholy Indian.

The room changed immediately. Adam now sported his Western jeans and plaid flannel shirt. The familiar log cabin walls of the hunting lodge appeared. A fire crackled in the cast iron woodstove. Bo lay stretched out in front of the fire, unharmed. He looked up at Adam, wagged his tail, and then put his head down contentedly for a nap.

Adam went to the window and drank in the pristine Western vista. Tall pines blanketed the nearby hills. A lone eagle soared through an intensely blue sky. He could hear the call of the eagle as it circled and wheeled. He soaked in the peace and beauty for a few minutes, until his hand suddenly flew to his head and he staggered against the window frame.

"No!" he cried out in protest. Another flickering, strobe-like attack had begun. Dark and ghostly buildings blinked in and out of the virtual vision prairie.

The flickering ended and his vision steadied. The frontier cabin was gone. Adam looked out over a dark city in decay. He saw ancient, neglected buildings, overlaid with jumbled networks of ducts and pipes. A few stunted evergreen trees struggled to find purchase in the small patches of earth revealed by broken concrete sidewalks and badly patched potholes in the ruined roads.

He stared out the window, struggling to understand what he was seeing. He had lived in this apartment for eight years and had never seen anything like this. Again, as in his office, things were in their right places, but they were the worst possible versions of themselves. What he remembered as a majestic oak on the corner across the street was now a spindly spruce. The postage-stamp lawns in front of the neighbors' bungalows were nothing but bare dirt and dry, matted weeds. None of the cute bungalows retained their coats of pale pastels; they huddled in a row, all dirty and gray. The only thing that looked "normal" was the VVN building in the distance. Its black and steel facade appeared even more starkly beautiful by contrast as it towered over the remnants of the ruined city that now lay before him.

His attention was drawn to a building across the street. Graffiti scrawled in very large letters screamed this cryptic message: "Madman, fly to the Bluebird Café!" It looked fresh, as though it had been left there recently, but his befuddled brain didn't register that fact. He couldn't process what he was seeing at all.

He left the window and went to the wall mirror. A stranger's pale, thin reflection frowned back at him. He rubbed his face with hands that looked like he'd been working in a coal mine. His hair hung to his shoulders in clumps. He kept blinking, hoping this was just a horrible nightmare, but it felt all too real.

When he could no longer stand to look at himself any more, he turned from the mirror and studied his living room. The room's air was thick and foul. Rotten plaster crumbled from the ceiling. Conduits and plumbing crisscrossed walls that were cancerous with rust and mold. Small brown finger-sized creatures scurried along the baseboards. He guessed them to be cockroaches, although he'd never seen one in person. In the corner, a much larger creature—about the size of his foot—dug at a loose carpet scrap. He wasn't sure, but he thought they used to call these animals "rats." He'd seen them in vidfilms, but he'd never seen them in real life.

A wave of nausea washed over him. His vision drifted in and out of Frontier Vision. The skin on his hands alternated between clean and normal and dirty and gaunt. They trembled uncontrollably as he held them both up and turned them over, examining their horrible appearance. Another wave of nausea hit and he groaned, cried out, and slid down the wall.

Slowly, his virtual vision returned. As he lay crumpled on the floor, whimpering in pain and exhaustion, the log cabin walls returned and Bo came to his side. The big dog licked Adam's face over and over. It was oddly soothing. This creature that didn't really exist offered comfort and compassion to a man who had begun to doubt his own existence.

TUESDAY

The Research & Development conference room was full. Adam, Brad, and a dozen other co-workers sat around a large black conference table in chairs that weren't meant to be comfortable, all eyes forward on the department head, Henry Jones.

Henry's bald head shone under the bright lights, partly from perspiration but mostly because he had given up trying to cover his shiny pate with the ridiculous comb-over that he had sported for years. The sides and back of his head still boasted a few strands of brown. He tucked them behind his tiny ears in a usually futile attempt to keep the wisps from drifting into his eyes.

Today, he had anticipated his role as showman, so had slicked it back with water just before he stepped through the door.

Henry loved these meetings. He got to be the one in charge, the one who shared the information and gave the orders. He especially liked using the laser pointer on the images as he spoke.

"You okay today?" Brad whispered to Adam.

Adam nodded without looking at his friend.

Henry lectured enthusiastically as a large wall-screen displayed a series of brilliantly colorful Shangrila motifs.

"VVN's newest premium channel, Shangrila, is expected to have wide market appeal." On the screen,

Henry pretended to casually point at the voluminous assets of a beautiful woman in a silken, diaphanous sari, lounging on a golden dais. Persian rugs covered the floor beneath her, and fringed velvet drapes hung from tall, gracefully arched windows.

"Subscriber Services anticipates it will be truly irresistible to many users, bringing them online 24 hours a day. We're promoting it as the luxury channel everyone can afford."

On the screen, a romantic couple in gold-embroidered caftans strolled hand-in-hand through a garden in full bloom. Behind them, Adam could see the Gardenia Jasminoides that he had recently perfected in his Simu-Strip. Its pearl white petals sparkled from the light dusting of gold. Adam would have smiled at the beauty he had created, had it not been part of the garish scene before him.

"Even subscribers with tight credit accounts will crave Shangrila weekends, at the very least. And why not? We'll promise them a 1000 credit illusion for only 80 credits a day!"

The R & D workers raised their eyebrows with surprise at Shangrila's low price. When the project had first been proposed, it had been promoted as the most elaborate channel ever created, and they had all assumed the price would reflect the complexity of the programming detail.

"In conclusion, we'd like to compliment the Research & Development Department on the terrific job you're doing on this project." Henry tucked the laser pointer under his armpit and applauded in the direction of the R&D people.

Behind him, on the screen, the Taj Mahal sparkled in all its glory. An ornate sign posted in front of the palace read: "Virtual Vision Network Presents Shangrila—Your Wish Is Our Command!"

Henry retrieved the pointer from his armpit and once again danced it around the screen. "The gardens, perfumes, and furnishings that I have had the pleasure of sampling are exquisite," Henry effused. "I know you'll keep up the good work until Shangrila goes on line... only two more months!" And with that pronouncement, he snapped off his laser light, signaling the end of the meeting. The room erupted in applause, followed by shuffling and murmuring as the assembly broke up. Adam rolled his eyes and turned to Brad.

"I bet Copley is already counting his millions on this piece of diamond-encrusted shit," he whispered.

"Come on!" Brad said. "Where's your sense of adventure? Shangrila is exotic, it's mysterious, it's..."

"Cheap and gaudy. This is one subscriber that won't be caught dead in a turban!"

Brad laughed and put his hands in a circle over his head as he pranced out the door doing a robotic belly dance. Adam couldn't help but laugh, too.

Later, Adam worked at the computer in his office, tweaking some of Shangrila's many exotic flower beds. Like it or not, he had a job to do, and the least he could do was try to bring some natural elegance and beauty to the settings.

The pain struck again like a steel-toed boot to the back of his skull. His hand flew to his head. Adam once more found himself sitting in the same dirty, unkempt office that he had seen during his first attack, but this time without the distracting flickering. He looked around at the disarray. He slowly and purposefully examined everything—the rusty metal desk, the crumbling walls covered in his drawings, the scratched and dented file cabinets. What the hell was all this? The place was never the neatest office in the building, but it wasn't this kind of pig sty either. It wasn't just messy, it was falling apart. Or was it? Was this real or was he hallucinating?

He made his way to the window and looked out on the same decayed city he had seen from his living room window. From this slightly higher vantage point he could see much further, and the city's decay was starkly apparent, even at a distance. Adam's eyes searched the horizon. He normally saw desert out beyond Appleton's perimeter—unending miles of sand and scrub. Now he was surprised to see that the city continued out beyond the old freeway that ringed its boundaries. Out there were collapsing buildings, blackened shells that had burned in unchecked fires, and mile after mile of emptiness beyond. What he had thought was desert was not, but it was definitely deserted.

Adam made his way back to his filthy desk. Something was very wrong. He didn't know what it was but he knew that without question, something was very, very wrong. He touched the corner of his monitor.

"Computer. Dial Dr. Freeman."

Now that the pain had subsided and his normal vision had returned, Adam regretted having scheduled a doctor's appointment. He perched nervously on the edge of an imposing, red leather chair in Dr. Jerome Freeman's consulting room. The seat was low to the floor and his knees felt like they were under his chin. It made everything else in the office appear so much larger, especially the doctor sitting across the big mahogany desk from him.

Doc Freeman was a gentle, fatherly type, the kind who really seemed to listen to what you had to say. Displayed on his desk were pictures of his wife and grandchildren. Adam recognized the frame around the grandkids' picture as the same type that housed Trish's holograph, and he knew one touch on the corner would bring the grandkids to life. He idly wondered how often the doctor called up the kids just to see their smiling faces and hear the laughter in their voices. He mentally shrugged. Certainly not as often as he called up Trisha's image to see and hear her. But then he had to admit to himself that there probably wasn't anyone as obsessed with a hologram as he was.

"Just relax and tell me what happened," the doctor said.

"I was just watching vidvision when it hit me. For a minute there it felt like my head was going to explode."

"Mmmmm hmmmm; go on."

"I steadied myself against the wall and... I don't know... everything looked different, ugly... Even the smell was..." Adam's voice drifted off. After a moment he looked up at the doctor. "That's all there was to it, really."

Dr. Freeman scribbled notes on a pad. "Has this ever happened before?"

"Yes, after a fall at work. I hit my head." Adam pointed to the spot on the right side of his head, behind his ear. "Here."

Dr. Freeman rounded his desk and stood in front of Adam. He felt Adam's head with both hands, flexing his fingers efficiently over his entire scalp. Adam winced when Dr. Freeman touched the site of his injury.

"You say your vision's been affected?"

"No, not now. Only once or twice." Adam tried to minimize his symptoms; he wished even more he hadn't come.

Dr. Freeman nodded.

"Almost like I was picking up some twisted new Virtual Vision channel." Adam leaned forward earnestly. "It's only a bump on the head, right?"

Dr. Freeman shook his head and smiled condescendingly.

"Possibly, but these are serious symptoms. I'm going to schedule a little vacation for you at Serenity Gardens, a chance to get away from it all and relax. Give that bump time to heal."

A look of alarm crossed Adam's face. "Serenity Gardens! I don't want to..."

Dr. Freeman interrupted and cranked up his condescending smile. "Who's the doctor here? Don't you worry. I'll call Serenity Gardens and put you on the schedule."

Adam continued to protest. "But... I..."

"Everything's going to be okay, Mr. Porter. You'll see."

Adam jumped up. "No! No, I'm fine. Thanks anyway." He turned to the door and started to leave.

"Wait, Mr. Porter! You must have that injury treated!"

Adam bolted out of the office. Dr. Freeman returned to his desk, now deadly serious. He dropped the country doctor act and punched the screen on his monitor with his stubby finger.

"Dial Serenity Gardens."

The monitor displayed a fluffy white cloud with "Serenity Gardens" written in ornate gold letters across it. A telephone operator in a white orderly's uniform quickly appeared onscreen.

"Serenity Gardens," she cooed. "Your cares are our concern. How may I direct your call?"

"This is Dr. Freeman. Connect me to Carl Thompson." He waited while the call was transferred and then barked into the monitor when the man appeared. "I have another Failure for pickup. And you'd better hurry. He's agitated as hell."

Adam walked home, lost in thought. The mention of Serenity Gardens had sent him into an immediate panic. The doctor must have thought this bump on his head was pretty damn serious to have suggested a visit to the hospital. But there was no way that Adam was going to voluntarily go to the one place in the city that held the worst memories of all to him. He could barely allow himself to think of it. The pain in his heart was almost physical.

He had just reached the front door of his apartment building when he heard a strange sound behind him. He looked back down the street and saw an old white vehicle moving quickly toward him. Across the front of the vehicle the word "AMBULANCE" was written in faded red letters. His first thought was "I wonder who died?" because that was the only time the ambulance came around. But it screeched to a halt right next to him. Two burly hospital orderlies jumped out of the van and approached him.

"Adam Porter?" asked the taller of the two men in a soothing voice.

"Yeah?" Adam said. He was growing increasingly alarmed.

"We'd like you to come with us, sir."

"What is this?" Adam said, backing away.

The orderlies moved closer to Adam, hemming him in.

From their porches across the street and next door, nosy neighbors first poked their heads out their doors and then, intrigued, began to congregate on the sidewalks and in the street. They talked in hushed voices among themselves as they watched the action.

"Let's make this easy, sir," the shorter man said. "Wouldn't want to alarm the neighbors."

"Alarm the neighbors? What are you talking about?"

The tall orderly stepped deftly behind Adam, catching him off-guard, and yanked back his wrists while the other one pulled out a pair of plastic handcuffs and slapped them on.

"This way, sir," the shorter man said, pulling him toward the ambulance. "Just a nice little ride to Serenity Gardens. Everything will be alright."

Adam tried to twist out of their grip, but they held firm. They pulled him roughly toward the back of the van.

"Get your hands off me! I'm not going!" he yelled frantically.

He stomped down hard on Shorty's foot.

"Shit!" the man cried out.

The tall guy backhanded Adam across the face. They both yanked him roughly toward the ambulance's back doors, one on each arm. Adam continued to pull and twist, trying to escape. Suddenly, his vision flickered and he felt the stab of pain in his skull.

Again, what had previously been his clean, familiar neighborhood with its pastel cottages and pretty green lawns now looked run-down and decayed. The neighbors looked thin and dirty, dressed in tattered clothes. Their faces appeared gaunt and their hair looked stringy and greasy. Their murmurs grew more animated as they watched the scene unfold.

"Don't let them take me!" Adam screamed to the gathering crowd. "Something's wrong here! Don't let them take me away!"

The gawkers shook their heads with pity for the poor, unbalanced man. One by one, embarrassed by the spectacle, they filtered back inside their homes.

The orderlies shoved Adam hard into the back of the rusty van and slammed the doors. He lay trembling on the steel floor, hands cuffed behind his back, as the two men got in the front seat and drove off. He was surrounded by old, smelly sheets and blankets, and a slim mattress that had once been a promise of hope for the sick and dying but was now a haven for small things that crawled about on six legs. He cringed as something tickled the skin on his hand. He tried to shake it off but his hands were bound too tightly behind him.

It was a short drive to Serenity Gardens. Although Adam couldn't see out from his place on the floor of the van, he knew what it looked like. The Gardens had once been a beautiful hospital complex and, in normal vision, it retained that beauty in its architecture and on the grounds. Neatly shorn grasses formed a lawn that swept gracefully around the curved driveway. Tall oaks offered deep shade to small patches of colorful flowers. Here and there a stone bench offered a resting place for whoever needed a respite from an afternoon stroll, or just wanted to enjoy the beauty and the shade.

The ambulance drove to the entrance marked "Emergencies" and stopped. The two orderlies jumped out and pounded the side of the van, laughing, as they passed to the rear and flung open the back doors. They grabbed Adam by the ankles and roughly hauled him out, dragging a stained and odiferous sheet with him.

They stood him up between them, holding onto both his arms so that escape was impossible.

Adam's heart was pounding as he looked around, recognizing the portico under which they stood. He could tell right off that something was wrong here, too. While the handsome brick architecture was reassuringly familiar, the grounds no longer appeared well-tended. Gone were the familiar gardens, lawns, and border hedges; in their place, just like his neighbors' yards, only bare dirt and trampled weeds remained.

He heard a squeaking noise and turned to see a very large orderly pushing an old, rusty wheelchair. The man had an odd look to him, with eyes that seemed too large for their sockets and a bulbous nose covered in veins that crept onto his cheeks. The overall effect was unpleasant enough that his thin lips carried themselves in a perpetual frown, even when he smiled, which was infrequent. His crudely lettered employee badge said his name was Carl Thompson.

"What the hell is that for?" Adam demanded, trying not to sound as frightened as he felt.

Carl scowled at him. "Patients ride in wheelchairs—hospital rules."

While the two van orderlies forced Adam into the wheelchair, Carl pulled a syringe from his coat and jabbed it into their prisoner's arm. Adam fought to rise from the chair but the hypo kicked in and his struggling became more and more feeble until he gave up altogether and surrendered to the drug.

"Okay, sleeping beauty," Carl said. "Welcome to Serenity Gardens."

The two orderlies pulled restraining straps tightly across Adam's chest and legs. His head lolled to one side, but his eyes remained wide open. He could feel the drug spread through his body, relaxing him until he felt as though his muscles were made of mush. He willed himself to strain against the straps but Carl saw his meager efforts and gave him a soft slap across the top of the head.

"Give it up. You ain't goin' nowhere, mister."

He would wait. Maybe an opportunity would present itself later. He sent his mind searching within his body to ascertain what effect the drug was having on his faculties. It appeared to be a relaxant but not a very strong sedative. And he could still see; but what he saw was almost beyond comprehension. What kind of nightmare was he living?

Carl wheeled him inside the swinging doors and through a large waiting room filled with sick men, women, and children. They huddled on rusted folding chairs, some of them coughing, some sleeping, some struggling to remain vertical. A nurse came in with a file, glanced at it and called out.

"Stone? Allan Stone?"

A young man in the back heaved himself up and followed her through the door. Carl also followed, pushing the wheelchair down a long corridor and then through a disorganized, dimly-lit hospital ward crammed with bed after bed of diseased and dying patients. Here and there families huddled in vigils near loved ones' bedsides. The patients and their bedclothes were filthy beyond belief. The smell of death, feces, and unwashed bodies was almost unbearable. Cockroaches scurried up the walls. One bold rat raced across his path and up onto a bed, stopping near a patient's unconscious face to lick an open wound. Adam's stomach churned. He swallowed hard, trying not to retch. The nightmare continued.

A ragged, toothless, middle-aged man sat nearby, holding a dead woman's hand. But to him, Serenity Gardens was cloaked in Chapel Vision. The man believed himself to be well-dressed, and his wife not dead but sleeping peacefully. The ward itself was as different as heaven and hell. For this man, and the other visitors and patients, there was no sign of rats and filth. In their place, row after row of sleeping angels floated in mid-air, cradled in billows of cottony clouds.

The man nodded his head and smiled at the big orderly pushing Adam's golden throne slowly up the aisle. Carl smiled back.

"How are you doing today, Mr. Buckman?"

"Just fine, thanks, Carl," the gentleman replied.

"And how is Mrs. Buckman today?"

"She's resting comfortably, thank you."

"Glad to hear it. You have a nice day now!" Carl's exchange with Mr. Buckman was not ironic, for Carl and the other employees of the hospital were also tuned to Chapel Vision. For them, Serenity Gardens was a pretty sweet place to work.

Carl pushed Adam's chair through a set of doors at the far end of the ward. The shimmering sign next to the doors read "Intensive Rest And Relaxation."

He parked Adam against the wall beside what appeared to be a floating angel asleep on a billowing cloud, then he sauntered over to check in with a golden-robed nurse at the desk down the hall.

"Hey, gorgeous. Got another one for you. Is the doc here yet?"

"Doctor Freeman will be here in a few minutes," she replied perfunctorily.

To Adam, the scene still looked grotesquely filthy and unreal. He would have suspected the drugs, but the distortion had begun long before the tall orderly had

43

stuck him with the syringe. He found himself now able to lift his head and look around.

He had spent a long, anxious day and night in a ward much like this when Trisha was in labor. He shuddered to think of the filth that might have surrounded them outside of their awareness. He wondered if these conditions were real or some demented hallucination of his own imagination. It felt to him like another VV channel, but perverse and horrible. Yet who would have programmed such a thing? And, if it was real, had it somehow led to his family's unexpected demise? No, it couldn't be real. He just couldn't believe such horrors existed. It had to be something else, something he didn't understand.

Suddenly, a grinning, ugly face loomed close to his own. Wild dirty-gray hair shot out from head, cheeks, and chin, bragging that it hadn't been touched by comb or razor for weeks. The old man's foul breath hissed from between cracked lips and rotten teeth.

"Pretty, ain't I?" the crazy-faced man cackled, but quietly lest he be heard. Still woozy from the hypo, Adam struggled weakly against his restraints.

"No use trying to escape. The only way out of here is dead or brain dead. They can't let you walk around talkin', ya know."

The old man laughed maniacally and shuffled down the hall. Chapel Vision and pastoral wall murals notwithstanding, this ward was an old-fashioned lunatic asylum, with half the inmates babbling crazies and the other half shave-headed zombies.

The weird thing was that, to everyone but Adam, they were all dressed like angels.

Adam noticed that the restraints across his chest and legs were frayed and threadbare. As he struggled against them, his nose was assaulted with a rotten stench coming from the gurney next to him. Phew. He had never smelled it before, but he knew it was the smell of death and that this man wouldn't "walk around talking" anymore. Again, he almost retched.

A loud commotion in the dayroom at the far end of the hall sent Carl and the nurse scurrying away. They burst through the doors as the yelling inside grew louder. It was followed by a ferocious banging.

Inside, an angry patient hung monkey-like to the golden grille of a stained-glass window. He was a young man in his early twenties with jet black hair falling over his face as he screamed and rattled the grille with all his angelic might.

"It's all a lie! A lie! You think I'm crazy but I'm not!" And then he sobbed, "I want to go home."

Carl joined another orderly who tried to pull him down. The patient kicked out with his feet whenever the orderlies reached up to grab him. They had to keep ducking and weaving like two boxers in the ring. A younger nurse stood nearby with a large syringe. She yawned and stared blankly at the hundred-year-old "Wheel of Fortune" episode playing on the dayroom vidscreen. The other patients huddled in the corner, unwilling to join their younger comrade's protestations.

Out in the hallway, Adam saw his opportunity to try to escape this nightmare. He fought hard against the drug in his body and pushed fiercely with his chest and legs against the chair's rotted restraints. Thread by thread, the decayed fabric broke as he slammed his torso against it over and over. His hands remained manacled behind him in plastic, so his efforts were slowed down not only by the relaxant but by the awkwardness of his position in the wheelchair. Beads of sweat covered his face and dripped down his neck. When the last piece of the strap finally gave way, he nearly lost his balance and fell out of the chair. He recovered quickly, willing himself not to feel the aching in his chest and shoulders.

With his upper body free, he struggled against the leg straps. They were even more frayed, but they still cut into his shins and calves as he jerked his legs around, all the while looking frantically down the hall toward the dayroom. When they, too, gave up their efforts to restrain him and fell to the floor at his feet, he sat for a few seconds to catch his breath. The exertion had made his heart pound, even while the drug was trying to calm him. His head was swimming.

Adam could still hear the screaming and cursing coming from the dayroom. Carefully, he half stood, easing his hands down below his rear and behind his thighs. He was still pretty woozy and it didn't take much effort to throw him off balance. He fell sideways to the floor but he only laid there for a second before continuing his struggle to get his hands down over his feet and up in front of him. Luckily, the nurses and orderlies were still fully engaged with the commotion in the dayroom.

The crazy old patient watched him closely from a doorway, grinning like a Cheshire Cat. Adam caught his eye and hesitated. Would this man who was obviously unbalanced reveal Adam to his captors? But Crazy Face motioned impatiently for Adam to continue.

Adam looked up and down the hall. The only two obvious avenues of escape seemed to be either into the dayroom or back the way he had come in. Neither seemed to make sense. He would be captured again and didn't even want to think about what they might do to him next time. They had been none too gentle with him earlier, and had even seemed to take pleasure in abusing him.

The screaming and yelling continued from the dayroom. He had to make a decision; they might return any minute. There was one other door nearby, right next to the gurney beside him; it looked to be locked. He turned to the corpse on the stretcher. "Can I do this?" he silently asked himself. "Shit, no choice. Gotta do something." He steeled himself against the smell and the touch of the corpse, then he quickly threw his manacled hands over the body, lifted the cadaver from the gurney, and plopped him into the wheelchair.

It was like a dream he'd once had, where every movement was in slow motion and he was barely strong enough to do what needed to be done. That, plus this whole, surreal, shit vision scene. He was tempted to think he really was just dreaming—actually, he wished he were just dreaming—but he knew he wasn't. He was thankful for the adrenaline coursing through his system, counteracting the effects of the relaxant. He hoped it would last.

Old Crazy Face watched with approval and nodded enthusiastically.

Suddenly, silence from the dayroom. Whatever drama had called his captors away had apparently played itself out. Adam looked down the hall. He had to hurry. He lay on the gurney and pulled the tattered sheet over himself. He looked one last time to Crazy Face, who danced down the hall, singing:

"Fly away little bird. Fly into the blue. Fly, fly, fly away."

Crazy Face passed the nurse and Carl on his way to the dayroom as they came back into the hallway.

"So what's to be done with them?" Carl asked, pointing back toward the dayroom. He liked this nurse and tried to chat her up as they walked together to the Nurse's Station.

"Most of them are too far gone to reimplant. They'll be sent to the SPA."

"The SPA? Geez. Poor bastards, eh?"

"Somebody has to, right?" She shrugged and left him alone in the hall. At the last moment, she called over her shoulder, "Take that sleeping angel to Cloud Haven, Carl."

"What happened to this one?"

"One of Dr. Freeman's special patients. That's all I know and all you need to know. Take him down, please."

Carl sighed and walked past the golden throne, whose occupant, slumped down with chin on chest, appeared to be sleeping off the effects of the hypo. Carl didn't even look at him and so didn't notice the swap. He moved to the foot of the sleeping angel's cloud and pushed it toward the locked door.

Adam held his breath, hoping that Carl wouldn't notice even the slightest movement under the torn sheet. Adam still saw the world in "shit vision," as he now began calling it. With one eye peeking out the side of the sheet, he tried to see where he was headed.

Carl pushed the gurney toward the locked exit. The nurse buzzed the door to let them pass. Crazy Face nodded so hard he had to stop his head with his hands. Ouch. Gave himself a headache. As Carl and Adam disappeared through the door, the old man giggled and did a jig up and down the hall, then danced himself into the dayroom.

Carl pushed the cloud through the bucolic halls of Serenity Gardens. He liked Chapel Vision quite a lot and was glad they provided it free every day at work. He found it so much more pleasant to see the place all clouds and angels and niceness, rather than as it really was in normal vision (which was just a plain, ordinary hospital, all white walls and stainless steel gurneys and bedpans—a far cry from the horror show of Adam's shit vision).

At home, Carl's choice was usually Cartoon Vision. He had no family so he had chosen the cartoon world because it cheered him up so much. Once in a while, when he felt like he needed a giggle or an afternoon energy boost, he'd secretly turn on the Cartoon Vision at work. What a hoot that was! The clouds all took on happy faces and whistled funny little upbeat songs, while long rows of zzzzzz's blew in and out of the mouths of sleeping patients. The best part of all was that the people turned into hilarious cartoon animals who bore about as much resemblance to the patients and staff as Chip and Dale did to the now-extinct chipmunks. If that wouldn't cheer a body up, nothing would. But he couldn't turn on the cartoons too often because his co-workers would give him shit about his uncharacteristically jovial mood. "Spoil sports," he muttered to himself, as a tug of desire for Cartoon Vision pulled at his mind.

He wheeled his "sleeping angel" through a door marked "Cloud Haven" and then over to what appeared to be a narrow aqueduct of water slowly flowing toward a wall display of a peaceful lake.

"Hey, Billy boy!" he called out. "You here?"

Twenty-one year old Bill poked his head out from behind a door and jogged into the room.

"Another one from Intensive Rest and Relaxation?"

"Yep. They don't come much more relaxed than this."

"Go ahead and slide him into the lake." Bill knew it wasn't a lake. He opted out of Chapel Vision most days. Too ornate for his tastes. "Cloud Haven" was the frou-frou name for the crematorium.

Carl tipped his end of the cloud up and slid the angel into the channel. The peaceful, winged form floated slowly toward the lake.

Except that Adam's shit vision revealed that he was actually on a conveyor belt slowly moving toward a large furnace twenty feet away. Flames roared out of the open furnace door.

Adam watched the two men until they moved well away from the conveyor and headed for the exit. He could feel the heat from the flames.

"Later, Bill." Carl pushed the empty gurney out of the room.

Adam quickly tossed the tattered sheet aside, but it got caught around his legs! He scrambled to kick free of it and tugged at it with his manacled hands. He frantically ripped it off his ankles and rolled off the belt just before it reached the gaping maw of the furnace door.

Bill turned around in time to see the corpse leap off the belt and land, although clumsily, quite firmly on the floor beside it.

"Hey! You can't do that! You're supposed to be dead!"

"Oh yeah? How's this for dead?" Adam, his hands still locked together, gave Bill a two-fisted, back-handed blow across the face, sending him reeling. Bill went down in a heap. Adam headed for the door. He poked his head out cautiously, then ran out into the hall. Bill had regained his feet and stumbled out into the hall behind him.

"Stop! Someone stop that patient!"

Carl heard Bill's yell from the far end of the hall. He put it in high gear and started running back toward Cloud Haven.

Adam turned the first corner he came to and slammed into a couple of orderlies pushing carts filled with food trays. Gray glop flew through the air. Trays clattered to the floor as the orderlies smacked against the walls.

Carl came careening around the corner and skidded on the sticky glop on the floor. He slid like a skater, arms akimbo, and fell on his scrawny behind.

Adam yanked a door open and found a stairwell going down. He took the steps two and three at a time, holding onto the railing with both hands, stumbling, knees weak, still woozy, still drugged. Once again, he had the feeling he was in a nightmare. Each time his legs gave out, he picked himself up and kept going. He could hear Carl crashing through the door up above him. He ran out into another hallway.

This hall looked unused. It was dirty and there were broken wheelchairs and gurneys lying on their sides and backs everywhere. A dozen doors flanked both sides of the hall. No time to explore, he picked up a loose piece of something unidentifiable and tossed it far down the corridor, hoping it would throw off his pursuer, then he headed straight for the door in front of him on the other side of the hall. Luckily, it was unlocked. He dashed through.

As the door closed behind him, he lost all of his sight. It was pitch black in the room. No light came in from anywhere. He stood totally still for a second as he heard feet running past the door outside. When it was quiet out there, he debated—should he go back out into the hallway and maybe run into a couple of goons, or feel his way around this room hoping to find another way out? He chose the unknown.

Slowly and carefully, arms stretched out in front of him, he shuffled around like a zombie, bumping into object after object in the dark. "Damn!" he whispered as his shin hit something hard and sharp. More shuffling, more reaching out into the blackness. The dark was disorienting and, to make matters even worse, the drugs were still fighting to take over his system.

He'd been feeling his way around for a minute or two—it seemed like an hour—when he turned too quickly and the side of his head smacked hard into what seemed to be a tall column or support. That now familiar pain shot through his skull behind his ear. He held still for a second then, hearing sound in the hallway, pushed onward, keeping his hands moving in front of him.

His manacled hands reached a wall and he felt something jutting out. It had the shape of a small lever. Maybe a door handle? He wrapped his hands around it and even in the blackness he knew it was the way to freedom.

"Come on, baby, don't be locked." He turned it and pulled. Nothing. Damn! Wait... But it turned. It did turn; it wasn't locked. He smiled to himself. He turned the handle again and this time he pushed instead of pulled.

Framed in the utter, complete blackness, the door opened outward, revealing the hospital grounds. Adam's vision had changed from shit vision back to normal when he had smacked his head earlier. He stepped cautiously through the door, closed it securely behind himself, and looked around. It was an unused exit; the grounds were dark and deserted. He ducked behind a bush, trying to get his bearings. He guessed that he was in the rear of the Serenity Gardens complex. He had become disoriented inside, with all the corridors and stairways, but he didn't see the entrance or driveway here, nor anything recognizable, so he knew he was probably in the back. The sound of pounding footsteps to his right alerted him to hide himself. He ducked further down, peering between the branches of a small evergreen bush.

Carl and the same two orderlies who had picked him up in the ambulance sprinted past, searching for him.

"Where the hell is that son of a bitch?" one yelled, wheezing as he ran.

Adam crouched lower, trying not to breathe. The one who had yelled stopped suddenly, hanging his head and resting his hands on his knees, trying to catch his breath.

"Move it!" Carl spat. The guy shook his head, cursing quietly. Finally, he straightened up, wiped his forehead with his sleeve, and joined the others. They ran out of sight around a corner. Adam waited to be sure they were gone, then he stood up and sneaked away, glad to be out of that place and glad to have his normal vision back. Behind him, the wall was solid and there was no door.

Governor Jonathan Copley sat at his black steel desk in the corner of the conference room. He shouted into his vidphone. There was no image there, no indication of who was on the other side of the call. Just a blank screen.

Copley was livid. "Over my dead body! There will be no negotiation! You people will be apprehended and reintegrated into the system. Virtual Vision will remain online and that's the end of it." Copley smacked the side of the screen to end the call. He stood and took a deep breath to calm himself. The nerve of those people! As if they had any right to make demands!

He was still furious when the vidphone beeped again. Dr. Freeman's visage appeared on the screen to replace the VVN logo that had automatically come into view. He could see Copley's anger.

"I've warned you about your blood pressure, Governor."

"I know, I know. But can you imagine the nerve of those rebels having the unmitigated gall to call me here and tell me, the Governor of Appleton and CEO of Virtual Vision Network, that I must shut down the system? How dare they!"

"Just wait till they get a load of the new Shangrila module, speaking of which, I'll be a few minutes late. I'm here at Serenity Gardens and one of our, um, test subjects is reacting strangely to the new implant. I'll be there as soon as I can."

Copley nodded and signed off. He hoped the problem wasn't a critical one. He was so close... so close.

He walked over to the round glass conference table in his very chic, avant-garde office. UltraModern Vision was his favorite premium channel. He had tweaked his office rendition of UltraModern so that it was a little less flash and a little more polish. He preferred the clean architectural lines—the black glass and steel exteriors that cloaked Appleton's otherwise hopelessly prosaic structures. Copley would have preferred to be the governor of a large city, but here he was stuck as the chief executive of a hick town. Since the great cataclysm, there weren't too many large cities left. At least UltraModern Vision helped him live with that fact a little easier.

One entire wall of Copley's penthouse office was floor-to-ceiling glass, which afforded him a panoramic view of the city. In reality, the VVN tower rose far above the other structures of Appleton, but in his version of UltraModern Vision it shared the lonely skyline with many other tall, futuristic spires. He enjoyed looking at the bright lights pouring from the windows of the phantom towers, imagining them bustling with life.

Copley strolled to the rear wall, admiring his collection of purloined art from earlier days. The Jackson Pollocks and Picassos stood out beautifully against the highly polished mahogany walls.

He reached up to touch a spot behind his ear. He felt the small bump yield under his finger with the sound of a tiny click.

UltraModern dropped away. The room was shabby but clean, nothing like the neglected messes Adam saw in "shit vision." Copley looked fit and well-groomed, though far from the handsome leader he was under virtual vision. As chief executive of the local Virtual Vision affiliate, Copley was one of only a select few people in Appleton with the ability to turn his virtual vision receiver off and on at will with a special, clickable implant. Even the fact that everyone in the city possessed an implant was a closely held secret. The infant dedication ceremony had been devised as a ruse long ago to ensure that everyone would be on the grid and, ultimately, controlled by the tiny nanotechnology that allowed them full sensory immersion in each of VVN's channels.

In the wall, beside the original of Picasso's magnificent 1911 cubist "L'Accordéoniste," a mirrored recess revealed itself. In it, a small bowl of fruit and a miniature rose bush, just coming into bloom, were reflected back by the mirror behind them, making it seem like there were two of everything. This small space was Copley's own private altar of reality.

He pulled out a shiny red apple, almost caressing it for a moment before putting it to his lips. He bit into it, savoring the crisp, crunchy taste and fresh aroma. He primped in the mirror as he chewed.

He went back to the window and surveyed his reality. As there were no other tall buildings in Appleton, he could see rooftops all the way to the city's boundaries. A ribbon of unused freeways lay decaying around them, like a noose rotting in the sun. His predecessors had long ago decided that the circular highway around their small city would be fortified by walls and fences, thus confining the citizens within and leaving those left outside to fend for themselves— meaning to starve and die. It hadn't taken long to construct the barriers and, after a decade or two, policing them became unnecessary. VV implants held those inside, and as for those outside, well, he didn't know, nor did he want to. In his mind, they didn't exist, if they lived at all. His main concern was the area contained by the freeway.

Beyond that to the north, he could see the factory that manufactured the food base for the citizens. The recipe had been based on an emergency nutrition paste developed for starving babies in Niger and other African countries in the early twenty-first century. It consisted of a peanut-based substance infused with sucrose and vitamins. This "glop" was all the citizens had to eat and yet, through the magic of VVN's sensory altering nanites and virtual vision programming, they were all fooled into enjoying everything from illusory steaks and apples to ice cream. Little did they know.

Next to the glop factory, the large Solar Panel Array, or SPA, generated all of the energy Appleton needed in one localized, easy-to-maintain facility. The electricity the SPA provided served the whole city; even the trains and the city's few motor vehicles ran on electricity. The old power plants that had once fed the nation via cat's cradles of wire suspended from colossal metal towers had fallen into disrepair decades before, leaving each surviving community to fend for its own energy needs.

A visit to the "SPA" was actually a life sentence of hard labor, living and working outside the relative comfort of the city and its premium channels. The pool of slaves that worked the glop factory and the SPA was drawn from assorted malcontents who had displeased the governor in some way, as well as patients who proved too difficult for Serenity Gardens to rehabilitate. The crazy old man who had been babbling at Adam would wind up there sooner or later.

Copley shook his head. So primitive. Such a horrible little town. Well, at least they weren't banging rocks together to make fire.

He heard voices and footsteps approaching out in the hall. He was expecting Markles and Branton, but they were early. It wouldn't do to have them catch him eating a real apple. He knew they'd be able to tell the difference between a real apple and a virtual apple and he didn't want them to know about his illicit food source. He swallowed quickly, put the apple in the recess, and stepped away. Click. He reactivated his Virtual Vision. The recess and its treasures vanished, leaving a smooth wall beside the Picasso. The room was once again enveloped in UltraModern Vision. Even his two executives didn't know the extent of his abilities to control his and their lives. They had no such capabilities, and wouldn't until the day one of them took over as governor, which he privately hoped might be sooner rather than later.

He was certain that his new Shangrila channel would be his ticket out of Appleton. Shangrila was no tacky small-time production; he and his programmers had pulled out all the stops. This channel was so perfectly rendered it made other VV channels look like old broadcast television by comparison. And he was secretly working with Freeman and a couple of trusted technicians on one or two unique additions to the program. He was convinced that once the major players at GovCorp saw it, they'd move him up to Central Network for sure. The timing of these latest threats from the local rebels couldn't be worse—he had to make certain they didn't interfere in any way with Shangrila's scheduled roll-out.

The door opened. The other two members of the VVN governing committee—Maxine Markles and Joseph Branton—blew into the room like a summer squall.

"Deaths are up. Births are down. Something needs to be done," Markles said.

Branton dismissed her concerns. "Pump more vitamins into that peanut crap they eat."

"Band-aids, Branton. God, you're an ass." Markles and Branton were thorns in each other's sides, and had been for years.

"Will you two stop bickering," Copley said, taking a seat at the large conference table. My God, he was tired of these two.

"We have work to do," he continued. "The daily truck deliveries from the food base factory are averaging an hour late each time. See what you can do about that, Branton. We also have a delivery coming in from D.C. with additional implants, mostly refurbished, and some electronics. The list is already here. We'll go over it after we look at the network."

Branton and Markles took up their customary positions across from Copley. This was their weekly meeting to review problems with the network. They turned their attention to the clear Plexiglas monitors suspended from the ceiling.

"Computer," Branton said. "Display defective subscriber records for the week of 14 June."

The three execs reviewed a dozen reports of mild receiver malfunction, each resulting in a decision to commit the subscriber to Serenity Gardens for routine reimplantation.

Copley quickly grew bored with the monotony of the file review. He left his chair and strolled around the room, obviously indifferent to the proceedings. He hesitated near his now invisible private fruit stash and then walked to the window and stared out. He stood looking out over the phantom city, hands clasped behind his back.

Adam's file and image appeared on the computer screens.

> **Case# 385-A-92**. Adam Porter;
> **Date**: 17 Jun, 2133
> **ID#** 862M-60-59Q84. Widowed.
> **Residence**: 3416 Sector Q, #25.
> **Workplace**: VVN Research & Development Department, VVN Headquarters.
> **Occupation**: Horticultural Designer.
> **385-A-93**: Subject experiencing dangerous, type A hallucinations. Serenity Gardens scheduled. Physician referral. Subject refused, taken forcibly.
> **385-A-94**: Subject escaped from SG before reimplantation.

Markles shook her head. She looked worried. "Another type A failure? We've had far too many implant failures lately."

As usual, Branton took the opposite position from hers. He countered her concerns with a dismissive scowl. "Don't go into hysterics, Markles." He hated the way the woman saw catastrophe around every corner.

Markles spoke directly to Copley's back. "I'm not prone to exaggeration, Mr. Governor."

Branton tapped his fingers annoyingly on the tabletop.

"I'm afraid we're losing control," she continued. "Need I remind you of the steady trickle of implant failures leaking from the subscriber network? In the past year alone we've misplaced over twenty-five subscribers! Gone. Disappeared. Vanished into thin air. And D.C. keeps sending us refurbished implants. They're still defective, sir. Something must be done to stop it."

"Hold everything," Branton said. "Look at this."

He drew his finger across his monitor, highlighting a line of text on all the screens. "385-A-94: Subject escaped from SG before reimplantation," Branton read out loud.

"What?" exclaimed Copley. He whipped around and hurried back to the table. "No one escapes from Serenity Gardens!"

Branton waved at his computer monitor. "Look, this Porter works right here in the building! My God. This failure's a VV designer!"

"Did you say Porter?" Copley asked. "Adam Porter?" His stomach went sour.

"Yes, sir. He works in Research & Development."

"I know where he works! The man is a trouble-maker. A pain in the ass."

Branton touched his monitor again, bringing a close-up of Adam's animated image to all the screens.

"What if he goes to the Underground?" Branton asked. "With Porter's knowledge, they might figure out a way to..." Branton's voice trailed off. He wasn't quite sure what Porter might be able to accomplish. They had never really planned for this sort of contingency.

Markles shook her head.

"If we'd spent more money on upgrading the system..." she said accusingly.

Now Copley's stomach was doing back springs. "I'm telling you the budget's already stretched to the limit with our new Shangrila Channel. Nothing and no one will stop it from going online."

Branton turned expectantly to Governor Copley. The chief would have a plan; he always did.

"Get the Recovery Squad on him," Copley barked. "I want him back now! And I want him fixed."

Copley leaned in close to the image on the monitor, his eyes fixed on Adam. This might actually be fun— hunting Porter down and fixing him. Perhaps Mr. Porter could test drive one of the experimental implants. Let's see how he reacts to that. Copley's stomach settled down. He smiled with anticipation.

"Relax, Markles my dear," he said. "Mr. Porter will soon be one of us again. And if he resists further, we'll rewrite his job description and pack him off to work at the SPA." *Or send him back to SG for a refit*, he thought, savoring the result.

Markles quietly fumed. Men were so stupid. All they thought about was the bottom line. She had suffered through their arrogance for years and couldn't understand why they didn't see disaster looming on the horizon. She remembered a little ditty her grandmother used to say: "A stitch in time saves nine." It was an anachronistic saying even then—people hadn't stitched clothes in ages; they just threw them away and replaced them with something new. And, since the advent of the virtual vision system, no one even saw the little rips and tears, let alone repaired them.

She knew the repair of the VV system would cost very little money. If they would just put a little extra into upgrading the receiver nanotechnology and improving the nutritional quality of the Universal Food Base, it would solve a lot of problems in the long run. They had finally started outfitting the new receivers with rudimentary tracking capabilities, but Copley said they couldn't afford to retrofit the older subscribers. That's why they couldn't find these Failures. To her mind, another idiotic decision in the early implants. GovCorp had never anticipated the need to be able to track subscribers since, basically, they had become like mindless sheep hiding in Virtual Vision. Now that they needed the old-fashioned GPS tracking technology, who even knew if the satellites were still in orbit? At any rate, without those tracking capabilities, Failures were disappearing all over the city, and possibly into the Underground. She had an especially bad feeling about this Porter fellow.

Back at his apartment, Adam frantically sawed at the plastic handcuffs with a rusty kitchen knife. On the way back from Serenity Gardens, his normal vision had failed and he was stuck with this shit vision again. The manacles snapped off his wrists and fell to the table. He went to the computer terminal near the window.

"What the hell is going on?" he wondered out loud. This confused the home computer, which usually understood his commands.

"Please redefine your question" the computer said.

"I asked for Frontier Vision," Adam snapped. "Where is it?"

He tapped some keys on the keyboard below the monitor, trying to... what? He didn't even know, but he had to do something. He was startled when the system beeped at him. An incoming call. It was Brad.

"Hey, what's up? Geez, you look like shit. Are you okay?"

Adam quickly ran his fingers through his hair and wiped his face with his sleeve.

"I'm fine. Just... jogged home today."

"You're kidding, right?" Brad laughed. "Okay, so listen. Suzie wants to know if you'll come for dinner tomorrow. She's making..."

"Shit." Adam glanced up and out the window. Down the street, a six man Recovery Squad was approaching in formation. They each carried stun guns and police batons.

"What? What's going on?"

"Nothing. I've got to go."

"Wait, what about tomorrow?"

"I can't. I have to go. I'll tell you later."

"But..." The screen went blank on Brad's puzzled face as Adam closed the connection.

As he ran toward the bedroom, his vision finally shifted to Frontier.

"Swell. Now you kick in."

He snatched Trisha's framed photograph from the table by the mirror and tucked it inside his checkered shirt. Bo materialized and bounded down the hallway behind him.

When he reached the bedroom, Adam looked out the window into the gathering darkness. The coast was clear. He opened the window and checked to make sure there was no one around. Bo jumped up and put his paws on the window sill, wagging his tail.

"Bo, stay!" The dog whined but obediently sat down.

Adam could hear the Recovery Squad breaking into the apartment from the front. They hadn't bothered to knock. The entry door sounded like it was being smashed into splinters. He didn't care. He didn't think he'd be coming back here any time soon. He slipped out the second floor window and carefully dropped to the ground below, then ran like hell into the dark night. Back at the cabin, he heard Bo barking at the intruders.

Bo wasn't the only one watching Adam make his escape. A woman stepped from the dark shadows at the side of the building. Her view of Adam was bright as day and tinted with an amber hue. She watched him run down the street, an infrared heat trail in his wake. She was very pretty, even delicate, with long, silken black hair. Except there was something just behind her eyes. Something always alert. Even wary. She hurried after him, far enough back so he wouldn't notice.

Brad Jameson was enjoying an evening in Cartoon Vision. He'd been doing this more often since baby Bradley was born. The living room was a comical cartoon rendition of itself, awash with vivid colors and exaggerated shapes. A sofa with animal feet. A coffee table with a smiling face in its center.

Brad's clothes looked ridiculously silly and fun. He was outfitted as a caped super-hero in red and green tights, and a bright yellow cape. A white "B" was emblazoned across his chest, encircled in a silver braided rope. His hair was a bright orange swirl on his head with one curl bouncing jauntily on his forehead. His freckles looked like they'd been drawn on by hand, covering his nose and cheeks with little circles of brown.

He held the baby above his head as he ran around the room. The one-year-old's matching yellow cape fluttered above him as he stretched out his arms as if he were flying. He squealed with delight.

"Able to leap cartoon couches in a single bound!" Brad shouted dramatically. Superdad and his baby bounded up onto the cartoon sofa and back onto the floor. Then ran around to repeat the process. Three times.

Just before the fourth go-round, Brad saw Suzanne come into the room, a caricature of curly blonde hair and huge blue eyes with lashes like spider's legs. He had picked a pretty purple dress for her with flowered buttons. Not as cartoony as his own outfit, but he knew that she only agreed to the Cartoon channel for his sake, and for the baby's.

"Be careful, daddy," she said. "Your little angel is still learning to use his wings."

Before Brad could think of a clever retort, they were interrupted by a frantic pounding on the door. Suddenly Adam burst into the room and slammed the door behind him. He looked silly in his cartoon clothes with huge buttons and clown shoes. The baby pointed at "Uncle" Adam and began to laugh. His startled parents raised their eyebrows.

"I need your help," Adam gasped. He bent over with his hands on his knees, trying to catch his breath.

"We were just playing super hero," Brad said, smiling. "Want to join us?"

Adam shook his head firmly. "No! And ditch the Cartoon Vision! This is serious. I might not have much time."

"Okay, okay," he replied. "Off line," he told the computer.

"Offline, Adam Porter," Adam added. He didn't want to be stuck in a premium channel with everything else that was happening.

Brad and Suzanne's living room immediately reverted to normal vision. Gone were the cartoon furniture and clothes in their brash colors. In their place was a tastefully furnished cottage.

Adam rested in this brief period of normalcy for about five seconds until another stabbing pain jabbed through his skull. He gripped his head. The pain eased, leaving shit vision in its wake.

He saw his friend as he actually was: dirty, gray, gaunt. He took Brad's arm and led him and the baby to the stained, sagging couch. As they sat, Brad balanced his son on his knee and smiled at him proudly.

Adam struggled to put his confusion and suspicions into the right words. He knew this was going to sound crazy, but there was no other way to say it.

"Something really weird is happening. I think something's wrong with our virtual vision."

Brad was growing increasingly concerned about his friend. Adam's behavior was stranger every time he saw him lately.

Brad spoke quietly to Suzanne and handed her the baby. "Honey, would you go change the baby or something?" He nodded toward the baby's room, hoping she would take the hint. Puzzled, she lifted the child up into her arms and left the room.

"What are you talking about?" Brad asked his friend. He had waited until he was sure his wife was out of earshot. He didn't want to worry her.

"I've been seeing a lot of strange shit since I hit my head," Adam replied.

"What do you mean? Like what?"

"I'm not sure, but..." Adam searched Brad's eyes as he groped for the right words. "Do you ever wonder if any of this real?"

Brad's face clouded. "Adam. What the hell is the matter with you?"

"I don't know! I mean, I'm..." Adam paused to think about how to put this. He didn't really know what was happening himself, so how could he describe it to someone else?

"Look, Brad, I don't think this is the perfect world you believe it is." He couldn't sit still. He jumped up and began pacing.

"Do you have any idea what you're actually wearing? Or how you really look?" Adam gestured wildly about. "This house is a friggin' disgrace! The walls, the floors, the ceiling—they're old and crumbling! Look!" He pointed to a hole in the plaster of an interior wall.

"Did you know there's a hole in the wall there? Come here! Put your hand here! Can't you feel the breeze?" Adam grabbed Brad's hand and yanked him toward the wall.

"Let go of me!" Brad pulled back, freaked. "And keep your voice down. You'll scare the baby, yelling like that."

Adam continued, "Do you know that underneath the virtual vision this house is rotten to the core? Do you understand me? Rotten to the core!"

From Brad's perspective, Adam was a raving lunatic, spouting nonsense. His living room was as bright and cheery as ever. Brad saw no hole in the wall, or anything else Adam described.

"Cripes, man! What the hell are you talking about?" Brad asked.

"Come over here. Look at this!"

Adam yanked Brad over to the window. He appeared to be hallucinating as he pointed out features of the shit vision landscape that Brad couldn't see.

"There aren't any trees out there, Brad! There aren't any real trees! Don't you want to know what happened to the trees?"

Adam pointed to a cute house across the way. Except that it wasn't a cute house to Adam; the roofline was sagging and looked like it would give way any minute. He tried to show Brad a dilapidated brick building with large graffiti written across it: "Madman! Meet me at the Bluebird Café!"

"Who would write that stuff? Do you see it? Who would write 'Madman' on a building? Who's the madman? Who's writing about madmen?!"

Brad couldn't see it, of course. He only saw the neighbor's house, with its tidy lawn and shade tree, same as always. "See what, for God's sake?" he yelled back at Adam, forgetting his own admonishment to keep it down.

"Right there! Meet me at the Bluebird Café!" Adam shouted, jabbing his finger at the air beyond the window. "It's right there!"

From the kitchen, Suzanne listened, worried and scared. Baby Bradley was beginning to whimper from the tension in the air. She hugged his tiny body close to her.

Adam continued his tirade. "Back there in the distance, the buildings are abandoned! Why? Why are so many buildings deserted? Don't you want to know why?!"

Brad struggled to loosen himself from Adam's grip.

"Shit, Adam! What's the matter with you? Are you going nuts or something?"

Adam abruptly realized the futility of trying to convince him. Brad yanked his arm away.

"You're freaking me out, man! Geez!"

Defeated, Adam visibly sagged as the fight went out of him.

"I know this sounds crazy, but something's happening to me. I'm seeing some bogus channel or something. I call it shit vision, so that should give you a clue. Sometimes I think it must be real, but... it can't be, you know? It has to be virtual vision. This is seriously bad, man. It has to be virtual vision."

"Did you see the doctor?" the Brad asked.

"Yeah. They hauled me off to Serenity Gardens."

"Gosh."

"But I lit out of there and now they're after me."

"Who's after you? The police? The police are after you? And you came here? What were you thinking, man?! I got a wife and baby!"

"I know! I'm going! But you gotta do something for me. You gotta try to find out about this 'shit channel.' Who's broadcasting it? And more importantly, how do I shut it off? Promise me, okay?"

"I don't know how..."

"Promise me! I don't have anyone else I can go to. Nobody I can count on..."

"Sure, Adam. You can count on me. I'll find out what happened. Somehow. But you've got to leave. Now! Find some place to hide out. Get in touch with me as soon as you can."

"I will, buddy. And, thanks."

Adam hurried out the door. Suzanne returned from the kitchen with the baby, whose whimpering had ramped up to full-blown wailing. She frowned at Brad as she bounced the baby up and down in her arms.

Outside Brad's house, Adam's virtual vision kicked back in to Frontier Vision. It hardly hurt this time, but it startled him. He hadn't called for it; in fact, he had gone offline when he had entered Brad's house, but now Frontier had popped in unexpectedly. He didn't really mind though. It was his comfort zone, the one place he felt good. He hurried away from the Jameson cabin, keeping close to building walls for cover. He no longer trusted the ability of virtual trees and bushes to hide him. He looked back and saw half a dozen frontier-type deputies running up to Brad's front door. He got outta Dodge as fast as his boots would carry him.

Dr. Freeman came into the room in the middle of the technician's explanation. Markles was gone. Branton sat quietly in the far corner, observing. Copley didn't like it, but thought it prudent to allow one of his staff the knowledge of his future plans. Not all of his strategies actually, but at least the plans for the new Shangrila channel.

"It affects the brain in a particularly addictive and sedative manner," the technician, Robert, said, pointing to a graphic representation of the human brain on the monitor. "A mechanical stimulation of serotonin, also known as 5-HT. 5-HT is associated with twentieth century drugs like Ecstasy and LSD, substances that cause a feeling akin to euphoria and general happiness. Well, LSD was a hallucinogen, but then, isn't that what we're offering in all our channels, programmed hallucinations?"

The doctor interrupted. "But too much can lead to a fatal condition known as serotonin toxicity, as we've discovered in some of our test subjects. So there is an inherent danger in getting the mix wrong. When the mix is right, it will make people very happy, very loving, very docile. A perfect populace and one that would love their fearless leader enormously. Gone wrong, though, the overstimulation of the 5-HT would lead to death."

"Then don't get it wrong," Copley said, glaring at Robert. "I want you to make it so addictive that people won't want to desert the subscriber network no matter what, even if their implants fail. It must ensure subscriber loyalty."

"What about the failsafe mechanism you asked for?" Dr. Freeman asked. "I've been working out how we can get defective implants to terminate the host via nanite intervention."

Branton hid his shock at hearing this. Freeman continued.

"Exactly forty-eight hours after the implant fails, nanites will target the brain's medulla oblongata, which is the nexus of all nerve functions of the entire body. The nanites will attack and destroy it, causing immediate death. This part of the brain is the only part of the human body that cannot be operated upon. It's the life and death regulator. We've been running tests at SG, with mixed results, but I expect we'll have it perfected in a week or two."

Robert smiled. "I came up with a jingle to get people in for repairs, sir, if you'd like to hear it." Copley nodded.

"If you're not feeling up to snuff," Robert sang, "we know life can be real rough, come and see us right away, we will help to save the day. Serenity Gardens."

"I'm sure they'll be as attentive to that as they are to the shave and bathe jingle," Copley said, shaking his head. "Use it. They'll learn to come in quickly enough when their friends start dropping dead all of a sudden."

The meeting broke up then, each promising to keep the governor informed of any developments. Only Branton remained.

"I can count on your discretion, right, Joseph?"

"Of course, sir."

"Good. Now go. I'm sure you must have something official to attend to."

Branton was out the door in seconds. Governor Copley strolled over to the wall and clicked his implant off. His partially eaten apple was turning brown, but he wouldn't waste a bite of it. He sunk his teeth into the juicy flesh and smiled. Things were going well. Except for Porter's escape, things were going very well.

Adam nervously paced the wooden deck of an old Santa Fe railroad platform, surrounded by commuters clad in 19th century garb.

As the steam-powered locomotive chugged into the station, Adam had another attack. This one came easier, with even less pain. His vision shifted and the quaint train and picturesque station transformed into a rust-bucket subway from hell. As the train squealed to a stop, Adam saw "BLUEBIRD EXPRESS" scrawled on the side of a dilapidated car. He joined the throng and boarded the train, head down, trying to look like just another anonymous traveler.

Seated on the filthy coach, Adam studied his bedraggled fellow passengers. Everyone, including him, wore identical, dirty tunics, some in brown, some gray, some black. Also identical was the length of their hair. Every one of them had shoulder-length locks, and most of them were long overdue for a bath and shampoo. The beards on the men were a revelation to Adam. He shaved every Saturday, as was the custom, and he naturally assumed most of the other men did the same. In virtual vision, all of them appeared clean-shaven, and yet now he could see facial hair to some degree or another on just about every one of them. And they all seemed oblivious to their condition.

As he waited for the train to begin its journey, Adam turned his gaze to look out the window beside him. All he could make out was a wrecked and lifeless city. What he could see in the dark was limited to a few windows lit from within, and empty, crumbling streets trying to hide their shameful disrepair from the pale street lights above.

He turned his attention to the torn upholstery of the seat he was sitting on, and then to the other passengers. He didn't notice the mysterious woman watching him, hidden behind a tall man. He tried to fade into the grimy upholstery, just another commuter on his way home. His vision suddenly blinked to Frontier Vision again. Geez! He was getting tired of this back and forth shit.

The passengers had transformed into robust, turn-of-the-century travelers on an Old West train. As the locomotive steamed out of the station, the view out the window was of endless prairie under a star-filled sky and a sliver of first quarter moon. No broken streets; no faded apartment buildings.

Adam tried to look casual as he strolled to the front of the train car to access a public glow screen. Rather than say his name out loud, he placed his palm on the screen for identification.

"Off line," he said softly, trying not to draw any attention to himself. He hoped it would work this time.

Adam turned from the glow screen to see a common city commuter train in normal vision. The passengers, now wearing ordinary tunics, were all facing forward and many of them were staring up at the guy next to the monitor. Staring at him! A wave of paranoia flooded him and he decided against returning to his seat; he didn't want to walk back through that sea of faces. He quickly turned away and yanked open the door to the vestibule between the cars.

The pretty woman watched carefully. In her bright amber vision, she saw him walk to the front of the coach, open the door, and step into the vestibule. She stood up and started to follow.

Adam looked back into the coach and saw a woman in a black tunic approaching, watching him intently. What the hell? He opened the door in front of him and hurried into the next car.

The train rocked gently side to side as it continued to pick up speed, clacking heavy steel wheels on thick steel tracks as Adam moved forward, pushing his way past a few people who stood in the aisle. He kept looking back over his shoulder, as fearful men do. He saw the strange woman in the vestibule behind him, just starting to enter this car. It didn't matter who she was, he didn't want to stop and chat.

The train slowed as it entered the next station. Adam jerked open the door at the front of the car. He looked out and saw half a dozen local police scanning the train windows as it approached. He knew he'd be caught if he left the coach with the other passengers. No choice but to get off now. He turned to the door on the side away from the station and waited for the train to slow, and then, screwing up all his courage, he jumped off before it got to the station.

Adam rolled down the embankment and quickly picked himself up. Nothing broken, just a scraped knee where he first hit the ground. He'd seen cowboys in the vidfilms do similar stunts but he'd never paid much attention to technique. Who knew he'd ever have to pull such a stunt himself one day?

He looked up to see the mystery woman at the train's door, watching him. He had no intention of waiting for her. He was more frightened of her than curious about her. He ran off in the opposite direction as the train pulled into the station, using its mass to hide him from the police who waited for the passengers to disembark.

When he was out of sight of the depot, he stopped to catch his breath. He wasn't used to being so physical. All this running and fearfulness was taking its toll on him. He knew he needed to rest soon, but first he needed a place to hide. He remembered the graffiti on the buildings. He guessed he qualified as a "madman" as well as the next guy. He grabbed a young man's arm.

"Which way to the Bluebird Café?" he demanded.

Irritated, the man gestured up the street.

"Left at the next corner. Can't miss it."

"Thanks."

Adam hurried to the corner and turned left as instructed. He saw it right away. The Bluebird Café. Above the door a blinking neon sign depicted a bluebird perched on a twig, with colorful neon musical notes rising from its beak. The vibrant blues, reds, and yellows shone brightly against the night sky. He stopped outside the door and suddenly remembered something that crazy old man had said to him just before his escape from Serenity Gardens. Something about flying away, little bird, into the blue. Could he have meant this? The Bluebird Café?

It looked like any other bar in town. Regular folks went in and out as he watched. He figured this had to be the place. He didn't really know why he was here, but he knew it probably wasn't safe to stand there in the middle of the sidewalk doing nothing. Finally, he yanked open the door and went inside.

Adam quickly scanned the gloomy little joint. It was ringed with intimate booths of dark, red vinyl benches flanking ancient Formica tables where a dozen barflies sipped their drinks, hoping to fade into the shadows. In the center of the room, couples hunched over half a dozen small, two-person tables. The front windows were covered in smoke-stained blinds that might have been white in a past life. It was the kind of place where nobody knew your name, and you liked it that way. On a small stage in the corner, a female singer did jazz riffs while she accompanied herself on an exotic looking instrument. Actually, she wasn't too bad, considering the venue.

The waiter, a slender young man of about nineteen, moved easily among the tables. He knew the regulars, even some of their rarely-disclosed names, and greeted them with a smile and an unspoken promise of discretion, if necessary. In a far corner, a decorative privacy screen partially obscured the entrance to the restrooms. Well, it might have been decorative at one time; now it was faded and stained from years of living in a low-class, low-life bar like the Bluebird. More than a few drinks had been tossed in anger, contributing to the unique pattern of browns and yellows that dripped down its length.

Adam, tense with anticipation, seated himself on a torn red vinyl stool at the bar and wrapped his feet around its rusted chrome legs. Jake, a large, well-muscled and well-mustached bartender, swabbed the bar in front of him. He had seen that twitchy look before, but he kept his mouth shut. For now.

"Good evening, friend. What'll it be?"

"Vodka, please."

Jake poured the clear liquid and set it in front of him.

Adam reached for the drink but was stopped when Jake slid his beefy paw between Adam's hand and the glass. He tapped his finger on a narrow slot on the bar's surface.

"Payment first," he said.

Adam was embarrassed. He knew that. He'd just forgotten. He wasn't thinking straight lately.

"Yeah, sure," he said as he pulled his credit disk from a pocket and put it in the slot. The slot replied "Thank you" in a pleasant, synthesized female voice. He pulled the disk back out and laid it on the bar.

Jake glanced under the bar to check the readout on the card. It offered a profile of a VR programmer named Adam Porter. He'd have to keep an eye on this one. Jake nodded, slid the vodka closer to Adam, then moved down the bar. Adam gratefully threw the liquor down his throat.

In Security Headquarters, somewhere in the VVN tower, an apathetic young agent monitored a computer screen. For a city this size, there sure wasn't much going on. From the vidvision flicks he watched at home, life used to be a lot more exciting. Back then there were blood and guts in every episode. Those were the days, man. He'd been with Security for three years and he had never even seen a gun, much less shot anybody.

Suddenly, he sat up straight in his chair and called out to the others on night duty. "Hey! I got him back! When he got off the train, he headed into Sector 7. He just used his credit disk at the Bluebird Café."

Two older agents rushed over to look at the screen.

"Good work," his supervisor said, clapping him on the shoulder. "Send the local cops over there. They can pick the guy up for us. It'll take too long for a Recovery Squad to get there—the perp could get away."

The young agent grinned, quite proud of himself, as he quickly dialed the police in Sector 7.

Back at the Bluebird, the mysterious woman in black quietly slipped in and slid into a dark booth with a good view of the bar. She watched Adam closely from the shadows. He didn't notice; he was too busy getting acquainted with his drink. He made quick work of his vodka and flagged the bartender. He held up the empty glass.

"Hit me again."

Adam slipped his credit disk in and out of the slot quickly; the velvet voice said "Thank you."

Over at the booths, one of the regulars, Doug, an unsavory character with a Napoleon complex and a non-stop mouth, sauntered over to the mysterious woman, carrying two drinks in his hand. He didn't ask permission to sit because he figured she'd probably say "no." He parked his bony carcass across from her and slid one of the drinks toward her.

"Hi. My name is Doug. That's 'god' spelled backwards, honey, and all wrapped around 'you'." He gave her his winningest smile, but it still didn't improve his smarmy looks. "What's your name?" he ventured.

The woman considered kicking his ass out of the booth, but on second thought, having him sit there might be good cover. "Raven," she said, keeping her eyes fixed on Adam at the bar.

Hmmm. He usually struck out by now with the good-looking ones. Doug trotted out his best pickup line. "Let's get drunk and take advantage of each other." No response. "Or, I could get drunk and you could just take advantage of me."

Raven shot him a withering look. He backtracked quickly.

"Or, you can stay here and get drunk and I can go home and take advantage of myself," he said. "Either way, it's up to you."

"For the moment, let's just sit here and drink. That okay with you, Dougie?" Her eyes never left Adam's back. Satisfied that he'd actually gotten this far, Doug started telling her the story of his entire boring life. It didn't matter that she wasn't listening, she was there, she was pretty, and she had allowed him to be there with her.

Adam drank this vodka slower, still anxious but not knowing what his next move should be. He idly watched the singer croon her tune. Nobody else paid her any attention. When that drink was gone, he ordered a third. Probably not the best idea under the circumstances, but he couldn't think of a better one. He carefully lined up his empty glass on the bar next to the first one. He used his credit disk again and laid it on the counter next to the empties. Jake brought him another. Definitely loose now, he sipped at his latest drink.

Raven barely listened to Doug rambling on about himself. Her attention remained riveted on her quarry. With her bright amber vision she saw Adam's right hand suddenly shoot out and knock his fresh drink off the bar. She watched closely as he shook his head slightly and rubbed the side of his head. She saw Adam look toward the singer onstage and then around the bar. Raven sunk back into the shadow of the booth. Adam's expression changed from drunken confusion to excited clarity.

In Adam's "shit vision," the joint transformed into an even darker dive. The singer had abruptly gone silent in the middle of a verse, so he looked her way to see that she had disappeared from the tiny stage in the corner. He hadn't realized she was a hologram until then.

Adam's eye was drawn to a large white arrow painted on the side wall of the bar. It pointed to a phantom door that suddenly appeared out of nowhere next to the men's room, partially hidden behind the decorative screen. A big, handwritten message read:

"MADMAN, ENTER HERE."

Raven followed Adam's gaze and studied the same wall with her bright amber vision, but she only saw the privacy screen in front of the brick wall and restrooms. No message, no door.

Adam rose from his stool and lurched toward the newly visible exit. Maybe he'd find some answers behind that door.

Before he'd gotten even halfway there, a dozen police officers burst into the bar. They fanned out and started rousting customers, looking for Adam.

Doug hopped up from the booth before the cops approached. "See ya later, beautiful," he said, and he was off like a shot.

Patrons yelled. Tables overturned. A full-out brawl ensued. Adam ducked down and sneaked toward the corner screen.

Jake shot Adam a dirty look and then he bolted for the privacy screen. "Bobby, let's go!" he yelled to the young waiter. Bobby hopped over a nearby table and hustled out the door.

Adam's spell passed just as Jake followed the boy through the phantom door. In Adam's newly restored normal vision, Jake and the waiter appeared to pass right through the solid brick wall as if it were no more substantial than the cigarette smoke that curled through the Bluebird's air.

Raven sprang to the corner where she saw them disappear. Unable to see the door, she entered the adjacent men's room. A drunk, taking a leak, watched her with a befuddled expression on his face. He shot her a stupid grin.

"Here to help, honey?" he asked.

Raven shot him a look that could freeze hot lava. The drunk fearfully zipped it up and beat a hasty retreat.

She rushed to a window in the dimly lit bathroom and looked outside. In her vision, the alley appeared as bright as day. And empty.

In the bar, a burly police officer exchanged punches with Adam. The cop landed a hard blow to the right side of Adam's skull. Adam went down with a thud. He grabbed his head and jumped back up.

"What do I have, a freaking bull's eye painted on the side of my head?"

His vision immediately flashed to Frontier Vision and the Bluebird became a saloon in the middle of a brawl. Cowboys, saloon gals, chairs breaking over people's heads. Suddenly, his dog, Bo, leaped up onto the table nearest him, barking happily.

"Bo, I thought you were at home!" he said, surprised.

Bo leaped from table to table, growling and barking like it was all a big game.

The holographic chanteuse reappeared, this time as a raucous saloon singer swishing her skirts of satin and lace onstage. She did a loud and bawdy can-can, turned, bent over and flipped her many petticoats up over her pantaloons.

Adam and the burly cop, who now looked like a Western deputy sheriff with a handlebar moustache and shiny tin star, continued to grapple and punch.

The deputy grabbed Adam and threw him at the entertainer head first.

Adam's eyes were huge as his face was about to smack into her ruffled gluteus maximus, but he passed right through it! He landed underneath her, twisted and looked up to see her smiling and winking at him from a few inches above.

"Wanna dance, cowboy?" she said. "You're kinda cute."

The deputy reached through her and grabbed Adam by the shoulders.

Adam's vision surfed again, this time into UltraModern Vision. Everyone looked like they were in an old Flash Gordon vidfilm. Silver lamé clothes, boots, ray guns. The bar looked like the inside of a 1930s science fiction movie space ship. The lounge singer was a two-headed, bug-eyed alien, and she played a Theremin-sounding alien harp.

The Space Ranger fighting Adam yanked him up and back through the singer. Then he leaned Adam against the bar with an arm pressed to Adam's throat.

Adam's vision slid again, this time into Cartoon Vision. Now it was a cartoon cop that had Adam pinned against the bar. Betty Boop giggled and sang up on stage.

The cop pulled a pair of wriggling plastic cuffs with little eyes and snapping mouths from the pocket of his bright blue, big-buttoned suit and was about to clap them on Adam's wrists when cartoon Raven stepped up and smashed an oversized liquor bottle across the cop's head. The cop's eyes crossed, little birdies tweeted over his head and, like a melted ice cube, he slinked down the bar, the bar stool, and into a puddle on the floor.

Adam twisted away from the collapsed cop and looked at cartoon Raven, surprised to find himself face-to-face with the mysterious woman from the train. He recognized her delicate face and intense eyes, despite the Olive Oyl get-up.

"Thanks," he said, puzzled.

"Don't mention it," she said as someone grabbed her arm to take a swing at her. She ducked and threw a punch that sent the guy sprawling.

Adam's vision wavered again to his own special brand of "shit vision." He tried to make his way to the phantom door but there were too many cops between him and that wall. One tried to tackle him. Adam ducked and scooted out of the way. He saw another door on a different wall and headed for it.

Raven, holding her own against the brawlers, watched closely as Adam seemed to clasp a doorknob. But in her amber night vision there was no door. She saw Adam pantomime opening a door and stepping through. She even caught a glimpse of the alley outside. Then the alley and Adam both suddenly disappeared.

Raven rushed over to the wall. She pushed and prodded the area with her fingers, searching for a secret door but, in the confusion, she had gone to the wrong place. Her search found nothing—the wall was solid.

Outside in the alley, Adam jammed the door shut and hunkered down in the recessed doorway, breathing heavily. He couldn't stop trembling. He hoped this was a safe place to rest; with any luck, no one else had seen this phantom door.

The alley in front of him was filthy and cluttered with trash and debris. It was also crawling with rats. One of the loathsome creatures turned and abruptly darted toward the doorway where he crouched. Suddenly, not twelve inches from him, it disappeared. One second it was tearing toward him, the next it was gone. He knew it had to be right there with him, but he could neither see it nor feel it. The space around him wasn't just dark, it was a well of utter blackness. Beyond this four by four doorway, the alley was plainly visible. But in this small space where he crouched, there was absolutely nothing there. Not even the feeble light from the alley crossed the threshold. It was as though he was suspended in space with nothing above or below him. He was completely removed from reality, and he felt utterly disoriented. Nothing made any sense anymore. Whoever said the madman should go to the Bluebird, sure had it right. Any more of this crazy shit and he'd go stark raving mad. And where the hell was that rat?

Inside, the bedlam continued. With her night vision on full, Raven scanned the room. In a corner, she saw three cops trying to pin down a very squirmy Doug, who was small and bony enough to squeeze out of their grasp, only to be tackled by two more of them. She ignored his predicament. Adam Porter had gotten out of there somehow and she wanted to know how he had done it. Raven ran out of the bar.

On the left side of the building, she found an alley. This had to be the one she glimpsed from inside the bar. She knew it was probably dark to anyone else, but she had no problem seeing clear to the other end of it. Even so, she entered cautiously. Thirty feet down, on her right, she saw the bathroom window she had looked out of earlier. That meant the door had to be near here somewhere. She picked up a piece of metal debris and tapped along the wall, looking for the phantom doorway. Tap, tap, moving closer and closer to Adam's position.

Adam saw only the darkness and filth of the alley in his "shit vision." He made himself smaller in the doorway, drawing back deeper into the void. Raven moved ever closer, tap, tap.

The disappearing rat made his presence known by crawling up Adam's leg. He swatted blindly at its warmth and weight. It squeaked and ran off. Adam froze. A sound would alert his pursuer to his whereabouts. Luckily, the noise of the bar fight bled out into the alley and offered some cover for the small sounds of his ragged breathing.

To Raven, even though it was bright as day, there was no sign of Adam or the doorway he was hiding in. The wall along there looked solid. But she was determined. She continued her tapping inspection.

She had nearly reached the doorway. Adam stopped breathing. Tap, tap, closer, closer. She was almost right in front of the recess! He thought she should be able to see him by now. Why couldn't she see him?

Raven whipped around at the sound of a yell. She didn't notice that the piece of metal in her hand had gone right through the wall in front of her. Adam saw its tip disappear as if by magic, and broke out in a sweat. He thought for sure that he'd been discovered. But her attention was drawn to the mouth of the alley where a police officer tackled her pal Doug as he tried to slink away. She didn't want the cops to see her tapping on the walls like that; no doubt they'd arrest her, too, and start asking questions she didn't want to answer, so she tossed aside her stick and hustled, unnoticed, out the back of the alley.

Another cop joined his partner and made a cursory inspection of the area.

"The alley's clean," he said. "Looks like our guy got away. Let's take what we've got and head back."

"Sarge is gonna be pissed we didn't bag the big fish."

"He'll get over it. Let's go; I'm hungry and Maggie's making pot roast tonight."

They snapped a pair of manacles on Doug and hustled him away.

Adam could finally breathe. He was alone, except for the filthy little rats, and had escaped detection, although he couldn't guess how. He didn't think it wise to leave just yet; his pursuers might be waiting for him at either end of the alley or out in the street. Better to give them plenty of time to give up and go home. He hunkered down to wait.

In the blackness, he pulled out the photograph of Trisha and ran his fingers across the front, imagining her face. Then he lowered the photo and touched the side of his head.

He was thinking hard, puzzled, trying to figure this out. Why was he dropping in and out of the different premium channels? Did it have something to do with hitting his head at work? Was he hallucinating? No, he didn't believe that. He was experiencing something that felt very real. So why was he popping into Frontier, Ultramodern, and Cartoon indiscriminately?

And why was he seeing things that weren't there? Or maybe, just maybe, he thought, the rats and the filth really are there. But how could they be? Why had he never seen them before? His confusion lasted until he fell into a fitful sleep, cradled in the black void of an abandoned doorway behind the Bluebird Café.

WEDNESDAY

Governor Jonathan Copley looked out his large picture window at a pristine futuristic cityscape. The morning had brought new problems. Adam Porter was still on the loose and every day, every hour that he was at large, the possibility of his causing an even bigger disruption in Copley's staff grew. Even now, Markles and Branton had squared off across the conference table. As usual, they went at it like squabbling siblings.

"I'm telling you it's not enough! They're not going to catch him!" Markles screeched.

"Take it easy, Maxine," argued Branton. "Recovery Squad will get him. Besides, what can happen? He's just another Failure. They're all crazy, you know."

"My God, you're stupid! What about New Pittsburgh?"

"This isn't New Pittsburgh!"

Markles turned from Branton in disgust.

"Mr. Governor, I implore you. Security Vision is fine for policing subscribers but it's useless for combating these Failures!"

Copley didn't bother to turn around. He didn't even want to look at them. They had become such a pain in the ass lately. If he hadn't been forced to work with them because of their appointment by GovCorp, he would have sent them packing a long time ago. He, too, had been appointed to his position as governor here.

His own anger and disappointment reminded him that Branton and Markles probably felt much the same about being stuck in this backwater town.

He thought about what she had said, and even agreed with some of it. There were a precious few trusted individuals with clickable implants like his own. The clergyman at the cathedral, who inserted the implants under the guise of a christening. Dr. Freeman, who reimplanted the Failures. The private gardener who grew his secret stash of real food. And a skeleton crew of city employees who had to run the utilities and at least make an attempt to do some minimal upkeep on the city's decaying infrastructure. But, aside from those essential personnel, he would never allow anyone else to see what the world really looked like, not even Markles and Branton.

"We can't risk contaminating Security with actual reality just to flush out the Underground," he finally said.

"I'll tell you about risk!" Markles snapped. "Risk is turning a blind eye to a growing army of malcontents!"

"You're suggesting we violate the very core of our Network mandate. No. We will not expose large numbers of our Security personnel to actual reality. Truth is a virus, and we can not afford an epidemic."

He shook his head pensively, gently touching behind his ear.

"Trust me," he continued soothingly. "The situation is not out of hand. Sooner or later Porter will expose the nest to the light, and then we'll be ready."

Markles fumed.

Copley gazed out over the city.

Somewhere in that city, Adam Porter was getting desperate for answers. His normal vision had temporarily returned after sleeping in the cold alley all night, but within minutes, his vision continually shifted from one channel to another. The pain associated with the change had stopped but the effect of the switching was still disorienting and confusing. Now he was walking and thinking, trying to decide what to do. By late afternoon, he found himself in a neighborhood he'd never been in before. A bench at one of the many train depots offered a place to rest for a while. He kept his head low, trying to blend in with the daily commuters, hoping no one he knew would happen by. Across the street, a small restaurant was busy with the dinnertime crowd. He knew there would be a vidphone inside, and he had an idea. He scanned the area for police. Satisfied there were none, he crossed the street and entered.

It was a typical restaurant, with a typically ravenous assemblage of young and old citizens, each enjoying a meal seasoned by the premium channel of their choice.

As Adam entered, his vision distorted to shit vision again. He cringed.

The restaurant was bright, but the sparkling clean fixtures now looked rusted and old. The diners, still contentedly chatting with each other and eating their food, seemed shrunken and pale. Rats and roaches scurried everywhere, stealing bites of food off unattended plates.

Adam saw that the restaurant food had all become just so many versions of identical gray glop. There were bowls of slopped glop and plates of sliced glop. There were sides of mounded glop and frozen glop for dessert.

He was repulsed by how gross it all looked and smelled, and he shuddered as a wave of nausea swept over him.

Dammit, pull yourself together, he thought as he headed for the vidphone booth at the back of the restaurant. He lifted the privacy earpiece off the hook and reached into his pocket for his credit disk. It wasn't there. In a flash, he remembered leaving it on the bar at the Bluebird Café. And he suddenly realized that was how they kept finding him yesterday; on the train he had put his palm on the screen to switch channels, then at the Bluebird he'd used the credit disk. *How could I have been so stupid?* he chided himself. He had to start being more careful. As for now, he needed a credit disk to make that vidphone call. How could he get his hands on one without stealing it or causing a scene? His surroundings suggested a clever plan. Clever if it worked, anyway. He might be putting a noose around his own neck but he didn't see any alternative.

He was right next to the kitchen door. He looked around, and then slipped into the kitchen. Just inside, dirty, tattered aprons hung on hooks. He made sure no one was looking and quickly put one on. He grabbed a plate of steaming sliced glop and swung through the door, back into the dining room.

Adam set the plate on a table as he passed. A prissy young woman glared up at him.

"Hey!" she said. "I didn't order meat loaf! I said a hamburger, you dolt!"

Adam ignored her. He scanned the room and approached a table where a nice, middle-aged husband and wife appeared to be finishing up. Despite their rundown appearance, their decency shone through. He was nervous, but he took a deep breath and stopped at the side of their table.

"Did you enjoy your meal?" Adam asked politely.

"It was delicious, thank you," the husband replied.

Adam rooted around in the apron's pockets.

"I have your bill here somewhere," he said. "Now, where did I put that?"

The husband reached in his pocket and pulled out his credit disk. He handed the disk to Adam.

"Before you total it, add a cup of coffee, will you?"

"Yes, sir," Adam nodded. "I'll be right back with that coffee." He hoped they hadn't seen his hands shaking when he took the disk from them.

He hurried back to the vidphone and inserted the borrowed disk in the slot, checking behind him to make sure the customer didn't notice.

"Dial Brad Jameson," he whispered into the phone. After a few moments, Brad came on the line.

Adam's image had popped into the corner of the screen while Brad relaxed in normal vision watching vids in the living room. He looked around nervously. Was it illegal to answer a vidphone from someone on the lam? But Adam was still his best friend, no matter what. He took the call.

"Brad, listen. I'll be Frank and you be Jesse. I'll meet you at the hideout in an hour. Got that, partner?"

"What? Oh! Oh, yeah. The hideout. Gotcha."

The connection ended and Brad turned to Suzanne, who had just come back from the baby's room.

"We used to pretend we were Frank and Jesse James when we were kids. We had a hideout in the trees in the back of the Porter's old house."

"You're not going to meet him, are you?"

Brad got up from the couch and went to her. He took her in his arms and gave her a kiss and a hug.

"Don't worry, hon. I know what I'm doing."

Suzanne frowned. She doubted very much that he did.

Adam slipped behind the counter and slopped rust-colored water into a chipped mug. He suddenly realized he was famished. He picked up a piece of something gray off a plate and cautiously took a bite. It tasted like nothing the programmers had ever designated as food. If he had lived a couple of hundred years earlier, he would have recognized what tasted a little bit like peanut butter, but mostly like wet cardboard and Elmer's glue. He made himself swallow it but it didn't go down easy. He decided against a second bite. He'd have to get a whole lot hungrier to eat this stuff.

He headed back to the customer's table with the coffee, checking over his shoulder to make sure the manager was busy and not watching.

"Your coffee and your disk, sir," he said, setting the items down on the table. "By the way, you and your lovely wife were our one hundredth customer today. Your dinner is on the house."

The couple's faces lit up. "Well, thank you very much," they said.

"No, thank *you*. You two have a nice day now."

Adam turned toward the front door, shedding the apron as he went.

"Hey! Where's my hamburger?" Miss Priss snapped as he breezed by.

Adam tossed the apron on her head.

"Here. Make it yourself," he told her.

Once again, Adam's vision had involuntarily changed back to normal. Keeping to the shadows of buildings and trees, he found his way to the quiet, suburban neighborhood where he and Brad had been raised. The small houses, still neat and tidy, looked exactly like he remembered. Exactly. Soft, green grass lawns were bordered with rows of yellow pansies and pink rose bushes. Each yard boasted a shade tree which kept the hot afternoon sun off the front porch swing. A little boy bounced a ball in his front yard. He looked up at the stranger as he passed by, and then went back to his game.

Adam approached the vacant house that had been the Porter family home. The place had been vacant since both his parents had passed away five years before. A few years earlier, Adam and Trisha had decided to move closer to the center of the city so he could start his VVN training in the horticultural sciences and follow in his father's footsteps.

David Porter had worked his way up to the head of his department and had encouraged his only son to pursue the same career so that he, too, could enjoy the increased salary and benefits he would get from working as a horticultural programmer at the Network. Adam had been eager to emulate his father, but after Trisha's death, he hadn't wanted to play the office politics game anymore and had accepted that he'd probably always be the guy in the little office on the fourth floor who lived alone in a small apartment in the city. And now, with the population steadily dwindling, no one new had wanted to take up residence here on the outskirts of town. One in every four houses stood empty, including the old Porter place.

He stopped in front of the house and looked at it fondly as memories washed over him. Young Brad, his untamed orange hair ablaze, ran out from behind a tree, shooting his freckled finger at ten-year-old Adam.

"Bang, bang! I got you, Frank James!" Brad yelled.

"You're not allowed to shoot me, you big dope! I'm supposed to be your brother."

Little Trisha Cummings ran from her house across the street and planted herself between the two boys. "I want to play! Can I play, too?"

Adam threw his arms up in the air in exasperation. "Aw, Trisha, girls can't play cowboys."

"They can, too, Adam Porter!" she insisted.

From the front porch, Adam's mother, Lily, called to her son. "Adam! Lunch is ready!"

"Mom, can Brad stay for lunch? Please, Mom? Can he?"

Brad piped in as he riddled Trisha full of imaginary holes. "Bang, bang! But not Trisha. She's a girl! Bang, bang!"

The voices in his memory faded as Adam slowly walked up to the house and onto the porch.

"It's been a long time, Adam," Brad said.

Adam turned to see his old friend sitting at the end of the porch. He walked over slowly, still nostalgic, taking in the wooden porch swing, the shutters on the windows, and the porch railing where he and Brad had dangled their legs and spun their dreams so many years ago.

"And nothing has changed. Except... Funny, I thought the three of us would be pals forever. Who knew?" Adam sighed and tried to shake off the old feelings. "Let's go out back to the hideout so we can talk in peace."

Brad nodded.

The "hideout" looked like the day it was first built. A six by six wooden shed with cowboy photos on the walls and kid-sized furniture to sit on. Adam and Brad squeezed their grown-up sized frames into the tiny chairs.

"Did you find anything out?" Adam asked.

Brad shook his head. "Nothing yet."

"Well, I think I've got an idea how I've been getting free premium channels along with that shit channel I told you about."

Brad leaned in.

"A scrambled signal?"

Adam shook his head no. "A scrambled brain. Look, I think I've got, every one of us has got, some kind of receiver or something implanted in our brains."

"What? Oh, come on."

"I can't believe we've been so dense," Adam continued. "You and I both program the damn stuff and yet we never even wondered how it worked. That's weird as hell, don't you think? It has to be a brain implant. I hate to tell you this, but at the christening..." Adam paused.

"What about the christening?" Brad demanded.

"I... I saw them stick a little metal cylinder into Bradley's skull. I thought I was hallucinating but now I'm pretty sure it was real. You remember? He was screaming bloody murder when they drilled it in."

Brad started to doubt, just a little. But then anger took its place. He refused to believe what Adam was saying. It was just too horrible.

"No. Not my baby. Not my son. They wouldn't hurt my son."

Adam sympathized with his friend. He probably would have felt the same way if the tables were turned.

"Look. I know this sounds like I've flipped my lid, but it's all starting to make sense now."

Brad jumped up and smacked his head on the low ceiling of the children's fort. It just made him madder.

"You're damned straight you've flipped your lid! You should be locked up, man! You should turn yourself in to Serenity Gardens so they can help you!"

Adam jumped up and grabbed Brad's arms, hard.

"Don't you get it, Brad? They killed my wife and my baby girl at Serenity Gardens!" It ripped his heart out to say it out loud. "They don't help people! They turn them into crazy loons, and then they kill them! I saw it! I know! Access the computers and see for yourself! Will you at least do that?"

Brad yanked free, practically screaming at Adam.

"Hell no! I won't! Leave me alone!"

Adam heard noises from outside. He looked out the small window and saw half a dozen Recovery Squad members trotting around the side of the house toward the rear. He turned to Brad in surprise.

"You called them! You told them!" he yelled at Brad.

"What the hell are you talking about?" Brad yelled back.

Adam ripped off the boards framing the open back window, enlarging it. He crawled out the window, then poked his head back in.

"I'll make this simple for you. I won't bother you with my paranoid delusions anymore, okay? Go home to your Cartoon Vision."

Brad watched him disappear into the trees just as the Recovery Squad ripped the door of the hideout off its hinges. A couple of them squeezed into the small space and looked out the back window, searching for Adam. Their special vision saw the woods brighter, clearer, with a slightly rose-colored tone.

Security Vision was a special channel reserved for those law enforcement officers who had worked their way up through the ranks in the various police departments and had been accepted into one of the elite divisions of either the Recovery Squad, VVN Guards, or Copley's Black Guards. It provided them with enhanced vision both night and day. In the daytime, deep shadows disappeared, allowing visual access that might not otherwise be seen. It also provided infrared tracking capabilities so that the increased respiration and body temperature of a sweating, nervous fugitive stood out from that of an ordinary, law-abiding citizen. By night, the infrared capability allowed them to see clearly in the dark and to follow heat signatures of someone who had passed by up to two minutes before.

"He's gone," Brad told them.

They trained their disrupter guns on Brad. Three of them ran back into the woods after their quarry. But Adam had doubled back. He ran around to the front of the houses, looking back over his shoulder to see if he was being followed. For the moment, he didn't see anyone. And he smacked right into the boy bouncing the ball, knocking him down. Horrified, he stopped to help the child up.

"Sorry, kid. You okay?" The scared kid backed away from him, opened his gap-toothed mouth, and let out a blood-curdling scream.

"Shhh!" Adam put his finger to his lips in the universal sign to be quiet, but it was too late. The Squad had already changed direction and ran out from behind the houses. Adam spotted them and started running.

He turned the corner at the end of the block and came upon a family gathering. A dozen people were leaving a party. They called out their good-byes as they walked away. He dropped in behind three of them and made it a foursome. His new date, a tall brunette, looked at him, startled.

The Squad rounded the corner and pulled up short for a moment when they saw all the people. It only took a second for them to register Adam's increased heart rate and respiration with their enhanced vision. Once they'd identified him, they started to run.

Adam, still in normal vision, looked over his shoulder and saw them getting closer. They were looking right at him, so hiding in a crowd hadn't worked. He quickly pushed his way to the front of the group and then made a run for it. One of his pursuers saw Adam running away and yelled out to his partners. They knocked over a couple of indignant party-goers as they took off after their fugitive, but the group had slowed them down.

Adam knew there was a train station three blocks away. If he could get there fast enough and hop a train before the Recovery Squad got there, he might be safe. He ran faster and found a train about to leave. Ahead of him, a few passengers crowded near the first car's door. The Squad followed about fifty yards behind him. One of them fired his disrupter. He missed his quarry and hit a woman bystander near Adam, who grabbed her head and went down. The man shot again, hitting another boarding passenger who fell to his knees on the platform.

The train doors slid shut before Adam reached them. He dashed in front of the train and down the tracks. The train began to roll, slowly at first, then faster.

The Recovery Squad tried to shoot, but the train blocked their view of the fugitive. Even Security Vision didn't help them here.

Adam ran in front of the moving train, which continued to pick up speed. He churned his legs as fast as he could, trying to outrun the steel behemoth. He sprinted along the rails into a narrow passage between two warehouses. The train followed, only a few car lengths behind. There was nowhere for him to turn! Its whistle screamed at him. He felt the panic rise as the train closed the distance between them.

As he reached the end of the short passageway, he saw a culvert immediately to his left. The train was practically nipping at his heels. He jumped and landed with a thud in the culvert as the train thundered past overhead. The ground trembled below him as he took a second to catch his breath and try to calm his pounding heartbeat.

But only a second. He had to get out of there fast, before the train passed and the Recovery Squad came in its wake. His aching legs protested as he quickly pushed himself to his feet and ran off.

He knew this whole area quite well, so he stayed on the side streets as he made his way back to the heart of the city. He used the time to examine what had just happened. Brad had been his best friend since childhood. How could he have betrayed him like that? How could he have notified the authorities like that? Granted, Adam conceded, Brad and Suzanne had a family now and, granted, Adam had put them in jeopardy by involving them in this, but why hadn't Brad just been honest with him and told him he wouldn't help? Why be a back-stabber like that? Adam had been wounded, emotionally, by Brad's duplicity. It hurt more than all the horror he'd been through the last few days.

It was going to be a long walk back to the Bluebird Café. He didn't know where else to go. Night was creeping up on him, the time when all the vibrant colors turned to muted shades of grays and black. Soon it would be mostly black, except for the pinpoints of stars in the sky and the garish neon signs announcing each restaurant, shop, and bar.

He walked for hours until, bone tired, he found a place in a dark alley where he could sit and rest unseen. He felt the little picture frame inside his shirt and pulled it out. Trisha's pretty face smiled out at him. He looked around to be sure that he was alone, and then touched the frame to activate the hologram.

"Happy Anniversary, darling!" her soft voice seemed to whisper as her pregnant image sparkled into life a few feet in front of him. He reached a hand out, wishing he could touch her. "For five years you've been a wonderful husband and I know you're going to be a wonderful father! You're the greatest! I love you, Adam! I love you so much."

Her image retreated into the picture frame and she was gone again, leaving as she had three years ago and a thousand times since then. This hologram, meant to celebrate both their thriving marriage and imminent parenthood, had ironically turned out to be the last recorded image of Trish. He clasped her to his chest and squeezed his eyes closed, hoping to shut out the pain. Instead, it shut out the night. He fell asleep.

THURSDAY

It was bright morning before he awoke. His whole body ached from sleeping on the ground, but mostly from too much action the day before—more running than he'd done since he was a kid, plus the big barroom brawl at the Bluebird Café. Despite occasional virtual fistfights in Frontier Vision, he was basically an office worker who sat around on his rear end all day. Now every muscle in his weary body complained, so he took his time stretching and trying to work the kinks out. It didn't help much.

Trisha's photo had slipped from his fingers as he slept. He carefully picked it up and, after tucking the frame back inside his shirt, he stood up. A quick check of his surroundings assured him that it was safe to continue on his journey. He kept to the shelter of buildings and trees, mostly remaining unseen along the way. It only took another hour to reach the Bluebird Café.

Raven was waiting for him. She knew he'd come back here since he couldn't go home anymore. She figured him to be smart enough to know that his friends, the Jamesons, were also under surveillance so he wouldn't go there, either. He'd come to this place again. She was sure of it.

She was watching from a doorway across the street when she saw his familiar form approaching. She pulled back into the shadows, her eyes glued to her quarry as he trudged cautiously up the street.

He was exhausted. Despite an hour or two of sleep, it had been a long walk from his old neighborhood to this place. He was hungry and thirsty, too. He didn't know if he had the nerve to ask for a handout from the bartender when he arrived, but it became a moot point when he got to the door and found a sign that read:

"CLOSED. OUT OF BUSINESS. GO AWAY."

He couldn't believe it. He tried the door anyway but it was locked. He tried to look in the window but the yellowed blinds were down, and even the small random spaces between a few broken slats showed nothing. It was too dark to see inside.

He was stumped. He had no backup plan, nowhere else to go. He intuitively knew the Bluebird was the end of the line, one way or another. He turned and walked into the alley on the left side of the building.

Raven crossed the road to follow.

Adam searched the alley for the doorway he had hidden in two nights before. He couldn't find it. The side of the building was solid brick. There was no debris, no trash, and there were certainly no rats. He was actually glad of that part. But he was frustrated. He knew that door should be here. He hadn't just imagined sleeping in the recessed doorway, shivering in the cold and sharing the space with those hideous furred creatures.

"Great," he mumbled to himself. "Where's the shit vision when you need it?"

Regretting it before he did it but knowing it had to be done, he smacked the right side of his head with the heel of his hand. Nothing. He smacked it again, harder. A searing pain shot through his head like a knife. This time it worked. Adam's vision obligingly popped into shit vision.

Now he could see the alley with its trash and debris. A couple of rats cooperated with his search by running in and out of the black void he had hidden in. He braced himself and stepped into the nothingness and, fighting the odd sensation of not quite vertigo but definitely disoriented, he felt for the far wall. It was smooth wood, not brick. He nodded slowly. It all made sense now. He felt for the doorknob in the darkness. It was locked. He pounded on it. Nothing. Damn.

Stepping back out of the void, he glanced toward the mouth of the alley and caught a glimpse of the woman in black pulling back out of sight. Oh, great. Her again. He didn't know what her agenda was but her presence hadn't harmed him so far. He walked quickly out the rear of the alley.

Night had fallen. A steady stream of bedraggled pedestrians in frayed tunics passed him on their evening commute home. Adam, still in shit vision, nervously paced the dirty streets near the Bluebird Café. He didn't know why he was still here. He just didn't have any other place to go. Somehow, he hoped that madmen like himself found an answer here and he was going to stick around until something, anything, happened, though he didn't have a clue what that could be.

A neighborhood policeman walked up to the corner. Despite the man's old, standard-issue tunic, Adam knew he was a cop by his badge, holstered disrupter gun, and baton. Adam quickly reversed direction, hoping he hadn't been seen. He didn't notice the woman, Raven, who also changed her course when he changed his.

Adam looked over his shoulder and saw that he hadn't been noticed. He slowed down his pace. The cop must have only been patrolling his beat. He strolled past the front of the Bluebird a half dozen times but nothing had changed; it was still locked down tight. He sighed, frustrated, and moved on. He didn't know where he was going, but he was beginning to think that it was pointless to stick around here. It didn't look like they were going to open the bar again any time soon.

A couple of blocks east of the café, Adam focused in on a pair of suspiciously healthy-looking, clean-cut men carrying rusty, green metal boxes in their arms. Unlike the indistinguishable tunics worn by the other pedestrians on the street, they wore blue jeans and colorful shirts, and their hair was short and clean. One of them looked a lot like the bartender from the Bluebird Café. What was his name? Jake, he thought he'd heard someone call him. So Jake, if that was him, was hauling old boxes somewhere with another guy. Adam was intrigued and decided to follow them.

From a discreet distance, Raven noticed Adam's maneuver. Despite her enhanced vision, she couldn't tell the two men looked better off than the run of the mill citizen. To her, everyone looked healthy and they all wore clean, look-alike tunics. But she could definitely tell that Adam was interested in them.

Adam tailed Jake and his partner while Raven tailed Adam. The two men turned a corner and headed out of sight down a narrow alley. Adam hurried to the top of the alley and peeked around the corner. He watched as they stopped about midway down the passageway and looked in all directions, including up above them, in the windows and on the fire escapes, as though hoping not to be seen. Adam quickly ducked back out of sight and then cautiously peered around the corner just in time to see them walk to their left and disappear through the brick wall of a building. They simply disappeared. One second they were there, and the next they were gone.

Adam knew what he had to do. He flew down the alley after them and, seeing the spot where they had vanished, plunged straight ahead into the dark shadow. But instead of crashing into brick, he went right through it and into a void. In an instant, he was totally blind. He put his arms out and tried to get his bearings. Turning back, he found that he could see the alley beyond the door, but around him, below him, and above him, there was blackness; there was nothing. Just like the doorway behind the Bluebird Café. As he looked toward the rectangle of light framing the alley, the woman in black ran up and charged toward him through the opening. Then she vanished, just like the rat.

Raven had followed Adam into the alley and right through the wall, against her better judgment. She was surprised when she passed through what should have been a solid substance. Once she had gotten through, though, she found herself completely blinded. Her immediate reaction was to roll into a crouched, defensive posture.

Max Mooney, a large, well-built man in his late 30s, and Jake Perkins, the bartender, quickly set down their precious Red Cross boxes and rushed forward to take hold of Adam and Raven. The men could see just fine in these surroundings and had no trouble grabbing the two helpless intruders and holding them fast.

"Somebody get Diana!" yelled Max. "We've got company!"

Adam heard the yell and then footsteps running off into the distance.

A moment later, Diana Ames, a fit and well-groomed natural beauty in tight jeans and a pink tank top, hurried into the hall. She was in her early twenties but life had been hard and she carried herself with the strength and confidence of a much older woman. She went over to the rectangle of light and quickly pulled down the sliding metal door. This plunged Adam into total blindness. He struggled to shake off Jake's grip.

"Hey, let go of me! Who shut out the lights?" he growled.

"Close your eyes and you won't feel so disoriented," Diana said calmly, walking around the two captives to look them over. Interesting differences—the man was dirty and tattered, and struggling against his captor; the woman was in a plain black tunic and at least had tried to improve her appearance a bit. Diana wondered who she might be, and why she stood quietly instead of fighting them, as the man did. They didn't look as though they belonged together, and yet here they both were.

"Okay," she said. "Who are you and what are you doing here?"

"This is the jerk that brought the cops down on my place the other night," Jake said. He took a good look at Raven. "She was there, too."

"Hold them till I get back," she said. "I think Dad needs to see this." She hustled out of the room, leaving Adam confused and more than a little afraid.

The storeroom in the secret complex was piled high with scores of ancient, dusty crates, the pickings of expert scavengers. Jason Ames, the leader of the

Underground, piloted his wheelchair slowly among the crates with his lieutenant, Javier Mendez. Like the others, they both wore jeans and shirts, not tunics.

"The medical supplies warehouse was packed. We spent most of the day cataloging and didn't even cover half the haul," Javier told Jason.

"This is good news," he replied. "What condition are the supplies in?"

They paused beside some open crates. Javier rummaged through one and pulled out a hypodermic syringe. He held it out to Jason.

"Pretty damn good," he said. "Look at the plastic on this syringe. You'd never know it'd been sitting so long."

Diana's arrival interrupted their inspection. "Dad, there's a couple of VV subscribers at the door. The one who escaped from Serenity Gardens and a woman who was upstairs at the Bluebird the night of the fight."

Jason wheeled his chair around. "Let's go see what we have."

While they waited for their boss, Jake patted down Adam and Raven, looking for weapons. They couldn't be too careful; it was rare that someone stumbled into the Underground like this. Raven's search turned up an intricately carved, bone-handled knife strapped to her ankle. Adam's pat-down revealed a five by seven photo in a frame.

"Pretty lady," Jake said, turning Trisha's photo over in his hands. "Kinda big though. I just carry my girlfriend's picture in my wallet."

"You don't have a girlfriend," Max said.

"Yeah, yeah. Just making a point. Hell of a big picture to carry around with you."

"Give it back," Adam said. Click. Out of the utter blackness, Trisha's hologram appeared. It was the only thing Adam had seen since the alley door had been shut. He gasped. Trisha's holo always punched him in the gut, but seeing her this way, as if she were the only other thing in an empty universe, was unbearable.

"Happy Anniversary, darling!" Her blue eyes had never looked more intense; her hair never more golden. "For five years you've been a wonderful husband."

Adam groaned. His heart felt like it was about to break.

"And I know you're going to be a wonderful father! You're the greatest!" In the inky blackness, Trisha pursed her lips to blow him a kiss.

"Shut it off, damn you! Shut it off!" Adam cried out.

Max and Jake couldn't see or hear Trisha. They could only see Adam's agonized responses.

"What's he talking about?" Jake asked Max. "Shut what off?"

"It's probably a hologram," Max said. He took the picture from Jake and tossed it on a table.

Jason, Diana, and Javier entered the room. Adam and Raven still stood between their guerrilla guards.

Javier was shocked to see Raven. He bent down and whispered something to Jason who looked at Raven, frowned, and nodded.

"Take the woman to Room 12," ordered Jason. "Diana, check outside and make sure these two weren't followed. Jake, you and Max keep an eye on Mr. Porter here until I return."

Adam listened helplessly as the guerrillas hustled Raven out of the room. Jason and Javier followed. Diana headed out the door.

Once they were gone, Jake grabbed Adam by the shoulders and shoved him against the wall.

"And another thing! You brought the cops to my bar, asshole!" Jake bellowed.

"They must have followed me! I tried to lose them!" Adam said.

"Yeah, right. How stupid are you, anyway? You used your own credit disk to pay for your drinks," Jake hissed.

"Sorry, man. I didn't think of it till later..."

"And they knew right where to find you," Jake spat out.

"Cool it, Jakie," Max said. "What's done is done. We'll find you another joint just as sweet and classy as the Bluebird. Let the guy go."

Jake abruptly released Adam.

"Your credit check says you work for VVN," Max said to Adam. "What do you do?"

"I'm a New Projects Designer. I make flowers, alright? Who are you people? What's going on here?"

Rather than giving out any answers, Max probed further.

"You must have figured it out, Adam, or you couldn't have found us."

Adam slowly nodded his head. "Yeah, I've got a sneaking suspicion that Copley and his pals have been pulling the virtual wool over our eyes."

"So you're not a total idiot after all," Jake said.

"The short and sweet truth is this: what you think of as off line is just another channel," Max explained. "Used to be called Basic Service. You haven't really been off line since they stuck that thing in your head."

Adam nodded his head slowly, his expression grim. He wouldn't have believed it a week ago, but now he had no doubt.

Raven sat alone in the small holding room, patiently, blindly, no expression on her face. She heard footsteps approaching out in the hall. They stopped on the other side of the door. She could just barely hear a murmured exchange but couldn't make out the words. A key turned in the lock and the door opened. Someone walked into the room.

Jason and Javier came in and closed the door behind them. Raven, with her eyes closed, tracked their every movement as they drew near. Javier stopped directly in front of her.

"Hello, Raven," Javier said. At the sound of his voice, she rose from the bench.

"Javier, you son of a bitch," she said.

"I'm glad to see you, too. Took you long enough to get here."

"And just where is 'here'?" she asked.

"That isn't something you need to know," Jason interjected. Raven turned to the new voice.

"Who are you?" she asked.

"I'm the one who's asking the questions," Jason replied. "Now that you've found us, what do you intend to do about it?"

"Not a hell of a lot, mister. I'm kind of at a disadvantage here. No weapon. No sight."

"He means," Javier said, "are you here as a cop?"

Raven sat down, pensive. She waited a few moments before speaking.

"I've always been a cop, and a damn good one. So were you, Javier," she said, nodding in his direction. "But things are changing out there and I don't know if I like it. Tell me about 'here' and I'll let you know."

Jason headed for the door. He turned to his friend. "Javier, not too much," he warned him. "We may have to send her back."

"Sure thing, boss. We'll catch up on old times. What do you say, Raven?"

"I'm listening, partner," Raven said, smiling. "Talk to me."

Jason wheeled out, looking over his shoulder at her. He knew not to trust any newcomers until they'd proved themselves. And despite his complete faith in Javier, a former member of Copley's elite Black Guard, he especially distrusted cops, even the "failures" that went on to choose actual reality. They had to prove themselves doubly.

In a nearby room, Jason joined Diana across a table from Adam, who had squeezed his eyes tightly shut, trying to convince his brain that he wasn't floating in a black void of nonexistence. Max and Jake had gone to deliver the Red Cross supplies to the infirmary. Before leaving, Jake had taken Jason aside and filled him in on the information that he had seen in Adam Porter's readout at the bar the other night. Max had then taken a minute to probe further and learned more on a nearby computer terminal that held business and personal data on almost everyone who had ever worked at Virtual Vision Network. As they left, they returned Trish's photo to Adam. He gently laid it down on the table in front of him, but kept his hand on it, afraid it would disappear in the void.

"Everyone is fitted with implants soon after birth," Jason explained.

Adam nodded his head. "The christening."

"That's what they call it," Diana said. "It's barbaric. Incredibly painful and cruel."

"Your implant seems to be malfunctioning," Jason said. "What happened?"

"I fell at work. Smacked my head back here." He touched his skull behind his ear. "I could see everything before; it kept shifting from channel to channel, but I could see. Why not here?"

"You can't see this place because it's not plugged into the Virtual Vision databanks," said Jason.

Adam nodded with understanding. "You mean any sector not programmed for overlays would appear as a black void?"

"Right," Jason said. "When the original programmers mapped out the city, they conveniently overlooked whole buildings, like the one you're sitting in now."

"And you can see these spaces, but I can't? Why?"

"No more implants," Jason said. "They've been yanked."

Adam was dumbfounded. "But then, you can't see virtual vision at all!"

"It's a choice people make, Adam," Diana said. "You can't have it both ways."

Jason leaned forward in his wheelchair. "Just so you know, if we remove your receiver, your ass is ours."

"What's that supposed to mean?" Adam asked.

"After the implant is out, there's no going back. No more virtual vision. No more Frontier Vision. No more..."

Jason's eyes fell on Trisha's photo lying on the table between them.

"No more holograms," he said. "You'll have the photo, but no hologram."

Adam shook his head. He was having a hard time wrapping his brain around the concept of no more virtual vision. "You can't expect me to just disappear. I have a job, friends."

"And Serenity Gardens waiting with open arms," interrupted Jason. "If they get you back, they'll put a new implant in you and you'll never get away from them again. The new ones have tracking capabilities. Even if they malfunction, Copley's goons will find you. Or maybe you won't be so lucky. Maybe you'll wind up a slave at the glop factory or the solar array. So make up your mind. It's time to choose, Porter. Truth or virtual vision."

Adam shook his head again, still reluctant, still resisting. The shock of the last few days, coupled with the stark realization that his whole life had been a lie, was almost too much for him. And who were these people, anyway. Could he trust them? Did they mean him harm? Were they just lying, too?

Diana couldn't understand his hesitation. If she had just discovered she had an implant, she'd want it out this minute. "Come on. Get real. What other choice do you have?"

Adam's hand lifted the photograph and clutched it to his chest. No more holograms. No more Trish.

"You don't know what you're asking me to give up!" he protested.

Jason reached across the table and gently laid a hand on Adam's arm.

"She was a beautiful woman, Adam," he said. "How long has it been?"

Adam hesitated. "Three years."

"It's time to let it go," he said, reaching out for the photo in Adam's hands.

Adam pulled back from Jason, clutching the frame even tighter to his chest.

"I can't," he said, his voice choked with emotion.

Jason gently repeated, "Let it go."

Adams bowed his head, eyes squeezed shut. Slowly, he eased his grip on Trish's photo. His hands drifted toward the table top. He hesitated. His hands shook as he laid the photo on the table and slowly pushed it away, out of reach. He took a deep, ragged breath. He didn't seem to have a choice—he'd have to trust them. For now.

Back in the holding room, Javier sat opposite Raven, who was also still blinded by the blackness of the void. He was fiddling with her bone-handled knife. He was pleased to see that she still carried it; he had given it to her on her birthday. The carving was of a raven, and she had treasured it.

"You've seen this decay with your own eyes?" she asked him.

"All of it. Without the implant, all you see is what's real. And it sucks, Raven. If it ain't fixed soon, you're looking at the end, baby. No more city. No more people. I kid you not."

"There must be something..." she protested.

"I'm telling you, there's no other way. We tried negotiating, pleading. Didn't work. That asshole, Copley, would just as soon see all of us dead. He won't compromise on virtual vision at all. He just wants to sit up there in his ebony tower and rake in the dough from all his idiot subscribers. Well, I'm not an idiot anymore. I know what's going on and I don't like it. What about you, babe? You need to decide. Are you with us or do we send Alice back to Wonderland?"

Raven smiled. Javier had forgotten how beautiful she was when she smiled.

"Javier, I spent the last six months looking for you. If you think I'm leaving now, you're crazy."

He was really happy to hear her say that. Happier than he'd been in a long time.

Adam reclined in an operating chair, eyes closed, his head clamped in a vice. There was an intravenous needle in his arm attached to a glucose drip on a pole. The medic, Flo, sewed his scalp shut. She was older than dirt but had the personality of a teenager. And more importantly, she was good at diagnosing and healing. She had started her career as a resident at Serenity Gardens. A faulty implant had revealed the horrors of that place, but her efforts to correct the problems had resulted in the termination from her position there. Had she persisted, it might have led to her ultimate termination, period. So she found her way to the Underground. Old Doc Morgan, since deceased, had removed her implant. She had never looked back.

She unclamped the head vice. "OK. You can open your eyes now."

Adam opened his eyes and looked at the ceiling. He blinked involuntarily at the bright lights until his eyes adjusted to his new environment. For a moment, he was unnerved to find himself in hospital surroundings, but a quick look around convinced him that this place was no Serenity Gardens.

The infirmary was a bright, cheerful place. The walls were white and lined with shelves and cabinets filled with medical supplies and equipment. The hospital beds on the far wall were empty, and made up with fresh white sheets and newly fluffed pillows. Although obviously old, the equipment looked sanitary, rust-free, and well-maintained. The place even smelled clean.

Flo raised the chair to its upright position.

"How do you feel? Are you dizzy?" she asked.

Adam gingerly touched the sutures on his head. He slowly ratcheted his head back and forth.

"No," he said. "Except for having half my brain yanked out, I feel just peachy."

Flo picked up her surgical clamp and pulled the VV receiver from the metal bedpan at his side. It was a small metallic cylinder with short, wire-like tentacles. She held the device out for Adam to inspect.

"Ugly little thing, isn't it? But the nanotechnology is a marvel. To think these started out as simple identity chips for dogs." Flo dropped the implant with a clang back into the pan. "Just so you know, I got this bugger out, but there's still a shitload of nanites traipsing around in your skull. They won't hurt anything, and without the implant they're just dancing in the dark. So, you won't be bothered by them and after that suture heals; you'll never even be able to tell you were implanted." She shook her head. "Amazes me that people out there don't even wonder how virtual vision works."

Flo removed the IV and covered the small wound with a piece of gauze and some adhesive tape. "I gave you a glucose drip because you were dehydrated. That ought to plump you up a little bit and tide you over 'til breakfast."

She poured Adam a drink of clear liquid and handed it to him.

"Here, drink this. This'll take care of that headache."

"Some kind of medicine?" Adam asked. He took a careful sip and then looked at the glass in surprise.

"Vodka," she said, smiling. "Isn't that what you drink?"

She poured herself a shot of vodka, too, and threw it back.

"Whew. Even real vodka."

"We distill it ourselves," Flo said.

"Tell me more about these implants," Adam said.

Flo settled back and poured herself another drink.

"At first they were optional so that people who wanted to hide from reality could forget about the pollution and ruined eco-system of The Cataclysm. But when GovCorp tried to make it mandatory for everybody, civil rights groups got their panties in a bunch and refused. That didn't stop GovCorp; they just started doing it secretly to the babies at a phony christening. After a generation or two, nobody remembered it being any other way."

Diana entered the infirmary. She smiled at Adam, who got his first look at her. She was quite attractive even without virtual enhancement, with dark curly hair that she pulled back to reveal a narrow face and large green eyes. Her tight jeans showed her compact, muscular legs, and the sweater she had put on over her tank top didn't hide her other attributes.

"How are you doing?" she asked.

Adam returned Diana's smile. Now that he could see her, he liked her look; it fit her voice well.

"Better all the time. What's next? My wisdom teeth?"

Diana took Adam's arm and helped him stand. He swayed a little.

"Whoa..." he said. He grabbed Diana to stabilize himself, and noticed how broad and muscular her shoulders were. He quickly pulled his hands away, a little embarrassed, but it didn't seem to affect her at all. She reached right out and placed a strong hand on his arm, at the elbow.

"You'll experience some vertigo for the next few hours, so you might as well sleep it off," she said. "Come on, we'll find you a place to bed down." She kept her hand firmly under his arm to steady him as they made for the infirmary exit.

"Good night, Flo," Adam said. "And thanks. The headache's gone."

Flo waved them off and poured herself another shot. Diana grinned.

"Most docs give you aspirin for a headache. Not our Flo."

"Whatever works," Adam said.

They walked slowly down a dimly lit corridor. His legs had steadied under him and his eyes were drinking in the "truth" as Jason had put it. Actual reality, with no overlays, no channels, no lies. The corridors were simple and unadorned, but, like the infirmary, they were all clean and orderly. Diana and, for that matter, everyone they passed along the way, looked healthy and clean. No one was wearing a tunic; blue jeans and colorful shirts were the choice for almost all of them. Diana even had on a touch of pale pink lipstick and a pink barrette in her hair. It was all so far removed from what he had known all his life, and especially from the shit vision of the past couple of days. *So this is reality,* he thought. *I could get used to this.*

Diana's sweater pocket began to squirm. A fuzzy little head suddenly poked out the top. Adam recoiled in horror.

"Shit! What the... ?"

Diana laughed and pulled out her pet rat. "Well, look who woke up." She scratched his gray head and kissed his nose.

"This is my friend, Boomer," she said, rubbing the rat against her cheek. Adam took a quick step back, disgusted.

"I've seen those running in the shadows. That's a rat, isn't it?"

"Yes, and as far as we can tell, they're the only other mammals surviving on the planet."

Adam suddenly thought of his pal Bo and realized he'd never see him again. Man, he'd miss that dog.

"Want to pet him?" Diana asked. "He won't bite." She held Boomer out toward Adam.

Adam carefully raised a finger and nervously scratched behind the rat's ears. The little creature felt warm to his touch. He let his finger stroke the length of Boomer's back, feeling each tiny vertebrae.

"It's so soft," he said, wonderingly. It looked different from the ones he had seen in the alley outside the Bluebird Café. Those were dirty, with nasty looking eyes. They looked wild, as they were. But this rat was clean and looked gentle and sweet. Its fur looked well-groomed and it was completely comfortable being held and touched by the two humans.

Diana brought Boomer back to her lips and nuzzled him.

"If it weren't for Boomer and his friends," she said, "we'd be all alone here."

They continued a little further up the hall and then stopped before a door. Diana pushed open the unlocked entrance.

"It's late. You must be beat. Here's your room for tonight. There's a snack on the cot. You'll have a proper breakfast in the morning."

"Thanks," Adam said. He paused in the doorway. He hadn't realized how utterly exhausted he was until that moment. The thought of a real bed under his aching bones, a pillow for his head; his legs were ready to give way under him, just knowing they were so close.

Diana gently touched Adam's arm.

"Adam," she quietly said.

"Yeah?"

"Welcome to the real world."

"Thanks," he said.

Adam entered the room and closed the door.

Brad sat in the dark, his face illuminated by the monitor on the computer terminal. He lifted his hands to the keyboard, hesitated a second, then tapped on a few keys. He had decided to use the keyboard instead of voice commands so that Suzanne wouldn't hear him. He looked over his shoulder to be sure she wasn't around.

He tapped a key and the VVN logo appeared. Tapped another key and the screen said "Accessing remote location." Tapped a couple of more keys. "Searching..."

Suzanne's voice rang out sharply from nearby. "What are you doing?"

Brad nearly jumped out of his skin.

"Lights," Suzanne commanded the house computer. The room lights came up and Suzanne walked over and looked at the monitor. The VVN logo was plainly visible behind the onscreen commands.

"I just thought I'd check a couple things," Brad said.

Suzanne's voice rose. "Don't tell me you believe him! How could you? He's sick. He hasn't been right since Trish and the baby died." Her voice dropped to a soothing tone. "Brad, honey, he just finally lost it."

Brad slowly shook his head. "I don't know. Some of the things he said made sense."

She sat next to him and took his face in her hands. She gazed thoughtfully into his eyes.

"No," she said, firmly. "None of it makes sense. I know he's your best friend but let's face it, he's asking

120

you to do something that could get us into a lot of trouble."

Brad reached up and clasped her hands in his, pulling them down to rest between them. He squeezed her hands reassuringly as he spoke. "I just want to check..."

"They'll know!" Suzanne protested. "And they'll come here again!"

"They didn't do anything but ask us a few questions..."

Suzanne threw his hands down. "No! You stop this instant! Your wife and baby come first, do you understand?"

Brad slowly nodded his acquiescence. Suzanne reached over and punched a key. The screen went blank.

"That's better," she said. "Now come to bed, please?"

She stood and headed for the bedroom. She stopped and turned. Brad still sat at the computer. He loved his wife and baby more than life itself. But Adam had been his best friend since childhood. He loved him, too, and wanted desperately to help him somehow.

"Brad?" she said. It was more a command than a question.

He slowly rose and followed her, his head hung low.

FRIDAY

Early the next morning, Adam tossed fitfully on his bed, moaning lightly in his sleep. Diana knocked gently on the door. No answer. She knocked again and then opened the door a few inches. She could see that he was dreaming. *Poor thing*, she thought. *It'll take a while.* She tiptoed in and shook Adam's shoulder as he tossed and mumbled.

"Hey, Adam. Wake up. Wake up!" she said.

Adam's eyes popped open. He didn't know where he was. His brain was still in that limbo place between the dream state and the waking state. The first thing he saw was Boomer on Diana's shoulder. His reaction was instinctual; he reached one hand toward Boomer and with the other hand grabbed her wrist.

"Trisha! Look out!"

"Whoa there, Adam! It's me, Diana." She stepped back quickly, pulling her wrist from his grasp.

Adam's eyes cleared as he woke up. He leaned up on one elbow.

"Sorry," he said, glancing at Trisha's photograph on the table a few inches from the bed.

He tossed the blanket aside and sat on the edge of the bed.

Diana spoke gently. "It's a cliché but it's true: Today is the first day of the rest of your life, Adam."

"Yeah. I know. I guess sometimes life grabs you by the balls and gives them a good shake. If you're lucky, it rattles your brain a little, too."

"Ouch."

"Thanks. I'll live."

"I know you will. You hungry?"

"Hell, yes. Except for those crackers you left me, I don't think I've eaten in days."

"Well, then, let's get a move on before the mess hall stops serving."

Diana pointed to a stack of neatly folded clothes on a chair.

"There's a clean change of clothes for you. I'll wait in the hall."

She left and closed the door behind her. He found a small basin of cool water and a piece of cloth on a table beside the bed. It felt good to wash up and actually see the grime dripping back down into the pan. He splashed the water over his hair and face, then he tackled the rest of his body. Cleaner and somewhat refreshed, he slipped into the fresh tunic. He found an old but still serviceable pair of brown loafers on the floor under the chair. He was just about to pull the door open when he noticed a small mirror hung on the wall. The last time he had looked into a mirror, he had been horrified to see the dirty, gaunt stranger staring back at him. He was still gaunt, but he was cleaner. He raked his fingers through his still damp, shoulder-length hair, trying to tame it into submission. He only half succeeded, but he was satisfied with his effort. Adam picked up the photo on the table.

"Morning, Trish," he said.

His fingers rested on the small, hidden button that would have activated her hologram. She wouldn't be saying anything back this morning, or ever again. He sighed and set the photo down, then pulled the door open to face the new day.

Diana smiled when she saw how he had cleaned up. "Well, look at you. Not bad at all. And I bet you're starving."

"There's an understatement," he said. He wasn't quite ready to return her smile yet, still trying to adjust to his new reality. But he appreciated her cheerfulness. "Lead the way."

As they walked through the underground complex, Boomer rode comfortably on Diana's shoulder. She sensed that Adam wasn't feeling very talkative, so they walked in silence. He was using the time to see, really see, everything around him. And trying to memorize the passage so that he could find his way back to his room. Suddenly, he caught the aroma of fresh vegetation as they passed the open door to the hydroponics complex. He stopped, closed his eyes, and took several deep breaths.

"Orange blossoms... Green onions... Sweet peas!"

"I'm impressed. We grow all our own food here. Real food, not the glop you've been eating."

Adam and Diana stepped into the huge hydroponics garden. Row upon row of thriving fruits and vegetables strained up toward hundreds of high intensity grow lamps hanging from the ceiling of what used to be an underground parking garage. The gardeners nodded to Diana and went about their daily chores.

Adam was delighted by the sight and smell of live vegetation. He paused beside the first plant they encountered, a tub of tomatoes, and buried his face in its leaves.

"Tomatoes! Wow! All my life I've been creating virtual gardens. I'm an expert on the smells of plants. But this! This is incredible!" He straightened back up and excitedly sniffed the air like Bo catching scent of a deer. "Where's that orange tree?" he asked, scanning the room.

He hurried to a potted orange tree in full bloom. He tenderly stroked its trunk as he inhaled deeply. Then he saw...

"Lemons! I see lemons!"

He rushed to the lemon tree and rubbed one of the dimpled, yellow orbs between his fingers, then took his hand away and smelled the fruit's oil on his skin.

"Wow. This is so great. But, how?"

"It took a lot of years of trial and error to find the seeds that were still viable."

"Seeds?"

"Mostly from abandoned hardware stores and gardening stores. Vegetable seeds, fruits, even bird seed from pet shops. We tried all of it. After over a hundred years on the shelf, only a few seeds were still good. A dozen or two of each species was enough for cross-pollination and continued propagation. We've even created a few hybrids."

"Bird seed?" He moved between the rows, watching the gardeners tend the plants lovingly. What he had done with his Simu-Strip in his office seemed pointless to him now. This was real and he wanted to hug every tree and bush in the place.

"Mostly millet and hemp," she said. "We grind it into flour for breads, and a lot of other things. In fact, you'll be having millet porridge for breakfast."

Breakfast. His stomach was telling him to go, but his eyes, his nose, his hands wanted to stay and drink it all in.

Diana touched his back lightly.

"We can come back another time; it will always be here. But the mess hall is about to close and I'm starved. And you need to eat."

Adam was clearly reluctant to go. He gazed longingly at the grow room before leaving.

There was seating for a couple hundred in the simple hall but, besides Adam and Diana, only a few stragglers remained. He wondered just how many people lived down here, off the grid. He had seen about two dozen so far, in the halls, the hydroponics lab, and now here. He expected he'd find out sooner or later.

On one side of the large room, a vidvision screen hung high on the wall. It was blank; no one had bothered to turn it on. His own vidvision at home was always on. It didn't come with an 'Off' switch. The too-peppy pitchman who touted VVN's channels continued all night, but in a whisper. It seemed ridiculous to him now. Nearby, there were a few cushioned chairs in an alcove. A small shelving unit had stacks of faded boxes that he didn't recognize. One said "Monopoly," another said "Clue."

They ate a breakfast of golden millet porridge topped with almonds and bright red strawberries. Adam was amazed by the feeling of the different textures in his mouth—the contrast between the little pearls of hot millet and the crunchy resistance of the raw almonds. And the strawberries! The strawberries were juicy and so sweet they were like nothing he had experienced before. There was no comparison to the ones he was eating just days ago before the gunfight in his little log cabin. Had it only been a few days? It felt like a lifetime ago.

Boomer nibbled a strawberry from Diana's bowl.

"This is incredible," Adam said. "And I thought nothing could top that grow room."

"We do the best we can with what we've got," Diana said, smiling. She always enjoyed watching newcomers eat their first meal. "Eat slowly," she continued. "This is your first real food. If you gulp it or eat too much, you'll get sick. And it's a far trip to the restrooms." An awkward warning, but better said than left for him to find out the hard way.

He nodded as he chewed, happy to take his time and savor every bite.

"How did you come here, Diana?" Adam asked around a mouthful of berries.

"Oh, I was born in the Underground."

Adam swallowed hard and looked at her, amazed.

"Does that surprise you?" she asked.

"Well, yeah. I just never considered the possibility..."

Adam looked carefully at the other people in the room.

"Are there others who were born here?"

"A few."

"So there are... children? Babies?"

"Our per capita birthrate is higher than out there. Better nutrition and hygiene. And better medical care. I'm sorry you didn't have that for Trisha."

Adam nodded and looked away. These people knew so much about him.

"Everything you need... right here," he said.

"That's right. Everything except freedom. It's home, but it's still a cage down here. And it's been that way for thirty-five years."

Just then, Jason rolled into the room and scanned the tables. At fifty-five, his dark hair was sprinkled with gray and his face was showing the lines and wrinkles he had earned from his years as a rebel. While his legs were thin from the paralysis, his upper body was muscled and strong. He could push his wheelchair faster than most people could walk (for which he was often teased by Jake to "slow the hell down.") He didn't see any point in taking his time when he had the advantage of speed to get him where he needed to be. He finally saw Diana and Adam, and rolled quickly to the end of their breakfast table.

"Good morning," he said. "How are you feeling today?"

"Not too bad," Adam replied. "Enjoying this food here. I'm impressed with your grow room. It's pretty amazing. You've accomplished some wonderful stuff."

"Thanks, we've learned to adapt. After you get settled, maybe you could work in there. Would you like that?"

"Hell, I'd love it. That would be great."

Jason smiled as he turned to leave. "I'll be happy to arrange it. Diana, I stopped by to tell you that we're on for tomorrow afternoon. Bring Adam."

"Sure, Dad," she said, frowning, as he disappeared out the door. She turned back to Adam. "He never rests. Thirty-five years on the go."

"Can I ask you how this all got started?"

"His implant failed when he was twenty years old. He didn't know what the hell was going on, or who to turn to. Implant failures were rare back then. He walked for days like that, in shock, thinking he was going crazy."

"I know how that feels." He tossed another strawberry into his mouth.

Diana continued. She had told this story to newcomers so many times before. "One day, he made eye contact on the street with a pretty girl and it was obvious that she didn't look as neglected as everyone else. She also recognized him as being different. Over the next year or two several more people joined them, including Doc Morgan, who figured out how to remove the implants. It was an amazing leap forward for them. No more wandering like lost souls out in the streets. They made incredible discoveries about the system, and they found these spaces, mostly all underground, that were unprogrammed and invisible to the others.

"At first they were happy enough just to grow their own food and live their own lives, but eventually they decided they needed to help everyone escape the clutches of the Network. So they cooked up different ways to cause trouble for the big brass at VVN.

"They called themselves the 'Keepers'. A bit pretentious," she laughed, "but it does accurately describe who we are and what our goals are. We try to keep the truth alive by preserving the culture, traditions, and knowledge of the time before The Cataclysm. And one of the fun things we do to avoid monotony is pull down VVN booster towers around town, disrupting broadcast services whenever possible."

"I never heard of any disruptions like that."

"Of course you didn't. The Network doesn't want the 'Sleepers' to hear anything about this kind of stuff."

"The 'Sleepers'?" he asked.

"Yeah. You know—the ordinary people out there who live their whole lives in a dream state, never waking up to the real world around them. You were one of them until last night."

Adam felt a bit overwhelmed by all the information. His brain was still adjusting to life without the implant. The 'Keepers' they called themselves. Who even knew they had a name? And they'd been at it since before he was even born.

"You say you were born here?"

"Yeah, that woman he met that day was my mother, Christine. Five years later, I was born."

"Where is she?"

"When I was three, Dad planned an elaborate raid through a maze of underground sewers and conduits that he had mapped, but the tunnels were old and corroded, and one collapsed on them before they could get back here. A rescue party found them hours later. Old Doc Morgan did the best he could, but Dad's spine was broken at the waist, and Mom didn't make it."

"Geez, I'm sorry," he said.

"Thanks, but it was a long time ago. Life goes on." Diana reached out and lifted Boomer away from Adam's strawberries and perched him on her left shoulder. "Hey, would you like a tour of the place? I could show you around."

"Sure, that would be great." He finished his porridge and, looking to see if anyone was watching, he self-consciously sneaked some strawberries into his tunic shirt pocket.

"Better watch out. I know a certain rat who's going to be paying a lot of attention to that pocket," she said, standing and grabbing her bowl. "Bring your dishes. We'll drop them off in the kitchen."

He picked up his bowl, spoon, and glass and followed her out of the room. They were the last to leave.

The kitchen had originally been part of the same downtown hotel whose underground parking structure housed the hydroponics grow room. Its stainless steel counters and sinks gleamed beneath rows of hooks hung with institutional sized pots and pans—relics of another era, before catastrophic food shortages put an end to luxury dining. An aproned food service worker was finishing up the breakfast dishes when they walked in. Across the kitchen, her assistant washed fresh produce at another sink and laid it on a counter to drain. Diana and Adam took their dirty dishes to the dish washer.

"Go ahead and drop 'em in the soapy water, dear," the large lady at the sink said.

She was the fattest person Adam had ever seen, and he could not help but stare at her in awe. It was physically impossible to gain that amount of weight eating the Universal Food Base, so everybody he knew was thin, almost skeletal. Of course, in virtual vision everyone looked perfectly fit and healthy. He had never suspected they all looked chronically anorexic until his implant had failed. It was all he could do not to reach out and experimentally squeeze her soft, pink arm.

"Gladys, Adam," Diana said, making the introductions.

Gladys gave Adam a welcoming smile. She dried her sudsy hands on her apron and stuck out her right hand. Adam extended his hand to shake hers and was surprised and actually delighted when Gladys took his hand and pulled him to her ample bosom for a hug. *My God, what a sensation,* he thought, as he sunk into her warm, cushiony embrace. She smelled good, too, like food and soap.

"We'll have to put some weight on you quick," Gladys told him with a wink as she held him out away from her. "You help yourself to double portions for a while," she said before releasing him. She turned back to the sink. "Now go on. I've got work to do. Stick around much longer and I'll have you two washing dishes while I go have a cup of tea." She let out a loud, boisterous laugh, fully as large as she was.

Adam's head was spinning, and he didn't know if it was a reaction to the implant removal, or Gladys, or the strangeness of everything here.

"I never gave much thought to food before," Adam told Diana as they left the kitchen. "I mean, I knew we enhanced the taste and appearance of food with our premium channels, but you naturally assumed that the basic food was ... well, hell, who would ever imagine it was just so many piles of gray glop? I just don't understand how it came to this," he said.

Diana explained that after The Cataclysm destroyed the crops, scientists were able to genetically engineer a mega-protein enhanced peanut crop that could grow under almost any conditions. When ground into a paste and fortified with vitamins, it became the basis for the Universal Food Base. It wasn't tasty but it was enough to stop the famine.

"The glop provides just enough nutrition to meet minimum daily requirements, but not quite enough for optimum health," she said as they walked along. "Which is why the birth rate is so low and so many babies die." Diana glanced sideways at Adam; she suspected he was thinking of his own still-born child and she wished she hadn't reminded him of his painful memories again. She hurried to change the subject.

"So, how about some new clothes and a haircut?" Diana asked, stopping at a door marked "The Everything Room."

They entered another cavernous former parking garage holding aisle after aisle of wide, floor-to-ceiling shelves punctuated by the occasional oversized table. On those shelves rested everything that discerning scavengers figured might come in handy someday. That was a pretty large category; there had been countless recycling missions over the years.

Scavengers returned with things that had weathered time well: quality furniture from abandoned homes and stores, household items like dishes and utensils, personal care and grooming items like combs and toothbrushes, tools of all kinds, toys for the kids, first aid equipment from clinics and drug stores. Metal, glass, and whatever wood and plastic that was still serviceable. The newest craze among the kids was skateboarding up and down the long corridors—a few older folks regretted the day those particular hazards were recovered.

The trick, of course, was accurately cataloging the incredibly varied assortment. That was the job of the property master, Fred.

"It don't do nobody no good if you can't find it on the shelf when you need it," the old gent told Adam when he asked him how he kept track of everything. "I got it writ down and, more important, I got it all up here," he said, pointing to his nearly bald noggin. "I know everything in this place like the back of my hand—lock, stock and barrel." He bobbed his head up and down. "So what are you lookin' for today?"

"We're just going back in the men's section to find some clothes that fit Adam here. We want to get him out of these tunics, once and for all," Diana said.

Fred smiled. "I expected you. Javier and his woman friend just came and went with an armful of fancy duds for her." He proudly pointed over his left shoulder. "Section 17C for the guys."

"Thanks, Fred." She gave him an appreciative smile.

Diana and Adam wended their way through the maze of aisles and sorting tables to the clothing racks of the men's section.

Although he had seen the variety of clothing worn by the Underground, (he couldn't bring himself to call them the 'Keepers' yet), he hadn't really envisioned a single place where clothing of every possible color and texture hung suspended from wire hangers. Back home they all wore simple tunics that only got "dressed up" through the magic of virtual vision. So, if you wanted to wear something special to a party, you viewed a virtual fashion show until you spotted the costume you wanted. Then, you selected it and *voila*—suddenly you're wearing it. Of course, the people you were trying to impress had to be on the same channel as you, otherwise they'd just see you wearing whatever generic costumes were standard for the channel they were viewing. But here! Real food. Real flowers. Real clothes.

"Back home," he'd called it. *Where? With the Sleepers?* He felt utterly self-conscious aligning himself with either term.

"How about this?" Diana asked, holding up a pair of blue jeans and a polyester Hawaiian shirt. "These are the materials that held up over the years, so you'll see most of us in faded denim jeans and synthetic fabric shirts. What do you think of this one? Red and yellow flowers?"

Adam laughed at the bold floral print. The brightness of the dye almost hurt his eyes. Actually, it *did* hurt his eyes. Diana looked at his pained expression with concern.

"Okay, okay. So you don't like Hawaiian shirts," she said.

"It's not that; it's my head. There's a stabbing pain here behind my eyes," he said, rubbing his forehead.

"That's natural for your first day," Diana said. "Your nerves are getting used to their new job of bumping up against the real world. It'll pass. Meanwhile," she held out the clothes.

"Jeans a definite yes," Adam said, taking the pants and holding them up to his waist. "The shirt... let's keep looking."

They pawed through the racks until he found a plaid flannel shirt that looked like it had just been taken out of its plastic envelope straight from the department store. He felt the soft flannel and knew this was the shirt for him.

Then his eyes fell on a lavender nylon Western shirt trimmed in white piping and mother-of-pearl rivets. He had seen such fancy duds in the old vidvision cowboy films, and here one was, hanging right in front of him. He couldn't believe people used to make and wear such beautiful clothes in real life. He was thrilled to find such a swanky western shirt. Adam reached for the hanger.

"Wow, this is great."

"You like the cowboy look?" she asked.

"Yeah, besides spending way too much time in Frontier Vision, when we were kids my best friend and I used to play cowboys all the time, well okay, outlaws—the James brothers."

"Like in the vidfilms!" Diana said. "I watch them, too!"

"Yeah, but I never saw one of them wear anything like this," he said, holding up the lavender shirt. "How much is it and how do I pay for it?" he asked.

"You don't pay for it. It's free. It's yours. Everything here is everyone's. We have no money, no credits. We share."

"But..." The idea was totally alien to him. "Free?"

"Okay," she said, "in order to pay for anything you take, you have to do two things: tell Fred what you've taken so he can adjust his inventory lists, and be a nice guy around here. Do something to help out, like maybe work in the grow rooms or something. Easy, right?"

Adam nodded and smiled. "I can do that." He draped the jeans and both shirts carefully over his arm. "Thanks."

They finished their "shopping" excursion with shoes, boots, a jacket and all the necessary toiletries. After checking in with Fred, they headed out.

"Next stop, haircut," Diana announced.

The barber shop was a small room set within the warehouse. Old framed and faded posters of models sporting long and short hair styles covered most of the walls.

It was run by a middle-aged woman, Judy, who had two actual barber shop chairs that had been scavenged just for her. A pair of authentic beauty shop mirrors hung on the wall in front of them. The silver was chipping from the edges of them, but she kept them clean and shiny so you could see what a good job she was doing while cutting and styling your hair.

She had learned her trade from old books and magazines, and practice had nearly made perfect. Her beauty books were her bibles. She thoroughly enjoyed making her "customers," as she called them, look good, especially the newcomers, whose long, stringy hair always presented a fresh challenge. How short? Where to put the part? How to make sure the cut flattered the shape of the head and face?

Diana had left Adam there with the promise to return in half an hour. She had said she'd drop his new clothes off in his room.

He sucked in the sights and smells of the place. It was nothing at all like what he was used to: a quick chop-chop by an angry guy with dull scissors.

Judy washed Adam's hair and scalp, carefully avoiding the stitches on the back of his skull. She patted his hair dry, draped him in a patchwork plastic cape, and began trimming off the shoulder-length locks worn by the Sleepers.

"You'll want to shave and wash your hair at least every other day," she told him as she clipped.

"Every other day?" Adam asked. "Not once a week?"

"The Saturday bath? No, we generally bathe every day or two around here. Living in such close quarters, we try not to offend our neighbors, you know."

The barber stepped back to check her work, then leaned close to his ear. "In fact," she whispered, not wanting to offend him herself, "you might want to shower when you get back to your room."

After leaving Adam's clothes in his room, Diana had bumped into Javier and Raven in the hall. They were both laden with jeans, shirts, and boots—far more clothes than she had in her own closet. She had been shocked to find Javier uncharacteristically giggling like a teenager and nuzzling Raven's neck as they carried her booty back to his room. He seemed pretty eager to get there quickly and help her out of her black tunic. Raven noticed Diana's look and poked Javier with her elbow. He looked up and smiled at Diana.

"Diana. It is my great pleasure to present to you my partner, Raven, no longer under the evil influence of virtual vision," he had said with a half bow and a sweeping gesture in Raven's direction. Raven extended her hand.

"How do you do?" Diana took Raven's hand and shook it, returning her courtesy. And that's all it was, a courtesy. Both women had sensed an immediate dislike of the other. Javier, of course, was oblivious to the tension between the two women. He had thrown his arm around Raven's waist and whisked her away with the promise of having her all to himself for an hour. As they walked away, Diana couldn't figure out why she had gotten a bad vibe. Maybe it was because Raven was still wearing her black tunic. Diana shook it off. She was probably a nice enough girl once she got out of that tunic and into a pair of jeans.

From there, Diana had gone on to seek out her father. She found him in the weekly meeting with the leaders of the five settlements. There was Elizabeth of the B Street Settlement; Cyrus of the 18th Street Settlement; Rachel of the Morgan Boulevard Settlement; Gary of the Crystal Road Settlement; and Peter of the Clark Street Settlement. They were just finishing up when Diana arrived, so she stood quietly at the back of the room.

"I like that idea of using the teens on skateboards as messengers and couriers," Jason said. "It will definitely improve communications between the settlements and the central complex."

"Yeah," Gary piped up, "and if they have a legitimate reason for being there, maybe I won't get so damned aggravated when they go whizzing by in the corridors."

The others laughed, nodding their agreement, as they gathered up their ledgers and stuffed them into their backpacks.

"We'll see you again next time," Jason said, smiling. "And Pete, if you can stay a minute?" Peter fastened his backpack and joined Jason at his desk. As the others filed out past Diana, she nodded to each of them, then she joined Peter and her father at the front of the room.

"Do you have the beat cop timetables?" Jason asked Peter.

Peter handed a paper to Jason, who carefully scrutinized the information on it. Jason nodded.

"Thanks, Pete. Our people will stop by your settlement on the way. Diana here will be squad leader on this one."

"We'll be waiting, and we'll let you know if anything changes between then and now." He turned to Diana. "See you at the rendezvous. Are you sure you don't need any of my people on this one?"

"No, thanks, Pete. We can handle it."

He shook both of their hands and picked up his backpack. As he left the room, Diana turned to Jason.

"Listen, Dad, are you sure we should bring Adam on this raid?" Diana asked. "He just got here. He's not even recovered from having his implant removed. Besides, most of the towers have been refortified."

"Adam Porter is a member of this community now. Let's find out what his capabilities are and where his loyalties lie. The Clark Street tower hasn't been upgraded yet. It ought to be a simple in and out operation. Porter will do just fine."

"Well, okay. I guess I can understand why you want Adam to go along. But I'm worried about Raven. You're not thinking of including her, are you? She was a member of the Black Guard."

"So was Javier. And I trust him implicitly. Raven goes, too."

That had shut her up, as it was intended to do. She had bid him farewell and returned to the barber shop.

Satisfied with her creation, Judy pulled off the cape, brushed Adam's neck and shoulders with a nylon haired brush, and spun him around to face the mirror. Adam liked what he saw. She had left his hair much shorter, but long enough that he could see that his blond hair was naturally wavy. A few curls kept falling onto his forehead. He shoved them with his fingers, then gave up. It looked fine. He was happily surprised by his image in the mirror. But Judy's last comment made him aware that his basin bath this morning had probably missed a few crucial spots. Suddenly, he couldn't avoid smelling the stink on himself. He hoped it was just his olfactory nerves coming alive. Still, he couldn't wait to take that shower.

He was glad to see Diana come in just then.

"Congratulations, Judy. Another masterpiece," Diana said.

Judy beamed, proud of her accomplishment.

"Ready to resume the tour?" Diana asked Adam as they left the shop.

"Can we take a detour back to my room and then find the showers?"

"I was hoping you'd say that!" Diana laughed. "Right this way, sir."

She led him back to his room, where he picked up a change of clothes, then took him through the corridors to the showers, a large, open room with decorative tiles embedded on the wall with the initials "YMCA."

"Leave the tunic in the basket over there. Someone will pick it up later. There are towels in the cupboard over here. Can you find your way back to the mess hall when you're done?"

"No problem," he said as she took her leave.

Adam stood naked under the hot water. The spray from the shower head felt like little needles bombarding his skin. Without the sensory deadening effects of the implant, he was experiencing the true sensations on the surface of his skin for the first time. He felt the hardness of the bar of soap sliding over his palms as he worked up a lather and spread it all over his chest and shoulders. It slid pretty nicely over the rest of his body, too, and after three years of mind-numbing depression, the removal of his implant had heightened all of his senses, especially a certain sensation experienced while washing parts of his body that he never thought would awaken to his (or anyone else's) touch again.

The exquisite intensity of the feelings quickly overwhelmed him and he had to step back out of the water for a moment. After a few deep breaths he stepped back in and continued lathering up. He slowly rotated under the water spray, then squeegeed the lather off his arms and thighs with his hands.

After a thorough rinse, watching thirty-plus years of dirt and grime go down the drain, he hated to shut the water off. It felt good just to stand there with his eyes closed, surrounded by the warmth of the dripping water, listening to it echo off the tiled walls. Reluctantly, he spun the knobs closed and stepped out. He was surprised to feel the chill of evaporating water on his skin even though it wasn't cold in the room.

He found the towels where Diana had indicated and, after drying off, he slid his legs into his new blue jeans and slipped on the flannel shirt. His skin still tingled, even under the clothes. After pulling on a pair of shoes, he combed his hair and tucked the short, black comb into his back pocket. Then he found his way to the mess hall and presented himself for inspection.

Diana was really impressed. "Wow," she said. "You look almost human, Porter."

He laughed and nodded his head.

"I do feel good," he said. "Where to next?"

On the fortieth floor of the Virtual Vision Network tower, Henry Jones was making his daily visit to Governor Copley's office. His arms were laden with stacks of drawings that could have been reviewed on the monitors, but Henry thought he'd look more industrious with a pile of physical evidence to present. Copley preferred the computer but, because the new Shangrila channel was so important to him, he humored the department rep. He was crunching on an apple as Henry went over the specs for the silk fabrics. It was a real apple, not virtual, but Henry wouldn't know either way. They all looked real to him.

"And so, Governor, while we've achieved the feather-light feel of the fabrics quite beautifully, we haven't reached the point where it, um, actually feels like silk yet."

"What does it feel like?"

"Well, sir, it's not far from our goal of..."

"What does it feel like, Henry?"

"To be honest, sir, it feels like burlap."

Copley sighed in frustration. Two months. At this rate, they'd never be done in time. His angry gaze bored a hole in Henry's rapidly fading bravado. Henry was getting frustrated, too, but he faked over-confidence each time he met with Copley. It was getting harder every day.

"We're having difficulty increasing the thread count," Henry continued.

"Make it work, Henry. I'm holding you responsible if we have to roll this channel out beyond our announced due date."

Just what Henry didn't want to hear, but had fully expected.

Copley's vidphone beeped. He waved Henry out of the room as he answered the call. Henry couldn't hear what the caller said, but he heard Copley roaring in anger as he quickly closed the massive doors and scurried away down the hall. Something about Adam Porter? He wondered what had become of one of his best programmers. Rumors were flying but no one knew for sure, not even Porter's best friend, Brad Jameson. *Apparently,* Henry mused, *our esteemed Governor doesn't know either, and is a bit peeved about it. And what the heck am I to do about that thread count?"*

Diana guided Adam through a maze of corridors. Next stop on the tour was the school. A dozen or so children, ages five to eight, were listening intently to their young teacher as two aides moved around the class, watching, helping, and occasionally policing the unruly. There was a blackboard on the side wall with a diagram that Adam quickly translated as a map to this underground complex. It was labeled "Escape Routes" with lines and arrows depicting entrances and exits. It looked like it had been frequently erased and redrawn. Diana pointed it out to Adam.

"Memorize it. Just in case," she whispered. "And come back here every day to keep yourself up to speed on the changes in it." He nodded. Apparently, access to the Underground changed often, as did this drawing of it.

They stood silently at the back of the room. Adam listened intently to the lesson being taught and then turned his attention to the map on the blackboard. He was unfamiliar with this type of seemingly fluid, hand-drawn blueprint, but his programmer's brain picked up the complicated pattern of rooms and corridors and he soon had it committed to memory.

A few feet in front of them, a precocious seven-year-old boy turned around in his seat and stared at Adam.

"You're pretty skinny," he piped up, loud enough for the whole class to hear. "You must be new here." All the other little heads spun around to gawk at the skinny visitor. Adam had seen children before, in the virtual world, but had never spoken to them, never interacted with them. He was a bit startled by the kid's outburst and didn't know what to say. He was relieved when one of the aides came to his rescue.

"Mikey! Eyes front please. Concentrate on your seed clusters diagram." He turned to Adam. "Sorry about that."

"No problem." But being around this many kids was a little unnerving. He forced his thoughts back to their lessons. The teaching methods and the subjects being covered weren't the same as he remembered when he had been in school. When they were out in the hall again, he asked Diana about it.

"You went to Sleeper schools," Diana explained, "where you were mostly fed propaganda. Kinda like educational glop. They actually kept you from learning anything that might stimulate your natural curiosity about the real world. The last thing GovCorp wants is innovation, because that would challenge VVN's grip on their 'subscribers.' So, in the Sleeper schools they encourage programming skills and a knowledge of natural history, but only enough old technology to keep the lights on and the water running."

Adam nodded. "We never even wondered how it all worked. Not even us programmers. Geez."

"That's because they also discouraged critical thinking, since GovCorp relies on Sleepers not asking tough questions."

Adam couldn't believe he'd been such a fool. He had actually taken it upon himself to do additional research into his own field of expertise, horticulture and agriculture, so that he could be the best VVN programmer he could be, perhaps even as good as his father had been, yet he had never questioned how the channels worked, how they created the images before your eyes and in your mind. He mentally chastised himself for his lack of critical thinking. How had he learned so much and still learned so little?

"What kind of stuff do they study here?" he asked Diana.

"Besides the basic skills of reading, writing, and math, like you had, our kids learn how to repair scavenged items from the past while learning about that past. And they have the advantage of studying the old books—there are books that teach just about every imaginable subject. We're finally getting to the point where we can fabricate some of the things we need from recycled materials. You can't do that without encouraging creativity and innovation from the get-go."

"Is that the only class? They looked pretty young."

"No, we have three age groups. This is the five to eight-year-olds. Then there's the nine to twelves, and the thirteen to sixteens. After that, they become apprentices in some skill or area that they have a talent or interest in."

"And the map on the blackboard?"

"If GovCorp ever finds out where we are, they'll try to take us by force. Everyone has been assigned an evacuation route, with certain duties to assist others in the evacuation. EvacPacks, or EPs, are stashed at every exit and in strategic points outside. They contain dried foods, water, first aid kits, and other basics. Each kit will sustain five people for five days."

"And then what?"

"And then either we'd better be able to come back home, or be real damned resourceful. Oh, and until you've settled in and found your place here, you're with me, which means when push comes to shove, if I say 'jump,' you say 'how high?'."

"Yes, ma'am!" Adam said, grinning.

"I don't mean to be a hard ass, but if it ever comes to that, there won't be time for explaining or arguing."

"No problem. I understand. It's cool."

"Good. C'mon, there's more to see."

She led him down another corridor and then turned at another one. He tried to figure out where he was based on the map in the school room, but quickly got disoriented. He gave up trying to guess which corridor he was in and decided it was simpler just to follow her.

She continued her tour guide spiel and explained that this underground facility was actually the basements and underground garages of a full city block in downtown Appleton, connected by tunnels and corridors that the Keepers had created by breaking through some of the walls between them. It included office buildings, a hotel, something called a YMCA, and various other buildings. They had decided that since everything below street level was unprogrammed, that would be their safe haven, their home. And it linked up to just about everywhere in Appleton through unused sewers, basements, and the narrow spaces between buildings. These were the usual routes used by the scavengers to bring loot home.

"Lucky for me those two guys decided to use the city streets yesterday," Adam said.

"Max and Jake," she said. "Two of our best scavengers. Jake owned the Bluebird Café until the cops tore the place up."

"Sorry about that."

"It's okay. We already have another place lined up."

They passed a room full of shelved books. The carefully hand lettered sign outside the door read "Library." Several people inside were intently reading at long tables. Adam stepped inside the door and was greeted with the musty smell of old books. It was a new smell, but one he'd remember and always associate with this wonderful room.

"Wow. Where the hell did you people find all these books?"

"Gov-Corp never wanted people to read real books, so when we found out that the city library was in an unprogrammed space, we created a tunnel directly to it for everyone's use, and we've brought many of the books here for easier access." She picked up a nearby book and reverently opened its cover. "Histories, biographies, politics, life sciences. There's an amazing selection available to us. We've gotten quite an education from them." She closed the book and gently laid it down.

"We also scavenge everything that was left to rot in the unmapped sectors of the city. There are some things too precious to leave behind. We're trying to preserve the books that are readable, and those that aren't, we recycle. We make new paper out of them for other uses."

"Like what?"

"Paper for the kids in school, towels and washcloths, and," she blushed, "toilet paper, among other things."

Adam gingerly picked up a book that was lying on a table, and was surprised by the weight of it. He lightly stroked the grain of the burgundy leather cover with his fingertips, then carefully opened the cover. He caught his breath at the sight of the full color lithograph frontispiece of the white-haired, bearded author. The name below the image identified him as Edgar Rice Burroughs. Adam ran his fingers across the surface of the paper and noted how the page with the picture on it was smoother than the pages with writing, but neither of them was as smooth as the plastic pages he was accustomed to.

He opened the book to its middle and read words in a style he'd never seen before, of things he'd never heard of.

> Squatting upon his haunches on the table top in the cabin his father had built—his smooth, brown, naked little body bent over the book which rested in his strong slender hands, and his great shock of long, black hair falling about his well-shaped head and bright, intelligent eyes— Tarzan of the apes, little primitive man, presented a picture filled, at once, with pathos and with promise—an allegorical figure of the primordial groping through the black night of ignorance toward the light of learning.

"What does this book teach?" he asked Diana.

"It doesn't really. That's fiction—it's read for pleasure," she said.

He wondered how reading for pleasure stacked up against vidvision. He didn't quite get it. So much of this place was out of his realm of experience; he felt lost. Adam set the copy of "Tarzan Of The Apes" back down on the table. Too much information. Too many differences. So much to learn. He suddenly felt bone-tired and more than a little sad.

Diana sensed his change in mood and suggested they swing back by his room so he could rest before lunch. He readily agreed. She had shown enough newbies around to understand the strain the first few hours posed for them, both physically and emotionally. They left the library and the silent readers behind as she lead him to his door and promised to meet up with him later.

Back in his room, he laid on his back, staring up at the ceiling. There were so many thoughts, images, and feelings racing through his brain that he couldn't sort them out. The past week had been so filled with discoveries, both frightening and exciting, that he was exhausted from it all. He closed his eyes and slipped into darkness.

He was walking with Trisha. They were holding hands. He helped her step over a boulder at the foot of a hill. An eagle screamed overhead. Bo looked up and barked at the great bird. Trisha sat on a large log and watched as he and Bo played with a stick. He tossed the stick for Bo to retrieve but the dog just sat down and, looking up at him, cocked his head to one side. He went to get the stick himself but whenever he thought he was getting close to it, it seemed even further away. When he finally reached it and picked it up, he smiled and turned to show Trisha and Bo. But they were gone. The meadow was empty. The boulder faded into the grasses. He was alone except for the eagle, which flew overhead, calling him, calling him.

He woke up. For just a moment, he wished he was back at work, still implanted and oblivious. But he shook it off and sat on the side of the bed. Her picture smiled up at him from the bedside table.

Despite his nap, he was still tired. And he realized he was hungry. With a last look at his wife, he left his room and, after a few wrong turns, found his way back to the mess hall.

The room was about half full. Adam spotted Gladys behind the counter filling trays with a large, long-handled spoon and handing them to hungry diners in colorful shirts. He could smell the delicious aroma beckoning to him from across the room. He headed over there, smiling at her friendly, familiar face.

Gladys looked up and saw the newcomer heading her way. *What was his name again? Oh, yeah. Adam.* She started scooping up double portions of everything onto a tray.

"Hello, Adam! I hope you brought your appetite," she said, handing him the tray and returning his smile. "Tofu goulash, flat bread, raw carrots, and an orange for dessert." She pointed at each selection as she named it; these newcomers were unaccustomed to real, honest food.

"Thank you, Gladys. It smells great." His stomach was growling as he took the tray from her. He couldn't wait to dig in.

Adam looked around the room. There were lots of people at lots of tables, but he didn't feel very sociable. As he searched for a place where he might eat alone, he heard soft music coming from one side of the room and was drawn in that direction. Two young people were sitting in the big chairs in the alcove, playing guitars in harmony. He didn't recognize the tune, but he thought he recognized one of the musicians. It was the young waiter from the Bluebird Café. They exchanged a slight nod. Adam liked the melody; it sounded pleasant and would provide a nice accompaniment to his meal. He found an empty table nearby.

Once again, he was surprised at the tastes and textures of the food in his mouth. The goulash was spicy, the carrots crunchy, and the bread was a perfect complement to both. He was especially delighted by the combination of sweetness and tartness in the juicy flesh of the orange, and the potent scent of the orange oil that lingered on his hands after he peeled it. He didn't think he'd ever get used to this and he hoped he never would.

Half an hour later, his stomach was deliciously full. He bussed his tray to the kitchen and was surprised to see a familiar figure just leaving. It was the woman in black who had been following him all over town for a couple of days, except now she was wearing a tight little yellow top and even tighter black jeans. Her black hair was tied back with a bright yellow ribbon and she wore big, golden, hoop earrings in her ears. She was in the company of a big guy in the ubiquitous Hawaiian shirt, who seemed to be more than just her tour guide in this new place. Adam hadn't even thought of her since he'd seen her disappear over the threshold yesterday. He still didn't know why she had been tailing him. With nothing better to do with his time for the moment, he decided to follow them.

He trailed after Javier and Raven at a discreet distance. They were holding hands by now and walking at a pretty brisk pace, like they were in a hurry to get somewhere. Every once in a while they'd lean into each other and make each other laugh. It didn't take long for Adam to lose track of them; the place was a maze and he'd been lucky to find his way from his room to the mess hall. He shrugged and decided to go off exploring on his own instead.

Javier and Raven rushed into his room and closed the door. Raven whipped off her yellow top and tossed it into the air.

"How about a little dessert, Officer Mendez," Raven said, cupping her ample breasts with her hands and offering them up to him.

It took Javier less than three seconds to strip out of his jeans and shirt and lock his lips onto a tender, pink nipple. She moaned as they fell backward onto the bed. He pulled her tight, black jeans down over her hips and threw them in a pile on the floor. He saw the bone-handled knife strapped to her ankle.

"Can we get rid of the blade?" he asked, smiling.

She looked at him, her eyes smoldering. "No. Leave it. Just in case you don't satisfy me."

"That, dear lady, will not be a problem."

Later, as they lay exhausted in each other's arms, their naked bodies glistening with sweat, Javier nuzzled into the side of her neck.

"I'm so glad you found your way here."

Raven and Javier had worked together before. In fact, they'd been partners for years and that close partnership had led to friendship and then intimacy. Although they had never spoken of marriage, they had assumed that they'd be partners for life, that is until Javier disappeared one night after a party. He'd had a few too many drinks and had staggered off to get some air, never to be seen again.

Raven had been worried beyond words. She had searched everywhere, but all signs of his passing had led to the same dead end. He had just vanished from the face of the earth. In the weeks and months that followed, rumors of the Underground had become more prevalent and something in her brain clicked. He might have been captured by the guerrillas. She was determined to find them, and in doing so, to find him. And she had done just that. Adam Porter had led her to the Underground and her man. She was pleased with her success.

"A trail of breadcrumbs from you might have helped," Raven replied.

"Now that you're here, you know why I couldn't do that," he said.

It wasn't what she wanted to hear. She had hoped he was being held against his will, but ever since they had talked her into removing her implant, she had seen that he appeared happy and had even been given a position of authority in the organization. She was beginning to have strong doubts that he would ever be willing to go back home with her.

SATURDAY

Adam roamed about for most of the day, becoming familiar with the place that was to be his new home. He stopped into the infirmary for a check-up. He wasn't having any problems with the site of his injury where Flo had removed the implant, but daily check-ups were required for a while, just to be sure.

"Come on in. I'm Victor," said the young medic. "You must be Adam." Victor's long, black hair was gathered at the rear in a ponytail. He was slight of build, with dark eyes and an easy smile and friendly manner.

"Where's Flo?" Adam asked.

"As dedicated as that lady is, we do insist that she take an occasional day off. Now, let me have a look at those sutures."

Adam sat in the chair while Victor carefully examined Flo's handiwork.

"I didn't know there was anyone else here besides Flo," Adam said, looking around.

"There are four of us here in the central complex that were trained by Flo, and another still in training. And each settlement has at least one medic, too. Lucky for you it's my day on duty—John's all thumbs and Lu Yi would talk your ear off if you gave her half a chance." He finished probing and went to the sink to wash his hands. "Looks like you're healing well. Come back in two days, okay?"

"Sure thing. Thanks. I'll be back on Monday." With that promise made, Adam left the infirmary to continue his exploration.

He found the other classrooms and several play areas for the children. Because it was Saturday, the classrooms were empty, but he took his time examining some of the books and all of the students' artwork distributed around the room, covering all the walls with colorfully drawn images of trees, flowers, birds, and even a few dogs and cats. He guessed that they learned of the animals from the library books, although some of the drawings scarcely resembled actual living creatures. He smiled at one particular piece labeled "Kitty" which was no more than a circle with eyes, and a stick figure body with five crooked legs. Seven toes radiated from each of those lightning bolt limbs. A true artist, Adam thought as he left.

In another corridor, he stumbled on a large work area where both men and women sat behind foot-operated treadle sewing machines, repairing scavenged clothing and patching together all manner of other cloth items for use by the population. Many of the articles were blue denim, both jeans and jackets. Even if the original item was a jacket, a torn or stained sleeve meant that a newly made vest or child's skirt would soon hang in Fred's Everything Room to be chosen as someone's favorite.

After wandering into a place simply named The Jewelry Store, he was reluctantly convinced to adorn his flannel shirt with a color-coordinated brooch. Nearly every jewelry store in the city had been picked clean by the scavengers over the years (what hadn't been looted and lost during The Cataclysm) and many of the

Keepers wore precious gems as easily as costume jewelry. The clerk, Athena, was festooned with gemstone earrings, necklaces, brooches, rings, and bracelets. Nearly every inch of her sparkled under the lights.

"See how nice that looks?" she said, admiring the brooch against his plaid shirt. "Now come over here and pick out a watch. Jewelry isn't mandatory, but watches are."

They were all old-fashioned wind-up watches and he picked one that had a simple style. Athena set the time at four o'clock.

"Wind it once a day or it will stop," she instructed, showing him how to pull the tiny stem out to set the time, and push it back in to wind it. "Dinner is between five and six. Don't be late."

He thanked her and continued his solo tour, a little self-conscious about the brooch on his collar, but quite comfortable with the watch and its brown leather strap.

He soon found himself back in the hydroponics room. Now, this was heaven. Jason had already mentioned to the gardeners that Adam would be working among them soon, so they welcomed him with open arms.

He spent nearly an hour getting acquainted with them, while they happily showed him the intricacies of an underground farm planted in fertilized water or nutrient-rich soil collected from their own compost piles, bathed in grow lights powered by stolen electricity.

The head gardener, Caryn, was a small, wiry woman, with a thick mane of prematurely gray hair that hung free almost to her waist. She had a ready laugh that crinkled her sparkling green eyes behind wire-rimmed glasses. She was dressed in a full-length denim skirt, topped by a denim vest over an earth-toned Hawaiian shirt. She wore multiple loops of beads and dozens of bangles on her thin arms that jangled whenever she moved. She took it upon herself to be Adam's social informant as well as instructing him on the state of their agricultural and horticultural endeavors.

"We tap into the city water system," she said, "for irrigating the crops using a basic drip irrigation system, with these black PVC pipes that you see snaking around the floor everywhere. Watch you don't trip. Then from here we pipe it throughout the central complex. The government never notices the missing power and water because, as you well know, Sleepers aren't billed for utilities anymore." Caryn chortled. "They don't have any way to keep track of the missing water! We steal all the water and light we need!" she laughed again.

"Central complex? Victor mentioned that, too. What's a central complex?" Adam asked.

"This is the central complex here—all the facilities and rooms in this city block. And there are several other underground satellites in other parts of the city that can be reached through tunnels that radiate out from here, like spokes on a wheel. We call them settlements. In our garden we grow all the usual fruits and vegetables, plus soy beans, almonds, millet, and a few other crops like hemp that are used in places other than the kitchen. The satellite grow rooms raise most of the same crops, but in much smaller quantities. And all the settlements have canning operations to preserve food in case of emergency. They also have medical facilities, although our infirmary is better stocked and staffed for anything major."

"I don't understand," Adam said. "Why are there satellites? Why doesn't everyone just live here?"

"There are too many of us, and it's too dangerous for all of us to be in one place. Copley and his goons would just love to squash every single man, woman, and child in the Underground. If they ever find out where we are, if they ever infiltrate one or more of the settlements, only a fraction of us will be endangered.

"But, not to worry; getaways are built in. If anything happens we have escape routes and booby traps to collapse the tunnels. If one settlement is compromised, or worse, captured, the others will still be safe."

"But what if the central complex is breached?"

"Well, then, our fannies will be caught in the wringer, won't they?" She laughed at the look on his face. "We'll be fine. Really, you'll soon learn all about our defenses and what not. But for now, let's meet your partners in crime."

As Caryn continued the tour, she introduced Adam to the other gardeners. They were a gossipy group, full of information about everyone and everything. From them he found out that the Underground numbered close to two hundred and fifty souls, over one hundred right here in the central complex, from a three-week-old newborn to one, very rare, ninety-four-year-old who actually remembered some of the times before. When she had been born, it was no secret that babies were routinely implanted. Her parents had been against implants and had home schooled her and hidden her condition from the authorities. She had lived her whole life pretending to fit in and had been thrilled to discover the Keepers when she was sixty years old. Her name was Savannah, but some of the Keepers called her The Oracle. Her wisdom had helped the community survive on more than a few occasions.

He learned more about Flo and Gladys and Jason and Diana. After a while, he began feeling as though he was learning too much. People were talking, they said, about Javier and that woman. Everyone had seen how they were behaving like teenagers and kept disappearing into his bedroom. Javier wasn't getting his work done or some such.

"You know how people gossip," Caryn laughed, knowing full well that she was doing that very thing.

A glance at his new watch gave him the reason he needed to excuse himself. Dinner time. As he walked back to the mess hall, he chuckled and thought he might have to reconsider his job choice here. As much as he loved horticulture, he didn't know if he could stand all the chattiness every day. Maybe he could just be the weird, quiet guy in the corner, experimenting with hybrid vegetables or something. He turned a bend in the corridor and found himself in a crowd.

That was odd. He thought he had just seen that woman, Raven, enter the busy corridor fifty feet in front of him, lock eyes momentarily, and then do an about-face and leave. After following him for days, now she was avoiding him? What the hell was that all about? He shrugged it off. Maybe it wasn't her. There were a lot of people in the corridor and he had only gotten a glimpse. Still, it bothered him. Should he follow? Try to talk to her? He finally decided against it. She was long gone and he'd have a hard time finding her down here. He still didn't know his way around very well. Besides, his stomach was churning and he couldn't wait to see what Gladys gave him double scoops of tonight.

Dinner was every bit as tasty as lunch. Gladys had a knack for making the most out of the limited ingredients she had to work with. She had a fairly good collection of scavenged tins of spices, salt, and sugar, plus fresh rosemary, basil, and other herbs from the gardens, and she put them to good use dressing up the simple vegan fare. Adam didn't know the name of the main course, but it was superb. Maybe he'd work in the kitchen, he decided, if he couldn't handle the gossips in the garden.

"There you are," Diana said, interrupting his reverie. She set her full tray next to his empty one and sat down. "I see you found The Jewelry Store," she smiled, pointing at his sapphire-studded brooch.

"Yep," he answered. He nodded over to the side of the room where four people were seated around a small table, engaged in what was obviously a recreational activity. From the smiles and good-natured bantering, it looked like they were having a good time.

"I think I've seen something like that on the vidvision," he said, turning to Diana. "Are they playing cards?"

"Poker, judging by the chips in the middle of the table. You want to get into the game?"

Diana introduced Adam to the poker players. He already knew Fred. "Take it easy on him—he's a greenhorn," she told them. "I'll pick you up tomorrow morning for breakfast," she said to Adam. "Seven o'clock." Adam nodded as he pulled up a chair to the table and smiled at his opponents. Fred pushed a pile of chips in his direction. This was going to be fun.

In ten minutes he learned the game, and an hour later he lost all his chips to the sharks at the table. They had given him a nickname–Fish. He didn't know what it meant, but it felt good to be accepted enough by the small group to have been tagged with a good-natured appellation. After a promise to meet regularly with them, he said good night and excused himself. It had been a long day and he was more than ready for it to end.

After his earlier explorations, he thought he knew his way back to his room, but maybe because he was tired, he took a wrong turn into an unfamiliar corridor. He mentally chastised himself for his mistake, when he heard a soft voice coming from an open door on his left.

"Come here, child. I've been waiting for you."

The room he entered was dimly lit with candles and draped with lush fabrics and tapestries in reds and blues and purples. Some of the candles were scented and filled the air with fragrances he didn't recognize but found soothing and pleasant.

She was seated in the center of the far wall. Her chair was overstuffed, and still she was surrounded with pillows to support her fragile frame. She was the oldest person Adam had ever seen. Her skin was translucent, the color of pearls. Her white hair was plaited and hung to her waist. Each bony finger was wrapped around the faded cover of a book whose title he couldn't make out. There were many more books on the table next to her. "A Brief History of Time," "Metaphysics And Our Perception Of A Fragile Life," "Cosmos." There were others, but most of the spines that he could see carried similarly unfathomable titles.

"Come sit with me," she said, putting the book aside and gesturing to a large pillow on the floor beside her. "Tell me about the dream."

He looked up at her, startled, as he settled into the pillow she had indicated. This must be Savannah. The Oracle. How much should he tell her?

"Trish and Bo were gone," he began.

"Trish and Bo *are* gone," she gently corrected.

He felt the tears suddenly well up in his eyes.

161

"The time for tears is long gone, child. Now is the time for now, and tomorrow will be for tomorrow. Give me your hands."

She reached out both of her fragile hands and he laid his hands in her palms. He felt both the physical weakness and the spiritual strength of her in the sweetness of her touch.

"Your pain and confusion are strong. You must put them aside. Healing will only come when you surrender."

Surrender? He didn't understand.

"I... I need more time," he stammered.

"You have all the time in the world, yet you need no time at all. It has been and already is."

Adam's eyes gave away his confusion. She smiled and tried to explain.

"The passage of time is but an illusion. Time, as you know it, is only linear within the confines of this three dimensional space through which our mortal bodies travel. But that pathway, my child, is a delusion. The essence of your true being, perhaps you can call it your soul, is free of those restrictions and occupies all of time, all the time. Therefore, you already are what you desire to be... whole, healed, complete. Healing will only come when you surrender. In the fullness of time you have already surrendered. You will realize this when you do it."

Adam looked at her, more confused than ever. She smiled softly.

"Go now. I'm a tired old woman and I must rest."

"But..." He wanted to know more. To stay with her in this room where everything was soft and beautiful and quiet. Mostly, he wanted to understand.

"Go. All will be clear to you when the time is right. Go."

Adam stood slowly, reluctantly releasing her hands. When she smiled at him, her eyes were lit from within.

He mentally memorized the route back to his room so that he could visit her again.

When he closed his door behind him, he looked around. Someone had put an alarm clock on his bedside table and hung an old painting on the wall. It was a landscape; a lone tree stood in the foreground, its leaves turning gold and red and brown. The meadow was empty except for low grasses and an occasional yellow flower. In the distance, tall gray and purple mountains shone in the sun, already sporting snowy caps of stark white. He stared at it for a long time. He was the tree, alone in a wide meadow, not knowing what those distant mountains held for him.

He pulled himself away and checked out the rest of the room. With his shiny lavender cowboy shirt hanging in the closet and Trish's photo on the table, it was starting to look and feel like home. He smiled as he thought about the frilly curtains she'd want to hang, if only there had been a window.

He picked up her picture and touched her cheek with his finger. Mentally wishing her a good night, he walked to the other side of the room and put the photo up on the dresser, then he took off his sapphire brooch and put it at the base of the frame. He liked the way it sparkled the same blue as her eyes. Then he unbuckled his watch, dutifully wound it up and put it in front of the brooch.

There were empty hangers in the closet for the jeans and shirt he took off. With nothing between his clean skin and a set of clean sheets, he fell into bed and slept, dreamless, until the alarm clock buzzed at 6:30.

SUNDAY

Diana caught him in the act of snitching a couple of strawberries the next morning after breakfast. He looked a little red-faced.

"Is it okay?" he asked. "I mean, you know, for later. They're pretty good," he said as he slipped them into his shirt pocket.

She laughed at his awkwardness. "Of course it's alright. Help yourself."

"Thanks, I will," he said, rising from his chair and taking his dishes to the now familiar kitchen. Diana walked with him.

"I wonder if you'd be interested in stopping by my martial arts class this morning?" she asked.

"Sure thing," he said. "I have to see Flo real quick, but then I'll be there. How do I find you?"

"Ask anyone for the dojo. They'll point you in the right direction." She waved over her shoulder as she left.

"Gonna go get an ass whuppin'," Gladys laughed as she took his dishes and slid them into the soapy water. "Maybe you should wait and see Flo afterwards instead."

Ass whuppin'? Martial arts? His puzzled look tickled her immensely and she let out a guffaw.

"You'll be fine," she reassured him. "Go on now. Go see Flo. Tell her to get up here and eat before it's all gone."

"Will do," he said and headed for the door.

Flo was in the infirmary, chatting with Lu Yi. Actually, listening as Lu Yi chatted on about a sprained ankle she had wrapped earlier that morning.

"I know Jason wants to use these kids as couriers, but skateboards are dangerous, Flo. He could have broken something, or worse."

Flo made short work of examining Adam's skull, patted him on the shoulder and silently shooed him out of there before he could pass along Gladys's message.

"I mean, what if he had hit his head or..."

Adam found the Underground dojo easily enough. He could hear the grunts and kicks as he approached in the hallway. He was surprised to find that Diana was the teacher of the classes. He didn't know why that should surprise him; he had no frame of reference for what was "normal" here.

She was instructing the young waiter from the Bluebird how to stiffen his fingers.

"Bobby, please, I've told you this so many times: in karate, you must focus your strength into a relatively small area of your body, because if you whack with an open hand, the force is dissipated over a broad area. But if you stiffen your fingers, hold them together straight and tight, and hit with either your fingertips or the side of your hand, that same force is applied to a much smaller area. See?" She demonstrated with a hit to his stomach.

He tried not to double over. Everyone was watching.

"Yes, sensei. Thank you, sensei."

"Remember what Nietzsche said: 'That which does not kill us makes us stronger.'"

"I thought he said 'Bet ya can't spell my name,'" Bobby muttered as she turned away.

She hid a smile as she walked to the front of the class. She knew she had to be tough enough for her students to learn the techniques that could eventually save their lives, but not so tough that they got discouraged. She put Bobby with Jake to work out, then, looking back over her group, she spotted Adam at the rear of the room. She waved him up to the front.

She put Adam through some basic offensive and defensive moves in both jujitsu and karate. She showed him how to dodge an opponent's attack and then grab the arm that held the weapon and apply a joint lock to the arm. The joint locks were intended to destroy the appendage by disjointing it and tearing apart the connecting muscles and tendons. He cringed as she explained the ripping muscles part. The follow-up kick or strike was supposed to target a vital area of the body and was designed to quickly kill or disable the opponent. Diana preferred the "disable" method but understood the necessity of teaching both.

Adam was clumsy at first, but picked up on a few of the basic moves fairly quickly. He was fascinated by her explanation of the four martial arts that she taught: judo for sport and competition; aikido, which was more spiritual; and karate and jujitsu for combat.

"Combat?" he asked.

"Hope for the best, prepare for the worst," she said. "Jake, come work out with Adam for a while."

Jake lumbered over while Bobby gratefully sat out. For a big man, he was fairly agile, but still hadn't mastered the joint locks and throws quite as well as Diana would have liked. He got a kick out of tossing Adam around on the mat for a while until Adam got the best of him and he landed on his back. He stood quickly and faced his opponent.

"Not too shabby, Porter." He couldn't help himself; he was starting to like this new guy. Porter learned quickly and he wasn't cocky. And despite Jake's best efforts to slam him repeatedly to the mat, Adam took the abuse without complaint, and did his best to perfect some of the moves. Jake figured he was okay, even if he'd been the reason for his bar shutting down.

Javier stuck his head into the dojo. Diana met him at the back of the room.

"Where've you been?" she asked. "I thought you were going to be here an hour ago. It's important that we're all ready, you know?"

"Don't worry about me. I'm as ready as I'll ever be," he said, smiling broadly. "I just wanted to let you know I won't be here for class but I'll see you later this afternoon when we go out. Is Porter coming?"

"Yes, and Raven?"

"Yeah, have you seen her? I'm trying to find her." He didn't wait for an answer. He took off down the hall, calling over his shoulder, "See ya later."

She shook her head and turned back to the class. She was worried about the raid this afternoon. Would they be prepared? And Bobby was asking if he could go along. He thought he was ready; she didn't. She hoped her father would tell him to wait a bit longer.

After lunch, Diana found Adam in the Library room, surrounded by an odd assortment of books on gardening and martial arts. He was reading in a book on hydroponics when she leaned over his shoulder, surprising him.

"Sorry," she said. "I didn't mean to startle you. I see you're learning about our growing methods. We learned from the books, too, but we've taken it a few steps further based on our experiences with it."

"I like the idea that some crops can grow in a water solution and don't even need soil. You have lots of water, but the soil isn't the healthiest."

"We're working on that by composting our kitchen scraps. We're doing pretty well with it, too."

"I'm guessing," Adam said, "that you're not here to talk gardening, though."

"True. I'm on my way to see my Dad. He'd like you to come along, too."

She helped him return all the books to their proper places on the shelves, then they left and headed up the hall. They turned down a corridor he hadn't yet explored and came to a door marked "The Machine Shop. PERMISSION ONLY." This was the first restricted area Adam had encountered in this place. He had begun to assume that there were no restrictions among these people, what with the freely shared goods and their apparent philosophy of openness and honesty.

They entered a large room where they found Max wearing goggles and busy working at one of several old-style machines that looked like they came from the industrial age. Adam had never smelled this type of oily, hot metallic odor before. He had seen machines like this in vidreels, but hadn't met anyone that actually worked in a machine shop.

The lathe made a tremendous racket as a young female apprentice slowly moved a piece of metal back and forth against a spinning cylinder. Max guided her hand, regulating the speed of the lathe and the sensitivity of her touch on the five inch tube.

Diana led Adam to the back of the large room. He was surprised to see a number of weapons among the assortment of metal items piled on the shelves. Most of the guns were foreign to him, but he recognized a Colt Peacemaker and a Winchester 200 rifle. There was no time to stop and examine them, though.

Jason and Jake were waiting for them, along with a very happy-looking Bobby. Max joined them, pulling his goggles down around his neck and sitting on the edge of a table. He was slipping tools into a small canvas bag. He passed the bag over to Jake, who tucked it under his arm and nodded his thanks.

"How are you settling in, Porter?" Jason asked.

"Good, thanks," Adam said.

After inquiring about Adam's adjustment to his senses without an implant, Jason told him the real reason for their meeting: a raiding party was forming up for a strike on a booster tower. They were to leave in one hour.

"Good luck with that," Adam said.

"You're going along," Jason told him.

Adam grimaced and shook his head. "Why me? I don't know anything about busting up booster towers."

"You'll follow your squad leader's orders," Jason said. "You can do that much, can't you?"

"But," Adam protested, "why the hell would you want me to go? There must be other people more qualified."

"Call it your initiation," Jason said.

Adam considered protesting more vehemently but, truth be told, he was curious about what went on during these booster tower raids. Plus, the walls were starting to close in on him a little and he felt like he could use some fresh air.

Javier and Raven finally joined them, just in time for Jason's mission briefing.

Six guerrillas set out for the Clark Street booster station through a sewage tunnel on the south side of the underground complex. Diana kept Adam close by her side. Jake, carrying the small bag of tools, walked behind them with Bobby, and Javier and Raven brought up the rear. They walked quickly but quietly, other than Bobby's frequent attempts to break the silence. As much as he had wanted to come on this mission, he was nervous. This was his first time and he wanted to prove to Jason that he was ready. Adam smiled to himself. He could hear the boy's mantra behind him.

"I'm gonna bust up that tower real good, wait and see." He must have said it a dozen times before they got there, each time they switched from tunnel to alley and back to tunnel again. "I'm gonna bust up..."

"Okay, kid. We get the picture. Now shut up," Jake finally said.

"Sure, Jake. Sorry, Jake." The pace was too slow for him. He wished they were running instead of walking so slowly. Oh well; he figured they'd be running like hell after they wrecked the tower.

Adam was nervous, too, but he kept it to himself. According to what Jason had instructed during the briefing, they'd be stopping at one of the Underground satellite areas before going on to their destination. Then, at the tower, Diana and Javier would climb up on the bunker and knock down the antenna, while Adam and Bobby would scavenge all the loose wiring that fell, leaving Jake and Raven outside the fence as lookouts. This was a routine strike; it should be easy. He didn't know what Jason had meant about "misdirection" and "This will keep Copley's eye on the suburbs for a day or two," but he supposed that if they'd wanted him to know, they would have told him.

After nearly an hour, they were met by a small group of people holding candles to illuminate the damp, murky passageway. They were strangers to Adam, but obviously well-known to Diana, Jake, and Javier. Peter was there to greet them.

"Pete, good to see you again," Javier said, extending his hand.

"You, too, Javier. Hey, Jake, Bobby."

After introductions were quickly made, Diana and Peter went over the beat cop timetable again. The local police were particularly punctual, and could be counted on to walk their beats at precisely the same times every day.

"No changes," Pete assured her. "You should have an hour; plenty of time. Are you sure you don't need anyone from our group?"

"Thanks, Pete, but we're good. Ten minutes from here, right?" Diana said.

"Less if you walk fast. Good luck. We'll be here if you need us." He put his hand on her shoulder and then he and his group retreated into the shadows.

The raiding party continued on their way. They were getting closer now. They were in the sewers under Clark Street, hunched down so as not to hit their heads on the conduits above. It had taken long enough that it should be dark outside now, offering at least some cover for them when they arrived.

Bobby turned to Jake and whispered, "Are we there yet?"

Jake pointed straight up and nodded. Above their heads, there was a manhole cover. Javier went up the ladder and carefully lifted the heavy metal disk. After a quick look up and down the street, he gave the others the "all clear" sign and they scrambled up the ladder behind him and out onto the cracked asphalt of Clark

Street, keeping low and watching in every direction as they ran toward their target.

The small booster tower consisted of an antenna that sat atop a ten by ten concrete bunker, enclosed by an eight foot high chain link fence. Years ago they had learned not to bother trying to get into the bunkers to sabotage the equipment inside. It took far too long and greatly increased the danger. Taking down the antenna was much faster and, ultimately, much safer. It was also sufficient to cause VVN major headaches for at least a few days. The actual antenna was only about six feet tall on this one. There weren't any high buildings in this area to block the transmissions. It was mostly residential.

The guerrillas approached carefully. Jake tossed his canvas tool bag down beside the gate, pulled out a heavy bolt cutter and made short work of the lock. He pushed open the gate while Raven took up watch, and Diana, Bobby, Javier, and Adam slipped inside. Javier boosted Diana up to the roof of the bunker and then jumped up there himself. They yanked on the antenna and had just started tossing wires and cables down to Bobby and Adam when Jake called out, "We got company!"

Two uniformed police, armed with disrupters and billy clubs, ran down the street toward them, one of them already shouting into his portable vidphone.

"Shit! Let's get out of here!" Diana yelled, as she and Javier jumped down from the roof of the bunker. Within seconds, more police were arriving from the other end of the street.

The first cops to arrive had already started shooting and, when they found their disrupters were useless, pulled out their billy clubs and started swinging. All six guerrillas were outside the fence now, trying to fight their way back to the street. Adam forgot everything he'd been taught that morning, but let out with a series of John Wayne fists to the face that seemed to work pretty well. This was his second real fist fight in less than a week. He was scared, but he kept swinging.

Bobby remembered to keep his fingers tightly together and did a good job of inflicting some damage to a couple of the cops before a billy club connected with his thigh. He heard the loud crack of the bone and his legs gave way beneath him. He dropped to the ground, but despite the pain he tried to stand and continued fighting.

Jake saw the courageous kid but couldn't go to him; he ducked and spun around as he snap-kicked one cop, sending him sprawling backwards into another. He only had a split second to admire the boy's chutzpah before he was confronted with two more cops, swinging clubs and fists at him. Out of the corner of his eye, he saw that a half dozen more cops were converging on the scene from all directions. It was apparent that none of the police had been adequately trained in hand-to-hand combat, but with these odds, the guerrillas didn't really have much of an advantage, despite their skill. Escape was their only hope.

Javier and Diana were able to incapacitate several more cops with their superior martial arts skills as they made their way out into the street and the open manhole. Raven demonstrated that she had some pretty decent defensive moves, too. Adam just tried to keep his feet under him, throwing punches at the nearest faces.

Jake fought his way over to Bobby and threw an arm around the kid's waist. "We gotta get outta here!" he yelled over the melee. He got his bearings in the crowded street and was dragging the injured youngster toward their escape when two cops grabbed Bobby and yanked him away. Two more were pounding on Jake, trying to bring him into custody, too. He was surrounded and it was all he could do to fight them off.

One by one, the other guerrillas fought their way out to the middle of the street and disappeared down the manhole. Diana followed Javier and Adam into the blackness. In the noise and confusion, they couldn't see that Bobby had been captured. Raven was last; she looked around to try to see Jake and Bobby, then dropped into the void and disappeared.

More police troops were approaching from the other end of Clark Street. There wasn't anything Jake could do. The cops were dragging Bobby away. If he went after him, they'd get him, too. Screaming in anger and frustration, he reluctantly gave up his attempts to rescue Bobby as he kicked and chopped at every cop in his path until he escaped down the manhole.

The cops stood around, staring at the spot in the street where the guerrillas had disappeared. The manhole cover had been replaced from underneath, leaving no sign of the off-the-grid escape route. Their instructions had been to bring back at least one, and they had done that. Like lions on the hunt, they had chosen the weakest of their quarry and had easily captured him for their leader. They picked up their wounded and headed back to the precinct house with their prisoner. From there, the Sarge would know what to do.

Down in the sewer, it was chaos.

"We have to go back for Bobby!" Jake insisted.

"There's too many of them," Diana said. "We can't take the chance of anyone else getting caught."

"Where the hell did they come from?" Javier spat.

"And they've got Bobby! You know what they'll do to him!" Jake continued.

Adam and Raven said nothing. Diana was the voice of reason.

"He doesn't know anything. We have to leave him," Diana said.

Jake started to object, but Diana cut him off. "We'll get him back, just not right now. Let's move out."

It took just over an hour to get back to the safety of their underground home. No one spoke on the way. Each one of them went over and over the events of the raid in their minds and wondered if they could have done anything differently; anything that would have produced a different outcome.

Jake felt especially responsible for leaving the boy behind. Rationally, he knew he'd had no choice, but emotionally, that didn't fly with him. He had a feeling of dread in his gut. The fact that Bobby didn't know anything might serve to prolong whatever methods his captors might use to extract information from him. The fear moved up into his chest and throat, making it hard for him to breathe.

Bobby's thigh hurt like hell where the police officer's billy club had cracked his femur. It was a couple of hours later and he thought he might have been brought to the VVN building. He knew that he was in a small room, flanked by two of Copley's Black Guard, but he couldn't see them.

They had stripped him of his jeans and shirt and put him into a dirty brown tunic. A thick cloth hood covered his head and was tied below his chin. With his hands tied behind his back, he struggled to stay balanced on the backless stool they had him sitting on.

Every once in a while, one of the Guards would reach out and give him a shove, trying to knock him off the chair. He was getting terrified every time he heard a boot move on the floor, not knowing if they were coming at him again.

Copley had stormed into the room shortly after Bobby had been delivered to VVN by the local cops.

"What's your name?" Copley had asked.

"Go to hell."

He didn't see the punch to the side of his head. The hood obscured everything. But he heard the explosion in his skull and saw stars for a few seconds. Someone held his arm so he wouldn't fall off the stool.

"Let's try this again. What's your name?" Copley asked again.

"Screw you."

The next punch came to his thigh, where it was broken. He screamed inside his hood. The world went away. Nothing existed but the tremendous pain and the shriek in the blackness surrounding his head. He almost passed out.

As if it were a hundred miles away, he heard Copley's voice telling the Guards that he'd return in the morning to continue. And he told them to keep him awake. The cold water splashed on his chest brought him around, but he hovered on the brink of slipping away into unconsciousness. He was both terrified and pissed off. His first raid. Not a good start for an aspiring guerrilla.

Late that night, in the infirmary, Flo worked to tend to their cuts and bruises as they all talked at once. Jason rolled in to find Flo stitching up Jake's arm where a billy club had split the skin just above his elbow.

"What the hell happened?" he asked.

They all answered together. All except for Adam and Raven, who sat quietly in the corner.

"Somebody ratted us out!" Diana said.

"We don't know that," Javier said.

"They were waiting for us!" Jake insisted. "They got Bobby! We have to go after him!"

"One at a time!" Jason yelled. "Diana, you were squad leader. What happened out there?"

"It couldn't have just been cops on the beat. According to Pete's intelligence, they weren't due for nearly an hour. Once they saw us, they called for backup. We were outnumbered."

"How could that be?" Jason demanded. "I thought we had a timetable. There weren't supposed to be any cops there. Javier, did they change their scheduling?"

"How the hell should I know! The Clark Street settlement told us the cops wouldn't be around for another hour. But they were there; they got Bobby. That's all we know."

Jake flinched as Flo pulled the last stitch tight on his arm. "We need to get Bobby back. How are we gonna do that?" he asked.

"We'll do it tomorrow," Jason said. "I have some contacts on the outside. I'll see if anyone knows where they're keeping him."

Adam watched each of them, including Raven, trying to read their faces, read their minds. Had someone betrayed them? Or had it just been a coincidence that the police had been there at the same time they were?

"I bet Copley's got him," Adam spoke up. "This stinks of GovCorp."

"What if somebody did rat on us, Jason?" Javier asked. "Somebody who knew what was going down and who to call about it." His glance went over to Adam in the corner.

"I know you're not talking about me, man." Adam stood tall, expecting a confrontation.

"Adam's not the only new person here!" Diana protested to Javier.

Javier was surprised at Diana's defense of Porter. Or was it an attack on Raven?

"Adam and Raven," Jason interrupted, "get out of here. Go to bed. Get some rest." He left no room for debate. Adam shot an angry look at Javier over his shoulder as he followed Raven out the door.

"Javier, Diana," Jason continued, "don't let them out of your sight." And when they hesitated, "Go! Now! They aren't to be left alone."

Javier left with an annoyed glance in Jason's direction. Diana touched her father's arm as she passed.

"Sorry, Dad."

"It's not your fault. You did the best you could. For now, just make sure Porter stays in his room all night. Put a guard outside his door."

"And Raven?" she asked.

"Javier will be with her. She won't be going anywhere."

Diana nodded and left.

"You think Copley's got the kid?" Jake asked after the three of them were alone. Flo had poured each of them a vodka. Jake was still pretty upset about leaving the boy behind. He tossed back the liquor and held out his glass for another one.

"Could be," Jason replied. "We'll know more tomorrow morning."

"We never had anything like this happen before those two got here," Jake said, "and both of them had connections to GovCorp and Copley." He held out his glass again.

"I know, but Javier vouches for Raven, and Diana, well, she believes in Porter. She doesn't think he's the one either. This puts us in a difficult position." Jason shifted in his chair. After twelve or fourteen hours, it started to get pretty uncomfortable in his chrome-plated cage on wheels.

"Are we still on for tomorrow?" Flo asked. She had been quiet until now. "It might be dangerous to go forward with the plan after what happened tonight."

"We have to," said Jason. "We've been planning this for months. And the only people who know about it are people I trust with my life. So, yes, we're still on for tomorrow."

"And what about Raven and Porter?" Flo asked thoughtfully. "Should they be included? Can we trust them?"

"It's possible Peter's timetable was off," Jason said. "Raven and Porter bring unique qualities to the team. Raven is a trained fighter, just as Javier is. And Porter knows our target inside and out. I can't see leaving them behind when they could be such valuable assets to the operation. But we'll keep an eye on them."

"Yeah, I'll keep an eye on them, boss," Jake said. "You can bet on that."

They sipped their drinks and talked about meaningless things, trying to clear their heads and calm their nerves. Then Jason checked his watch and, with a quick turn, he left the two of them to finish the vodka. He had to talk to someone in particular about tomorrow and it didn't matter that it was the middle of the night. He'd have to wake him up. New plans had to be added to the schedule if Bobby was to be rescued.

Max was still awake and was waiting for Jason in his machine shop. He was putting some finishing touches on a small, square package. Satisfied, he slid it to the back of a shelf as Jason rolled in.

"Are they finished?" Jason asked.

"That was the last one," Max said. "I heard what happened. What's the plan?"

"Have you seen your brother lately?"

"Sure. I went to Georgie Jr.'s seventh birthday party a few days ago."

"Get in touch with him. We'll need his help tomorrow. We have to find Bobby and get him back home."

"I'm already gone." With that, Max yanked off his heavy work apron and strode out the door.

Jason's next stop was Javier's room. He knocked softly, hoping that he'd awaken his friend but not the woman who slept by his side. Javier answered the door, zipping up his jeans over his naked body. Jason motioned for him to join him in the hallway. Looking over his shoulder to be sure Raven slept undisturbed, Javier stepped barefoot out into the corridor. He closed the door softly behind him.

"I'm going to cut to the chase," Jason said. "In the six months since you've been here, I've come to know and trust you implicitly. I would have put my life in your hands without question. Until now."

"What? What are you talking about?" Javier was more than a little surprised.

"Since Raven's arrival, you've neglected your duties in favor of spending time in her company. I didn't say anything because reunions with loved ones can be great and wonderful things. So much to catch up on, so much to talk about."

"Your point?" Javier was getting suspicious about where this was going.

"Did you tell Raven about the booster tower raid?"

"I might have, but don't think for a minute that she betrayed us. I know that woman inside and out. She's tough and won't pull her punches, but she's loyal to a fault. There's no way she's an informant or spy. I'd bet my life on it."

Jason shook his head. He wanted to believe him.

"And no," Javier continued, anticipating Jason's next question, "I didn't tell her about tomorrow."

"Okay," said Jason, "you're squad leader on this one, and it's vitally important that I can count on you."

"You know you can, Jason. I've pledged my life and my loyalty to you and this community. I won't let you down."

"Thank you, Javier." Jason offered his hand. After a hearty hand shake, Javier went back into his room, satisfied that all was well. Jason went to his own room. He knew he wouldn't sleep well, if at all.

After a quick shower to wash off the evidence of his trek through the city sewers, Adam slept fitfully. His dreams ran from the one with Trish and Bo disappearing to others where he was being chased by the governor in a blood-covered police uniform. His legs were leaden and Copley was getting closer and closer. He could hardly breathe, as he struggled to get away from the murderous look in Copley's eyes.

MONDAY

Adam awoke the next morning in a sweat. As horrific as last night's adventure had been, he had a bad feeling that today would be worse.

He dressed in his new jeans and flannel shirt, said a quick hello to Trish's picture over on the dresser, and was about to pull the door open when Diana knocked and stuck her head in.

"Let's go. We have time for a quick breakfast and then we need to see Dad and the others. We found out where Bobby is."

He snuck his extra strawberries into his pocket after gulping down a small bowl of Gladys's millet porridge. Diana didn't eat. She looked worried and preoccupied. She checked her watch a dozen times before finally jumping up from the table.

"Let's go. It's time." She started for the door. "Leave your dishes. Gladys will get them."

"Hey, wait up!" he said to her back. She didn't reply. She walked fast enough that he almost had to jog to keep up with her. She turned into The Machine Shop, entered with him, and closed the door behind them.

Diana and Adam pushed their way into a room bulging with a couple of dozen men and women, including Max and Jake. Flo, Victor, and two other medics stood off to the side, checking their medical bags and talking quietly among themselves.

Adam stood on his tip-toes at the back of the room, straining to see over people's heads. Charts and maps hung on the walls. A diagram of a floor plan was propped on an easel beside a large table in the center of the room. Jason sat beside the table, which was loaded with several handguns and boxes of ammunition. Next to those, there was a large pile of ordinary gray and brown tunics that looked like they could have used a spin in the washing machine.

Fred came in just behind Adam and Diana and made his way up to the front of the group. He carried four heavy canvas backpacks that were well worn and had obviously been recently patched in the sewing room. He tossed the packs onto the table, nodded to Jason and Max, and stood to the side. Max immediately reached deep into the dark shadows at the back of the shelves and pulled out a number of small, square packages. He carefully stuffed them into the backpacks.

All eyes were on Jason. "And as you can see," he said, gesturing to the items on the table, "Max has completed assembly of the explosive charges."

Max stood near the backpacks, staring sternly at the group. When he spoke, his voice was loud enough to reach every person in the room.

"We've been over this before, but I'm gonna say it again. Only four of us will handle the explosives," Max said. "Me and Jake, Javier and Diana. The rest of you we're counting on for cover and back-up. There will be four staging areas in alleys around the Virtual Vision tower, each with nine guerrillas and a medic." He nodded in Flo's direction and heads turned that way to see their chief medic and her staff standing at the ready.

"Most of you will filter into the building earlier," Max continued, "as members of tours and stuff. The main team with the explosives will go in last, after most of the employees have gone home. But there will still be a lot of people there, and a bunch of Security Guards. Watch yourselves, okay?"

Max took a step back, relinquishing the floor to Jason.

"We've pulled out the antique handguns. They've all been reconditioned and tested." Jason said.

Adam threaded his way through the crowd to get a closer look at the weapons. He knew a little about guns from his times in Frontier Vision. Mostly Colt Peacemakers, but it piqued his interest to see other guns, real guns, here in front of him.

"What's going on here? What are the explosives and guns for?" he asked Diana.

"We're going to take out the Network's central transmitters," Diana said.

"You're going to crash the entire system?" He stared at her in disbelief.

"You got it," she nodded.

"I thought you were going to rescue that kid today."

"We are. That's first on the agenda. We have someone planted inside VVN who will help us get Bobby back, then we blow the modules. All of them."

Adam was shocked at the plan. These people were nuts. After last night's fiasco, he had hoped to be sent to the hydroponics room with a rake and a bucket of plant food. Why was he even here? Did they think he was some kind of guerrilla or something? Jason raised his hand to call the room to attention.

"Comments? Problems?"

Diana raised her hand.

"Yes, Diana?"

"Ever since we recovered those antique weapons, I've been concerned about putting them to use. We know Security Guards don't use projectile weapons anymore. They use implant disrupter guns which have no effect on us anyway."

"Your point?" Jason said.

"Those Guards are essentially unarmed. I don't think it's right for us to fire on them. I propose we go in without the guns."

The room buzzed with discussion. Diana spoke louder, which quieted the crowd. "VVN Security isn't the enemy! The system's our target, not the guards!"

Jason turned to look his daughter straight in the eyes. "Look, Diana," he said. "I know what you're saying, but we only have one shot at pulling this off. We can't afford to fail."

"How are we going to convince the subscribers we're on their side if we start killing defenseless people?" she countered angrily.

Adam shook his head. He didn't care if he was a newcomer here. These folks needed to be set straight.

"Pardon me for jumping in, but you people are whacko if you think you can waltz in there and blow up the whole Network Control Center." Every eye in the room was on him. "I'm not kidding. What kind of trip are you on here? I see your floor plans tacked up all pretty on the walls, so you know the modules are spread out all over the place. How do you figure to get to them past dozens, maybe hundreds of guards without getting your asses shot up? And shooting back?"

Diana glared at him. "You don't know what you're talking about. We have this carefully planned. And they only have disrupters! They won't even have..."

A woman's voice interrupted from the back of the room. "Network Security has projectile weapons," she said firmly.

People looked back with surprise as Raven stepped into the room. No one had seen Javier bring her in. It was quite unusual to have not one, but two newcomers, especially at a meeting like this. Javier folded his arms and smiled slightly. Adam frowned. Despite her apparent acceptance into the group, there was something about her that he still didn't like. He had hoped to have an opportunity to talk to her and ask her why she had been following him. All he could do now was rely on the judgment of Javier and the others who had accepted her as one of their own.

Raven continued speaking as she made her way to the table. "And they won't hesitate to blast a hole in your chests when their disrupters don't stop you."

Her claim caused a stir in the room. Jason wheeled out to the center.

"Some of you will be carrying weapons," he said, "but they're only to be used as a last resort. Remember that our goal is to take out the modules that run virtual vision with a minimum of bloodshed. This isn't the OK Corral. Now, are there any more objections?" He looked pointedly at Adam, then around the room. No one had anything else to add. He nodded.

"We've tried to negotiate and we've been ignored," Jason continued. "I see no reason to postpone the operation any longer. Unless anyone knows something I don't, we move out in ten minutes. Here are your tunics." There were a few groans from around the room. "I know some of you hate the idea of wearing them again, but we need to blend in with the citizenry when the system crashes. Your parrots and birds of paradise shirts aren't the best camouflage."

He started tossing tunics into the crowd. The guerrillas murmured among themselves, stripping off their jeans and colorful shirts. They each took a moment to drape their real clothes over the back of a chair. They had great respect for the individuality that the clothing stockpile in Fred's Everything Room offered them. Despite the lack of undergarments, none of them were shy about changing in front of the others, and soon the room was a sea of brown and gray. From Keepers to Sleepers in a matter of minutes.

"Good. Go to your stations and begin preparations. We'll meet at the east door in ten minutes."

The room cleared quickly.

Adam and Diana stayed behind. Adam approached Jason, who remained seated at the table.

"Is all this really necessary? You have to blow up VVN?"

"How do you cure someone who doesn't know they're sick, Adam? Do you think people will voluntarily give up their perfect illusions for this?" He gestured around him at the plain room.

"Why should they have to?"

"Because they'll never clean up the rot and decay unless they're forced to see it."

"But crashing the system will cause total chaos. There'll be panic, madness!"

"We'll do everything we can to smooth the transition. But it must be done," Jason said. He looked pointedly at Adam. "And we need your help."

"My help? No friggin' way. I just got outta there. I'm not going back."

"Fine," Diana said. "We don't need you."

"Yes, we do, Diana," Jason told her. He looked back at Adam. "Diana has done recon in the building already. And Javier has given us what he can. But we need to identify more voids to use as staging areas— places that can't be seen by people with implants. You'll be able to see these unprogrammed spaces now where you couldn't before and you can point them out to Diana on one final sweep. Plus, if necessary, you have her back while she goes in and gets Bobby out."

He had been nervous last night, with no anticipation of trouble. Now he was being asked, no, *told*, that he would be going into a dangerous environment on a dangerous mission. He glared at Diana. She scowled back.

"Okay, I'll help spring Bobby. But then I'm out of there. You people are going to get massacred, and so are some of the people I worked with. I want no part of it."

Jason nodded and turned to his daughter. "Diana? Take him on reconnaissance and then bring him back out."

"If all he wants to do is save his ass, it's none of my business. Sure, I'll take him."

"Good. Here, Adam. Put this on." He held out a tunic. Adam hesitated. He had only been wearing his jeans and flannel shirt for a couple of days and the last thing he wanted now was to be back in a tunic and part of some cockamamie plan to get a lot of people killed. Before taking his shirt off, he reached in the pocket and pulled out the strawberries he had stashed there. *Probably my last*, he thought, and popped them in his mouth. Then he stripped and put the tunic on.

Jason unrolled a plastic map of VVN headquarters and began to explain the plan for rescuing Bobby. Diana pulled up a chair and joined him. This would be a stealth operation. If just one or two people could sneak in, they might successfully extract their young comrade without tipping Security before the larger, more important mission began. She leaned forward to listen. Adam only half-listened as he scanned the floor plans on the walls. At least they seemed accurate enough.

In an alley not far from the Virtual Vision Network tower, nine guerrillas worked quietly to unpack their gear. Flo checked her medical bag. Max, Jake, Raven, and Javier carefully checked the explosive packs and the weapons. Raven and Javier had worked together before, so words were unnecessary as they prepared.

Nearby, Diana and Adam geared up for their foray into the tower. Diana pulled a plastic half-mask out of her canvas bag and handed it to Adam.

"Here, put this on," she said. "Security won't be looking for these new faces."

Adam stared at the Groucho Marx-like glasses with attached fake nose, mustache, and bushy black eyebrows like he'd never seen one before. And he hadn't. He turned it over in his hands.

"What is this?"

"It's called a mask," she said. "People used to wear them in the days before virtual vision."

"What for?" he said, still not getting it.

She pulled another mask out of the bag and looked at it. It was the same mask. She hated stupid questions, especially when she didn't know the answer.

"I don't know! To hide your face! What does it matter? Put it on."

Diana hooked the side pieces of the mask's black plastic glasses over her ears to hold it in place. She looked ridiculous. The big, black, bushy eyebrows and bulbous nose covered most of her otherwise pretty face.

"What do you need one for? I'm the guy on the lam," Adam said.

"I've been in there a few times as myself. It might look suspicious if I show up again. Better to be safe."

Adam looked at her and chuckled. "You look funny."

Diana shook her head. "Only to you and me. In virtual vision no one should even be able to tell we've got them on."

"Yeah, but you might catch a few stares at that big shaggy mustache! Are you sure that part's right?"

Diana ripped her mask off and looked at it. She shook her head. "Oh, yeah."

She snapped the mustache and eyebrows off from the glasses and stuck them back in the bag. She put the mask back on. It was just a big nose, now, and black-rimmed glasses around her eyes. It would simply have to do.

Adam placed his mask carefully on his face and lightly explored his new "features" with his fingertips.

"I sure hope you're right or this is going to be a short trip," he said, turning to her.

"You should know as well as I do that people don't really see what's there, they see what the nanites in their brains tell them is there. Haven't you noticed how your senses have come alive since the implant was removed?"

Adam blushed, remembering his first shower the other day.

"They're not going to notice a thing," Diana continued. "Trust me."

She hefted her small canvas shoulder bag and nodded to him. She hoped he was ready for this, and that she could count on him if it got rough in there.

"Let's go."

Adam and Diana left the quiet security of the alley and joined the other pedestrians going about their daily business. On the next block, the big-nosed couple with black-rimmed glasses stopped and looked up at VVN Headquarters. Adam shook his head. This was ridiculous. He didn't want to be doing this. Diana poked him with her elbow and they walked through the massive glass doors. They entered the busy lobby and approached the guard desk.

The VVN lobby hid its age and decay better than most buildings because of the timeless durability of its marble flooring and walls. In fact, if it weren't for the plain gray tunics and pasty skin of the VVN employees, in actual reality the lobby would look a lot like a Basic Service view.

A placard on the counter announced: "TOURS ON THE HOUR."

The desk guard, in his sharp blue uniform, looked up from his computer log as an attractive young woman in a pretty red suit and pageboy flip nervously approached his counter.

"Hello, my name is Penelope Penny. I'm here to apply for a job."

"What department?" the guard asked.

She reached into her pocketbook and consulted a note.

"I'm supposed to see Mr. Watson in Touch and Textures."

"Ninth floor," the guard said. "Sign in."

She was anxious about the interview and accidentally dropped her ID card on the countertop. She quickly picked it up and forced it into the little slot, then slipped it back into her pocketbook.

"Elevators," he said, pointing to his left.

Miss Penny walked away, leaving Adam and Diana next in line. The guard looked them over with a bored, disinterested glance. In the guard's Security Vision,

Adam and Diana looked like the masks "come to life." Not an attractive couple. Though, in his old eyes, no one looked attractive anymore. So many anonymous faces filed past him in an endless parade every day.

"Cards, please," he droned, scratching his grizzled jaw.

Adam and Diana handed their fake IDs over to the guard. He ran them through the mag-reader and handed them back, then glanced at the read-out.

"Francis and Jessica James," he read. "Please state your business."

Diana went into her disgruntled customer act.

"We have an appointment with Billing" she whined. "Do you know they charged us 300 credits for a 30 credit service? As if prices weren't already high enough! Well I won't stand for it!"

The desk guard tuned out Diana's bellyaching. He heard this a hundred times a day. "Yeah, yeah. Sixth floor."

Adam and Diana headed for the elevators.

Adam shot Diana a look. "Frank and Jesse James?"

"Shut up," she said without looking at him.

Adam stared at her back as she forged on ahead of him and into an open elevator.

They exited on the twentieth floor and walked casually up the hall. Adam showed Diana a virtual vision-invisible door in an otherwise featureless section of wall. He whispered near her ear, "That wall should be smooth. I never saw that door before." Diana nodded. She glanced around to be sure they were alone and then turned the door's handle and pushed the door open, revealing a long forgotten utility closet. Glancing around once more, she and Adam quickly ducked into the closet and entirely out of view.

Alone in the conference room, Copley faced the Security Captain's vidphone image. He had just returned from an unproductive interrogation of the young prisoner. If he didn't hate him and everything he stood for, he might have admired the boy's resolve. Instead, he feared a possible rescue attempt from the Underground.

Out of the vidphone's view, the governor gripped a pearl-handled revolver as he spoke.

"There is the very real possibility that there might be unwelcome intruders in the building who plan to attack our employees. Keep a wary eye out for them and if you find them, bring them to me. Put every person you have on the search."

The Security Captain nodded crisply. "Yessir!"

"Contact me the minute you apprehend them. Oh, and Captain, issue projectile weapons to the search teams. You may discover your disrupter guns are not," he paused, searching for the right word, "... reliable."

The Captain looked surprised. This was a first.

"Yessir."

"Disconnect," Copley ordered the computer.

Copley turned from the computer screen and sighted down the barrel of his gun.

From inside the virtually invisible closet, Diana cracked the door inward a quarter of an inch so she could keep an eye on the hallway. She watched as a skinny guard walked toward them down the hall. She knew he was a guard because of his badge and holstered disrupter gun; otherwise, he looked like any other employee in a tunic. But in Virtual Vision, that badge on someone's chest changed their ordinary tunics into guard uniforms. It was the same for the beat cops. Wear a badge, and the tunic becomes a uniform.

As the guard passed just inches from their position, unaware of the guerrillas' presence, Diana popped out of the closet just behind him. She quickly pulled the startled man into the closet where, before he had a chance to react, Adam cold cocked him with a fist to the jaw. The unconscious guard slid silently to the floor.

"Did you have to hit him?" she hissed.

"I suppose you were going to talk him into sitting quietly here in the closet while you go blow up the place," Adam hissed back.

"You idiot! He's one of us. George Mooney, Max's brother. Dad arranged for him to meet us and take us to Bobby." Diana rooted around in her bag looking for something, anything, that might help revive the man. As she was searching, she heard a moan and looked down to see him regaining consciousness.

"George, are you okay?" She rubbed his wrists then checked his eyes. "Talk to me, George."

Just then, a couple of Network employees walked past them in the hallway, only inches away from their position. She quickly covered George's mouth so he wouldn't speak and give away their position. Once they passed, Diana turned to Adam.

"Look," she whispered. "I don't go for that macho shit, got it? There's too much at stake here for you to make like John Wayne in a barroom brawl."

"Okay," Adam said. "I guess I kind of admire your determination to end life as we know it without hurting anyone, but it just amazes me that you live in the real world without understanding the real world at all."

Diana paused a moment before replying. "We have to try, Adam. It means a lot to us, to do this without hurting people if we can."

Adam looked into her eyes and saw her sincerity. She had a habit of saying "we," but he suspected it was her own heart she spoke for. He nodded.

George sat up, rubbing his jaw where Adam's fist had connected. He was still implanted so he couldn't see anything but blackness in the void, but he spoke in the direction he thought Adam was.

"Yeah, that's why I love this job so much. Damn. You must be the new guy," he said. "Where'd you learn to punch like that?"

"Did you get the stuff?" Diana interrupted.

"I got two extra badges but I could only get one disrupter. They keep a pretty close eye on 'em. They have Bobby in the basement. Don't want to take a chance of any employees seeing him. We can take the main elevator down, then I know a back way out."

He reached into his pockets and pulled out two Security Guard badges and blindly held them out. Diana and Adam pinned them onto their chests. He then pulled out the lone disrupter.

"Who gets this?" he asked.

Diana took the disrupter and slapped it onto her hip.

"I'll take it. Looks like the cowboy here can take care of himself."

Diana picked up her bag and watched the hallway outside the closet, waiting for a break in foot traffic. With their masks in place, Adam and Diana left the closet, with George right behind them.

At the elevators, they looked each other over as they waited for a car to reach them. They felt ridiculously exposed in actual reality; Diana's badge and disrupter gun looked out of place on her plain tunic, and the fake noses and glasses looked transparently phony. They both jumped when the elevator announced its arrival with a loud *ding*.

Inside the elevator, in "Normal Vision," Brad Jameson and Henry Jones, the R & D Department supervisor, were returning from an unpleasant meeting with Security.

"Well, I didn't appreciate their whole attitude!" Henry complained. "You'd think we were the ones suspected of something! What's Porter done, anyway?"

Brad was uncomfortable with his question. He knew far more than he wished he did, and he wasn't about to share it with old Henry.

"I don't know any more than you do, Mr. Jones," he lied.

The elevator doors slid open to reveal three blue-uniformed Security Guards—a female with a large nose and eyeglasses, another who could have been her brother who sported a moustache and the most amazing eyebrows, and one quite plain. Brad and Henry looked right at Adam. Nothing about the tall man in front of him looked even vaguely familiar to Brad, which was exactly as the guerrillas had hoped—that his disguise would hide him from even his closest friends and co-workers. But even so, Adam's heart did a somersault in his chest at the sight of Brad. He wanted to say something to him, but stopped himself.

After their recent run-in with Security, Henry was a little unnerved to be faced with three more of their guards just two feet in front of him. He hesitated in the car before disembarking. He was torn between being rude just for the sake of being rude, or disappearing into the carpet. The female guard decided for him.

"Please move along, sir," Diana barked in an officious tone. "Thank you." She, of course, didn't know

Brad or Henry and only wanted them to get out of the way.

Adam, Diana, and George stepped in as soon as Brad and Henry exited the elevator.

"Pompous asses," Henry said loud enough for them to hear as they walked away.

Inside the elevator, Adam leaned heavily against its filthy wall. Seeing Brad had been hard. Despite their argument in the "hideout," he still missed his good friend a lot. Brad was his only connection to the life he'd known before. His whole life, growing up in that house, marrying Trisha, losing her and the baby, everything, every memory, rested with his best friend Brad, and seeing him suddenly like that had brought all of it flooding back. And with it, the knowledge that it was irretrievably gone. He had no idea what this new life would bring, and so far it wasn't all that great. What had he gotten himself into here?

Adam touched his mask and laughed nervously. Brad had looked right at him without knowing him, all because of a few pieces of plastic and a badge on his chest.

"What's the matter with you?" Diana asked.

He shook his head. "Nothing. I just..." he let the sentence hang. He didn't want to get into it with her. It was a long story, better saved for another day.

Diana turned to examine the grimy, illegible elevator control panel. Adam reached around her and punched the button on the lower left. The one with a faded "B". "Basement, I presume," he said.

The elevator stopped twice on the way down, each time letting passengers on and off, and each time Adam held his breath, expecting someone to see through the silly plastic disguise. The final *ding* of the doors opening in the dark basement was no comfort. It signaled the beginning of a fear that gripped his stomach and tied it in knots.

In all the years he had worked in this building, he had never been below the lobby floor. There had never been a need. Supplies showed up on his desk when he put in a requisition on his computer. He had no idea who fetched them, or where they came from. The basement? He hadn't even noticed the faded button on the bottom of the panel. And now he'd be going down there for the first time. He had no idea what to expect.

The three guerrillas slipped off the elevator and dropped into the shadows. The basement was typical of a large office building, with shelves loaded with plastic boxes and bins of office supplies. It was a maze of corridors, all of them dark, lit only with the smallest lights at the corners. For the moment, no one else seemed to be down there. George led the way to the left and started turning left and right, left and right. Diana and Adam were immediately disoriented.

Suddenly, they heard footsteps and voices. They ducked behind a tower of boxes and crouched in the dark shadows, holding their breath. Two of Copley's elite Black Guards were shuffling past.

"Man, I'm glad that shift is over. Geez, I could sleep for a week."

"Yeah, me too. I thought that kid woulda cracked by now. Copley's a mean son of a bitch, isn't he?"

"No shit."

Their voices faded off in the distance. Diana clenched her teeth to keep from screaming. Poor Bobby. She nudged her two companions and they continued on their way.

A door on their right caught Adam's attention. His sensitive nose picked up a scent. He stopped and put his hand on the door knob. In the dark of the hallway, his shoes were illuminated by the bright light that streamed from under the entrance. He slowly turned the knob and opened the door a few inches. He knew what he would see.

It was a grow room. Much smaller than the one in the Underground, but complete with grow lights, fruits, and vegetables. *What's this doing here?* Adam wondered. He stepped into the room and walked up to a dwarf apple tree heavy with fruit. There were other fruit trees and a few vegetables, too.

Diana and George stepped through the doorway. Although Max had been supplying his brother and his family with real food, George had never seen live plants actually growing like this. And, like the other employees of the tower above, no one had a clue there was a grow room in the basement of VVN.

"Wow! Would you look at this!" George exclaimed.

"Come on, Adam," Diana whispered loudly. "We've got a job to do."

Hearing voices near the door, the lone woman gardener strode angrily out to the center aisle and shook her fist at them.

"Get out of here and close the damn door! How many times do I have to tell you jerks? This is a controlled environment!" she barked sharply at them.

"Sorry, ma'am," Adam replied quickly. "Wrong door."

All three of them hastily shuffled out into the dark hallway. Adam closed the door and looked at Diana. They were all surprised to find such a facility here, but they didn't have time to investigate. George tapped on

Diana's shoulder and pointed silently further down the corridor.

They came to within thirty feet of another doorway when George stopped them.

"No guards posted outside," he whispered, "because Copley doesn't want anyone to know he has a prisoner. But there will be at least two of his Black Guards inside with Bobby. What's the plan?" He had gotten them this far, now he turned to Diana for instructions. She was squad leader on this one.

"Walk in, tell them Copley wants the prisoner upstairs, walk out with Bobby," she whispered.

"You're kidding, right?" Adam said.

She spun on him, and had to stop herself from shouting lest she give away their position.

"Listen, cowboy, we'll try it my way. If it doesn't work, feel free to use your fists since you don't seem too eager to use your brains here, okay?"

"Happy to oblige, ma'am," he hissed back at her. He couldn't decide if he hated her for being naïve, or liked her for her ideals. What the hell, he'd figure it out later. For now, they had a job to do and he was pretty sure it wasn't going to go as smoothly as she thought.

He was right. The two guards weren't buying it when Diana tried to talk them into releasing the prisoner to her. It broke her heart to see the bruised and bloody condition Bobby was in. He still sat on the stool but his shoulders drooped and his hooded head hung low on his chest. He recognized Diana's voice but said nothing and tried not to move at all.

The guard nearest her looked at the three of them suspiciously.

"Stay where you are," he ordered as he sidled over to the vidphone on a table. "I'll check with the

Governor, then I'll let you know if you'll get our little package here or not."

"Screw that," Diana said, and in the blink of an eye she pulled her disrupter out and shot the man. He fell in a heap on the concrete floor. His partner was quick though and jumped behind Bobby, grabbing him around the neck.

"Shoot me and I'll twist his head off as I go down."

Suddenly, Bobby lifted his head up and smashed the back of his skull into the guard's nose. His bound hands, still behind his back, reached out and, tightening his fingers together, he jabbed at whatever body part he could reach, which turned out to be the Guard's balls. The man stopped screaming abruptly when Diana shot him, too, and he dropped, unconscious, next to his partner.

"So," Adam said as he rushed over to release Bobby's bonds, "I guess you didn't need me after all." He was pretty happy about that, actually. Despite her idealistic and ridiculous hope to talk her way out of here, she hadn't hesitated to shoot when she needed to. His respect for her stepped up a notch.

She ignored him and turned to George.

"Can you manage him by yourself?" she asked.

"No problem. He's a little guy," George said, yanking off the hood and reaching for the last ropes around Bobby's wrists.

"Hey," Bobby's voice was raspy. "Not so little, and man, am I glad to see you guys. Let's get out of here. Copley said he'd be back soon."

The three of them half carried Bobby to a nearby exit that George assured them was little known. Bobby's legs were rubbery but he could support his weight on the unbroken leg with assistance. Diana hugged the boy and whispered in his ear, then, with a tear in her eye, she waved them off and pulled Adam back the way they had come.

After a few wrong turns, Adam and Diana found their way back to the elevator and slipped into the car when it arrived. She punched the button for the 20th floor.

They left the elevator and Diana headed for an unmarked door at the end of the hall. She motioned Adam through.

"Was this door visible before?" she asked after she had closed the door behind them.

"I saw this one every day. I just don't know what it's for."

"I do. Let's go."

She led the way up a narrow stairwell, walking softly, cautiously. At the top of the stairs, there was another door. She opened it a crack and looked out to see if it was clear. Satisfied, she stepped through and crouched down. Adam followed.

They were on a narrow catwalk that ran the perimeter of the large Module Control room. Forty feet below them, six major computer modules were tended by a dozen techie geeks. The modules were various sizes, but all had a mass of wires, pipes and conduits rising from their tops, reaching to a conglomeration of spaghetti that coated the whole ceiling. A metal grid work supported it and was accessible from the catwalk.

The module nearest them was for Frontier Vision. In plain block letters a stainless steel plaque affixed to the machine identified it as the "Frontier Vision Control Module." Behind and to the side, another module was labeled "Cartoon Vision." Two techs worked on an open panel in its front. One of them, Governor Copley's secret technician, Robert, laughed as the other got zapped with a slight shock from crossing the wrong wires. He patted his co-worker on the shoulder and headed back to the Shangrila module to continue his clandestine programming activities.

The plaques on the rest of the modules were too far away to read, but he knew that they were UltraModern, Chapel, Security, and, where Robert was now hunched over a circuit board, Copley's new baby, Shangrila.

"Ever been in here before?" Diana whispered.

"Sure, but not up here. I've been down there a lot. I know most of those guys. Buncha geeks, but they're okay." Adam pointed toward the main doors into the room. "Look over there," he said.

A tour group streamed in, about twenty men and women all agog at the immensity of the modules and in awe of the system that brought them their premium channels. They stopped in front of the closest computer tower.

To the tourists, in what they thought was normal, offline vision, the Frontier Vision plaque looked heavy and impressive, with raised letters rising up from a polished brass base. And although they saw the walls and ceiling as being a little brighter and cleaner than Adam and Diana did, they still saw that the computer towers dominated the room, draped with an abundance of wires and cables. They marveled at the Virtual Vision technicians bustling about in their bright orange jumpsuits.

The tour guide, Heidi, a plucky girl of nineteen, launched into her spiel. She was one of those kids that could say the same lines a thousand times and still get as excited as she had the first time she'd pinned on her tour guide badge and lead a group around.

"Here we have the control module for our most popular channel, Frontier Vision. About 75% of our subscribers select Frontier Vision every week." She surveyed the group.

"How many of you requested Frontier Vision in the last ten days? Let's see a show of hands."

Nine smiling tourists raised their hands. Up on the catwalk, Adam raised his hand, grinning. Diana rolled her eyes.

Heidi continued down below. "And how many have never tried Frontier Vision?" There were fewer hands this time.

"Well, have we got a treat for you. If the four of you—oh, what the heck, all of you—would step over there and place your hands on the screen, we'll give you a two minute taste of the Old West right here and now. Cowboys, horses, the great open plains. Come on, right over here. Give it a try."

When Adam heard this, he was touched with a little bit of sadness. As he watched them file over to the monitor, talking excitedly, he recalled his many days in his favorite log cabin, the great fun of the gunfights with the ugly desperadoes, and especially his loyal dog, Bo. He'd never get to see Bo again now that he'd agreed to have his implant removed. He envied those tourists their two minutes in the frontier.

Diana saw the look on his face and softened. She knew it was still hard for him to accept. But she also knew they had to get back to the business at hand. She tapped him on the arm and headed back out the door to the stairwell.

As they tiptoed back down the stairs, Diana whispered, "Each of those modules will need its own explosive charge. Did you see anything down there that we should know about?"

"Yeah, I think you should know that those are regular guys, with families and friends. Guys I don't want to see get hurt."

"Adam..."

"No." He turned away from her. He knew she didn't want them hurt either, but she was determined to carry out her mission, with or without his help. "Nothing hidden that you can use."

After leaving the VVN Control Center, the tour group followed their guide down the twentieth floor hallway. Heidi continued her memorized patter as she pointed out various quasi-interesting areas for her charges. As they passed the nondescript door to the catwalk, Adam and Diana removed their badges and tossed them into her canvas bag. Then they slipped in at the rear of the group. Mimicking the tourists, they "oohed" and "aahed" at each thing they were shown.

Around the corner, a couple of guards strolled down the hall from the other direction. Adam held his breath as he and Diana tried to appear inconspicuous in the group. He hated this spy stuff. What if they were caught? Back to Serenity Gardens for reimplantation? Or worse? He wished he'd never agreed to do this. He didn't start breathing again until the guards passed them without a backward glance.

Midway down the hall, they spotted Miss Penelope Penny wandering around, looking quite lost. She approached them with a sheepish look on her face.

"Pardon me," she said. "Is this the ninth floor?"

"No," Adam replied. "This is twenty."

"Oh, dear," she said, glancing at her watch. She hustled back toward the elevators.

"Where to now?" Adam asked after she had gone.

"Basic Service," Diana said. "It takes up the entire fourteenth floor."

Adam nodded. Fourteen had always been off limits to employees and like so much of his previous life, he had never questioned why.

"Because," he added, still putting the pieces together in his mind, "even though they don't know it, everybody in the city is on that system, aren't they?"

"Yes, but it's much too heavily guarded for a frontal assault. We'll go to fifteen and prepare an access route through the air ducts."

Outside in the alley, the rest of the strike team waited. Javier smiled over at Raven. She acknowledged with the barest smile back at him. Flo watched Max, Jake, and the others recheck their ammo for the umpteenth time. She took Javier aside.

"How much longer?" she asked.

"Everything is set up in each of the staging areas and we'll go as soon as Diana comes out—maybe half an hour," Javier replied.

Flo nodded. "I spoke to Jason just before we left. He said, and I quote, 'Tell everyone my thoughts are with you. Be careful, and try not to get anyone hurt, including yourselves.'"

"Thanks, Flo. I'll tell them." Javier patted her shoulder and she sat down, worried about all of them.

He relayed the message to the others and added, "Remember, they might have projectile weapons in there, so don't play the hero. Do what you have to do, then get out. I'm going further into the alley to check it out. I'm gonna make sure we don't have any problems like we had on Clark Street. Max, come with me."

"No, I'll come," Raven volunteered. "It'll give me something to do."

Javier nodded and gave the barest of smiles to Raven. The two of them left to reconnoiter.

Jake elbowed Max and pointed his chin in their direction. He made a crude gesture depicting Javier's and Raven's supposed tryst.

"Some guys have all the luck," Jake said.

Approaching the fifteenth floor of the VVN Tower, Adam and Diana checked each other's disguises as they waited for the elevator doors to open. He looked at Diana in her funny nose and big black glasses and realized that, like it or not, this was his life now. This is what he'd gotten himself into and he had to pull himself together. He remembered what Diana had said to him the other morning about doing the best you can with what you've got. He mentally shook off his sentimentality about the past.

The elevator doors slid open in front of them and they stepped out. They found themselves alone in the hallway. Adam looked around and spotted a virtual vision-invisible air duct halfway up the wall. There was no sign of the grate that must have once covered the gaping hole. He showed the duct to Diana and they made their way toward it.

The entrance to the air duct was dark and dusty. Adam and Diana looked up and down the hallway to make sure no one was around before hoisting themselves up into the duct. No sooner had they entered the duct than an office door opened and three employees walked out into the hall. One of the group glanced in their direction.

For a moment there, he thought he saw a foot sticking right out of a solid wall, but it quickly disappeared. Puzzled, he moved toward the spot, but all he saw was a totally smooth, clean wall. He decided against telling his pals; if he did, he'd never hear the end of it. His two friends grabbed him and moved on down the hall, laughing and talking with each other. He glanced over his shoulder one last time and walked on.

Inside the air duct, Diana breathed a sigh of relief and removed her mask.

"That was close," she said, watching the group leave the hall. She stuck the mask in a pocket. "We won't need these for a while."

Adam followed her lead and also removed his mask.

"But you look so darn cute with that big nose," he said.

"Save it, lover boy."

She crawled off down the air duct, pushing her bag in front of her. He followed. They crawled through the twisting ductwork until they located a downward turn that dropped to the floor below. She took a length of sturdy rope out of her satchel and tied one end to a beam with a double figure 8 knot. She gave it a yank, then reached out and grabbed it firmly with her hands. She swung her legs until she had wrapped the rope around both calves and ankles tightly. Then with the pressure of her legs to slow her descent to the floor below, she lowered herself hand over hand.

Adam stared at her from above, wishing he'd paid more attention to that nifty maneuver.

"How do I do this? What do I do first?" he called softly.

"Hands first, then legs. And use your legs as brakes to slow your descent."

Adam did as he was told and began the careful slide down the rope. Halfway down, the beam shifted under his weight. The rope jerked! Adam dropped a couple inches before the rope grabbed again. From below, Diana gasped.

"Hang on tight! Don't fall!" she called up to him.

"The woman has a unique talent for stating the obvious," he muttered to himself.

He gripped the rope hard and slid down it quickly, lest the beam shift again. When he got to the bottom he blew on his hands and gave them a shake. Diana grabbed them and turned them palms up. They were red but not torn or bleeding.

"Just a little rope burn. Nothing serious; you're fine. Let's go."

They crawled along the duct until they found a vent opening that overlooked the Basic Service control floor. The "Basic Service Central Processing Unit" stood like a giant octopus in the middle of the floor, fed by dozens of thick tentacles connected to a network of smaller units ringing the tower. A few technicians in their faded orange jumpsuits tended the enormous machine like clown fish darting around a bed of sea anemones.

"Bingo," Adam said. "Geeks and all."

"That's it, alright. The Fountain of Lies. The BS-CPU, or the "bull shit computer," as we call it. Damn, it's going to be tough shutting that monster down; you can bet it's got plenty of redundant backup systems to ensure it never goes down. We'll need to blow it all to hell to take it out. Okay, let's go back to the alley," she said, glancing at her watch. "They're waiting for us."

Jake, Max, and the others were growing impatient. This sitting and waiting stuff was getting on everyone's nerves. They'd run out of small talk, and no one really felt like talking anyway. Despite running over the plan so many times that they would be dreaming the details for weeks, they were still tense, even a little scared. They had gone on plenty of raids, some more dangerous than others, but all had been scavenging raids or just plain nuisance raids. Nothing this big, nothing this important, nothing that could result in more people getting hurt and dying than ever before. Some of them picked at their finger nails. Some just stared into space. Jake had taken to playing mumbledy peg with his pocket knife and had narrowly missed amputating his own toe.

"Oh, there you go, Jakie," Flo admonished him. "That's being real careful. You listen real good, don't ya."

Jake yanked the blade out of the ground and flipped it closed. "Well, shit. Where are they, anyway? How much longer do we have to wait?" He just wanted to hear that Bobby had been rescued and was safely out of that place. He shoved the knife into his pocket and crossed his arms.

Max ignored Jake's sulking. They'd be on the move soon enough.

"Just a couple more minutes," he said, looking at his watch.

"And what about them?" Jake jabbed a thumb toward the back of the alley. "They've been gone a while."

Javier and Raven had scoped out the rest of the alley. Satisfied that all was well, they found an open doorway and decided to check it out. They found themselves in the back room of what used to be a clothing boutique and had known immediately it was an unused space because of the racks of rotting clothes and the undisturbed dust that layered every surface.

Raven suddenly turned and kissed Javier hungrily. He resisted at first, but then kissed her back, just as hungry for her. He knew he probably shouldn't be here with her just before such an important raid, but ever since she had arrived, he had taken every opportunity to be alone with her, naked and sweating and wrapped up in her arms and legs. It was how they had spent most of their off-duty time before his disappearance. He couldn't resist her then; he couldn't resist her now. His kisses became more demanding.

She stopped and looked up at him, her arms around his neck.

"You were gone so long. Why did you stay away so long?"

"Because I chose reality. I stayed. Simple." He laughed, his arms still tight around her. "Why, did you miss me?"

She pulled away for a moment. Her eyes pierced his. "More than you'll ever know," she said quietly. His answer wasn't what she had wanted to hear.

Adam and Diana finally reached the mouth of the duct on the fifteenth floor. Diana pulled out her mask and put it on.

"Okay, the rope is secure for later. I should have run it over two beams in the first place. It'll hold now. Let's get out of here," she said.

Adam squirmed in the small space, searching his pockets for his mask. "I can't find my mask!" He searched the same pockets again. "I must have lost it in the ducts. Shit, now what? Should I go back and look for it? Do you have another one?"

"No and no." She pushed her mask up out of the way as she sat back on her heels to think.

211

"This is trouble, Adam. You can't just go walking around VVN Headquarters. Security will spot you in a minute. How the hell are we going to get you out of here?"

"I'll make it out on my own."

She looked at him a moment and then shook her head.

"No, if they catch you, the whole operation is in jeopardy. We can't risk months of preparation and all these lives. We have to find another way."

Diana slipped her mask back into place. Suddenly, she reached in her bag and rummaged about.

"Wait! The mustache. It's not much, but maybe it'll help."

She pulled out the fake mustache she had removed from her own mask. She rooted around in the bag, shoving things aside until she came up with a small roll of medical adhesive tape sealed in an airtight tin. Old, but still usable. She ripped off an inch or so, turned it into an inside-out loop, and stuck it on his upper lip. Then she stuck the mustache on it.

"Do this," she said, demonstrating by sticking her upper teeth out, looking buck-toothed.

He tried it. Major overbite. He looked ridiculous. She couldn't help herself; she almost laughed out loud.

"Now you're the one who looks funny."

"Leth hope ith funny enough to fool the Guardth."

"You just be careful, okay? Walk weird, with a limp or something, and keep those teeth out there where I can see them."

"You got it. Diana..."

He looked at her for a long moment. Unspoken potential crackled between them. Okay, maybe it was just a tiny sputter, but it was something. It was there.

"What?" She felt it, too.

212

"Nothing. Let's go." Now wasn't the time.

"Badges?" he reminded her.

"Oh yeah. Thanks." She reached into her bag and took out the two Security Guard badges. They each pinned one to their chests.

They waited for the hall to empty out, then lowered themselves out of the duct. Adam stretched his long legs, glad to be vertical again. He threw his teeth out over his lip as far as he could and headed for the elevators, throwing in a pigeon-toed limp for good measure.

Javier pulled Raven even closer and kissed her again.

"Just like old times. I've missed you, Raven. I'm glad you're here."

"I'm not," she replied.

"What do you mean?" he asked, surprised.

She pulled away from him and, with her fingertips, she picked up a rotted, filthy piece of cloth that had once been a silk blouse with pearl buttons. It disgusted her.

"I hate this. I want to go back to where everything is clean and looks the way it's supposed to. I happen to like blue skies and green lawns—is that a crime? And I want you to go back with me. Please, baby." She dropped the cloth and surveyed the rest of the room. "How can you stand this? Don't you miss the life we had before?"

Javier sighed. "Sometimes; but mostly I don't. Sure, we had sharp uniforms, all black and sexy with shiny gold buttons, but it wasn't real. Those green lawns and pretty skies weren't real, either, baby; nothing was real. And, Raven, listen carefully—if you were to go back, it's not like this would disappear. It would all still be here, still ugly and crumbling and dying."

"But I wouldn't have to see it!" She quieted down suddenly and looked closely at him. "Nothing was real? Not even us?"

"That's not what I meant..."

"Javier, the only reason I followed Porter for three days was because I hoped he would lead me to you. Not the Underground, just you. I thought... what a fool I was, I thought you had been abducted by them, captured and held against your will. Stupid me—I thought I was going to rescue you and bring you home. Instead, I find out you prefer this filth and these losers to me." She could feel the anger welling up inside her chest.

"No, Raven. It's not a case of preference. It is what it is, and neither of us can ever go back. There are hundreds of people in the Underground now, and they depend on their leaders—Jason, Diana, Max, and yes, even me—to keep them safe. This is our life now. I'm here; you're here." He looked at her pleadingly. "We can make it good, together."

She hated the idea. Terror and rage suddenly engulfed her like a thunderstorm. She couldn't breathe; she was suffocating. She had to get away.

"I was afraid you'd say something like that."

A slight movement passed between them. His face suddenly registered surprise, and then shock. She stepped back, away from him.

"You bastard," she said coldly.

Javier looked at her, then down to his belly. The bone-handled dagger stuck out of his gut. Suddenly he understood. The booster tower raid. He dropped to his knees, his fingers grasping the knife.

"It was... you? The... raid..."

"Me."

"Why?"

"The idiots were supposed to capture all of us, especially me and you. They only caught the little boy. Stupid fools."

He knew he was dying. "But... we could have been happy here."

"No, not me. Give me virtual vision any day. I want my sexy black uniform back. And I guess I want that a lot more than I want you." She yanked the dagger out of his body and stepped back as the man she had once thought she loved pitched forward onto his face. She wiped the blade on an old dress hanging nearby, then tucked it out of sight in her ankle sheath.

Looking around to be sure she hadn't been seen, she quietly hurried toward the front of the store and onto a nearby street. She checked to be sure she was out of sight of the alley where the others still waited. Sure that she was safe, Raven walked calmly away, blending in with the crowds on the sidewalks.

Half a block away, she felt something on her cheek. She angrily reached up and swiped the tear away with the back of her hand. She despised tears as a sign of weakness—and there was no room for weakness in her life. Love! Talk about a weakness! No way she'd ever fall for that load of crap again. She knew she should turn back to the tower, but she kept walking away. She needed to regain command of her emotions before reporting in.

It was the end of the work day. Diana and Adam stepped out of the elevator into a crowd of day-workers heading for home. They exchanged a look.

"Come wiff me," he lisped, then adjusting his teeth, he spoke properly. "Let's just get out of here. This is nuts."

"You know I can't." She looked in the direction of the Guard Desk. "You go on. Tell the others to begin. I'll take care of the guard."

"Diana..."

"Please..." She looked up at him, pleading for him to go. Behind the black plastic glasses, her dark eyes touched a little part of him in a way that he had thought long dead.

Adam nodded then limped out the main doors with the other workers, teeth out there for all the world to see. As soon as he was outside he unpinned the badge and slipped it into his tunic pocket.

Diana approached the desk guard. He looked up at her with a puzzled expression on his face. His Security Vision showed him an unfamiliar female guard with thick-rimmed glasses and a big nose.

"Can I help you?" he asked.

Diana moved around the counter to stand beside him. "I was called in from transport duty to help out. I understand you're having some troubles around here today."

The old guard eyed Diana uncomfortably. "I wasn't told about this," he said.

"I'm telling you now." She pulled her disrupter gun and silently shot him. He slid to the floor behind the desk. He'd have one heck of a headache when he came to, but otherwise he'd be okay.

Outside, Adam entered the alley, still buck-toothed with a mustache. Max and Jake grinned at his disguise. Suddenly self-conscious, Adam ripped off the mustache and straightened his mouth.

"Bobby's safe. George got him out okay." Jake breathed a sigh of relief. "And we've secured void spaces all the way to the twentieth floor," he told them. "Diana's at the Guard Desk now. You'd better get a move on."

Max said, "Someone better go down the alley and find Javier and Raven."

"I'll go," Jake said.

He lumbered off to the rear of the alley, out of sight. It was another minute before they heard his frantic shout.

"Flo! Get your bag! Max! Aw, shit!"

They all ran down the alley, following Jake's voice to the open door. Flo led the way into the room, medical bag at the ready.

Jake was kneeling next to Javier, holding his limp body in his arms. Dark red blood had spread over the front of Javier's tunic. Flo quickly knelt down and felt for a pulse in Javier's neck. She looked up sadly and shook her head.

"He's dead," she said.

"Raven!" Adam spat out. He had always felt something odd about her. Never truly trusted her.

Max nodded his head and looked around the room. It was easy to see Raven's tracks in the dusty floor. He followed the tracks to the storefront and onto the street. As he had expected, there was no sign of the traitor. He made his way back to the team crowding around Javier's body.

"She's long gone," he said.

Jake was still holding onto Javier. "Geez, man. Javier!"

"He vouched for that woman. He loved her," Flo said, shaking her head. "This is bad, people. This is really bad."

"I'm not sure we can pull this off without Javier," Max finally said. "Do we still go in?"

Jake gently rested Javier on the ground and got up. He looked pointedly at Adam.

"Don't even think it," Adam said, shaking his head.

"You know the building better than any of us," Jake said.

Adam backed up a step. "Wait a minute. I didn't sign up for this."

Max looked from Adam to Jake. "Diana's been here a few times," he said. "Maybe she can lead us in."

"She doesn't know the place like Javier did," Jake snapped. He stared at Adam through narrowed eyes. "Or like you do."

Adam stared down at Javier. Flo had just finished draping a crumbling old jacket over the body.

"Screw you," he said. "I'm not getting myself killed."

Adam bolted out of the building and into the alley, leaving the others grieving and confused. He walked quickly, aimlessly. He was angry. Not one damn thing had gone right since he had smacked his head. And now here he was feeling like an alien on another planet, unsure of the rules, or the expectations. He just wanted to be left alone to... what? Sulk like he used to? Cry over his dead wife? "Geez, Porter," he thought, "get a grip." But it was easier said than done.

Suddenly, he heard a child's voice. Turning a corner, he saw a grimy little girl of about four or five, sitting on the ground near her mother's body, unaware that her mother was dead. The smell assaulted him, even from that distance.

"If I fold it just like this, and this, and this..."

She folded a dirty piece of plastic, apparently trying to make some origami type thing.

"No! It's not working, Mommy. Oh! Okay, you fold it over this way. Right, Mommy?"

To the little girl, Mommy just looked like she was asleep. She didn't notice the man approaching. Her concentration was fixed on getting the plastic correctly folded.

Adam stopped to watch, incredibly saddened by the macabre spectacle.

"No, no, that isn't the way at all!" She reached over and shook her mother's stiff arm. "Mommy. Mommy? I can't do it!" She shook her mother's arm harder.

"Mommy, help me! Mommy? Mommy, wake up!" She forgot all about the folding as she shook her mother's lifeless body, trying to wake her up.

Adam wondered how long she had been sitting there and how often she had tried waking her mother. Where the hell were the police when you needed them? Why hadn't a van come around?

"Please, Mommy! Wake up! Mommy?" The little girl started to cry.

Adam couldn't stand it anymore. He kneeled down and touched her arm, startling her badly.

"Honey," he said gently. "I think you should come with me."

She pulled away from his hand. "No! I have to stay with my Mommy. She's napping! I want her to wake up now and help me fold my toy!"

Adam grabbed her arm and tried to pull her up. She pulled back, trying to escape.

"Please, I'm trying to help you. Your Mommy isn't..." How could he tell her? "She won't..."

The little girl yanked from his grasp and threw herself on her mother's dead body, screaming.

"No! I want my Mommy! Go away! I want my Mommy!"

Tears filled his eyes as he slowly backed away and dropped to his knees. All the pain, heartbreak, confusion, and anger washed over him like acid, burning his skin, his heart, his very soul. And in doing so, it cleansed him somehow. He saw with clarity for the first time. He knew who he was, and he knew he couldn't let this travesty continue. He couldn't bring Trisha back, and he couldn't bring this woman back, but maybe, just maybe, he could help make sure no one else died on the street again. Maybe little girls could grow up playing with their mommies instead of crying over their stinking, bloated bodies.

After a minute, he stood up, turned, and quietly walked away. He dried his face with the sleeve of his shirt as he picked up speed. He knew what he had to do.

It was a big risk, but he pulled his hair down on his face and stuck his teeth out. He pinned back on the badge that would allow others to see him as a guard, then he limped over to a police officer walking his beat and pointed him toward the little girl. Next, as he headed back to the hidden alley, he composed himself.

Adam found the guerrillas still in the alley, still grieving and unsure what to do.

"Okay, let's go," Adam said as he walked up to them. "I'll take you in." He grabbed a gun from the nearest back pack. He checked the cylinder then hefted the weight of the gun in his hands. It felt good, familiar. He twirled it around his finger.

Flo was duly impressed by his skills with the gun. He looked over at Flo's wide-eyed reaction and said, "Frontier Vision; turns out it was good for something after all."

Max checked his explosive charges one last time. The others stood around, reluctant to follow his lead.

Adam tucked the pistol into his backpack and looked up to see that they were all still just standing around.

"Pick up a gun, Jake. You, too, Max. And the rest of you, too."

They still hesitated. He had stormed out of there a few minutes ago with a "screw you" and then had suddenly returned barking orders at them. What the hell?

"Yeah, I know. I'm an asshole. But I'm here and I'm ready to do the job. So pick up those guns or you can go home right now with your tails between your legs and all your fancy talk about saving the planet will be just that—fancy talk.

He grabbed a gun and tossed it to Jake. "Look," Adam continued, "I don't want to shoot anybody either, but we might not have a choice. Let's just go do what we have to do, okay?"

Jake looked to his team members, then back at Adam and nodded. They all grabbed their guns and their gear, then quickly headed toward the front of the alley.

Adam reached in his pocket, pulled out the mustache and slapped it back on. He grabbed a backpack, stuffed another gun in it, and started out of the alley.

Flo stayed behind with her triage equipment. She called after them, "Be careful now. I don't want to have to be sewing on arms and legs later. And you better all come back!"

By the time Raven got back to the Black Guard locker room on the fortieth floor of the Virtual Vision Network tower, she had rationalized the murder of

Javier Mendez in her mind. She had decided, and firmly believed, that he had been a traitor—to her, to the city, and to the Black Guard. He deserved to die.

No more tears. She was angry with herself for being weak, first in loving him and then in taking a leave of absence to try to find him. She would never be weak like that again.

The locker room was empty. She walked up to locker #38 and saw for the first time that the paint was chipped and faded. She pulled the creaky metal door open and reached inside to lay her hands on the badge and gun that she had placed in there just over a week ago. She slapped the badge onto her chest. She couldn't see it anymore, the sexy black uniform with the gold trimmings, but at least for a few minutes, until the guerrillas destroyed the computers, others would. After that, she didn't care any longer. She threw her shoulders back and strapped on a holster. After checking her gun and slipping it into place at her hip, she turned to leave the locker room. She deliberately avoided looking at locker #10 as she went past it. It didn't exist in her mind anymore.

In the Virtual Vision Tower, Miss Penny approached Diana at the Guard desk. She felt relieved to finally be back in the lobby.

"Excuse me, do I need to sign out?"

"Sign out?" Diana asked, confused.

"Yes. I signed in for a job interview," Miss Penny said.

"Oh! Certainly. Card, please."

Diana nervously inserted the card into the slot on the counter. She handed the card back.

"Here you are, Miss Penny. How did the interview go?"

Frankly, it hadn't gone too well. For one thing, she was ten minutes late because she had somehow gotten off the elevator on the wrong floor. And then, Mr. Watson had been a lecherous old fool who took the title of Touch and Textures too literally. She didn't even want to work for the old creep.

"It went just great," she lied.

"Oh, that's nice. You have a pleasant day."

Miss Penny put her card back in her purse and headed for the door.

Diana watched her walk away in her plain gray shift, her long hair hanging stringy and straight over her thin shoulders.

As Miss Penny went out the door, she passed the guerrillas coming in. The men all carried backpacks and satchels. Adam led the group over to the Guard desk.

Diana was startled to see Adam and just as surprised not to see Javier. She stepped out from behind the desk and stuck her right hand out to Adam in a friendly greeting. They shook hands.

"Welcome to VVN Headquarters. My name is Diana, and I'll be your escort today. Please follow me." She adopted the same persona, voice, and stride as this afternoon's tour guide, as she led the group off toward the elevators.

They all filed into the same car and the doors closed behind them. They had the elevator to themselves. The atmosphere was especially grim. Diana ripped off her mask and quickly hit a high floor button on the unreadable panel to get the car moving.

"Where's Javier?" she demanded. "And what's he doing here?" she asked pointing at Adam.

"Raven killed Javier," Max said.

"Oh my God," she gasped. "What happened?"

"She shivved him," Jake answered.

Diana punched the clearly marked Emergency Stop button. The car jolted to a full stop.

"Where were all of you when this happened?"

It took a moment before Max spoke.

"They went on recon together. When they didn't come back, we went looking for them and found him dead."

"And where is Raven now?"

Adam jumped in.

"Who the hell knows? We're going to have to be fast, and real damn careful. If she's in cahoots with Copley..."

"Oh, shit," Diana said.

She'd heard enough. She quickly unrolled a plastic map of VVN Headquarters and flattened it against the wall of the elevator. Adam held the corners as the guerrillas looked on. Diana circled several locations with a marker.

"These are the void spaces we'll be using," she began. They all listened intently as Diana outlined the plan of attack. When she finished, she nodded to Adam and said, "Are you up for this, Porter?"

Adam's reply was to punch the Emergency Stop button to start up the elevator again. Then he correctly punched in the fifteenth floor from memory. His eyes met hers and she was reassured by the resolve in his steely gaze.

The fifteenth floor hallway was deserted. Diana, Adam, Max, and Jake got off there. The others went ahead to the twentieth to wait for these four to rejoin them after blowing Basic Service. Adam led their small group to the ductwork opening that he and Diana had used before. They stood near the wall, keeping watch as, one at a time, they disappeared into the small opening. Adam and Diana were the last to go. Diana took one last glance back into the hall to make sure they weren't spotted. Satisfied, she crawled after Adam and the others until they reached their objective.

Adam was in the point position, just inside the duct. From his hidden vantage, he watched the movements of a few technicians and a handful of armed guards on the floor around the Basic Service tower. Behind him, Max removed a bundle of explosives and a handgun from one of the bags. He tried to give the small revolver to Diana, but she waved it off. She mouthed the word "no" to him. Max shrugged and stuck the extra gun in his waistband.

Max and Jake stole quietly out of the duct with the explosives, keeping low to the floor. Adam remained posted just inside the mouth of the duct, gun in hand.

"Poor Javier," Diana whispered to Adam's back. "Dad is going to be heartbroken."

Adam didn't know what to say. He just nodded.

"I'm... glad you stayed."

"Yeah, well, let's see if we live through this, and then I'll let you know if I'm glad, too."

Jake and Max crept across the large room, keeping out of sight behind equipment and computers as they went. Their progress was slow. Jake was a big man. Like an elephant hiding behind a telephone pole. But somehow they went unseen by the orange-clad technicians with clipboards who milled around everywhere. Once they reached the shelter of one of the network's computers, there was only ten feet of open space between them and the Basic Control module. They looked at each other and nodded. Max prepared the dynamite, exposing the adhesive on the back so that he could quickly slap it onto the module. After a careful check to make sure the immediate area was clear of techs and guards, Jake covered Max while he dashed across the last few feet of open space to the base of the unit. He fastened the bundle of explosives to the behemoth's side.

From thirty feet away, a technician spotted Max crouching beside the control tower.

"Hey, you! Get away from there!" he shouted.

Max saw the technician yelling at him. He had to hurry. He pushed a small, red button and activated a ten-second timer on the explosive bundle, then jumped up and ran like hell away from the control tower.

A guard on the other side of the room heard the technician shout and caught sight of Max running from the module.

"You there! Halt!" he yelled, running toward the intruders.

Jake and Max ran at full speed toward the duct opening, visible only to them. There was no sense trying to hide anymore. The only thing that mattered was getting out of there alive.

Other guards heard the commotion and joined in the pursuit. The guard closest to the Basic Service module pulled a disrupter gun from his holster and fired in the direction of the fleeing intruders. It didn't phase them. Normally he was a crack shot. Anyone he pointed his disrupter at dropped senseless to the ground. But these two kept running. He aimed again, but before he could fire...

Kaboom! The massive Basic Service control tower erupted. The force of the blast knocked down nearby equipment and almost everybody in the room. The guard who had been shooting at Max and Jake cartwheeled through the air, his now lifeless body slamming into a thick column of cables. Smoke, small fires, and sparks popped up everywhere. Seconds later, an alarm wailed and the automatic halon gas extinguisher system kicked in, adding to the chaos and confusion. In seconds, the fires were out.

Max and Jake had also been knocked over, but they quickly scrambled to their feet. They had expected to feel the blast's impact, but were surprised it had been that powerful an explosion. They raced toward the duct in the wall, with guards close on their heels. Adam and Diana backed out of the way to give them room to make their escape. Jake was the first to dive into the open duct and seemingly vanish into a solid wall. Suddenly, one of the guards tackled Max, knocking him down inches from the opening. Two strong arms materialized and grabbed onto Max, pulling him away from his captor. As the guerilla's body disappeared through the wall, the guard let go and he jerked back in fear.

The other guards stumbled to a halt near the wall. In Security Vision, the wall was real; there was no opening, no way for the impossible to happen, yet they had seen it with their own eyes. Two men had passed right through it like ghosts in a nightmare.

Although all the technicians had been thrown into actual reality when the Basic Service module was destroyed, the guards' Security Vision remained unaffected by the blast. A nearby technician could now see the guerrillas dive into the duct as the guards stumbled and stopped their pursuit. He ran to the opening and shouted at the guards.

"Why are you stopping? Go after them!" He could still see Max's backside crawling away, deep into the dark duct. He turned in frustration back to the guards, screaming and pointing.

"They're getting away! Shoot! Shoot!"

227

The guards turned their heads in confusion from the technician to the spot on the solid wall he kept pointing at. One of the guards hurried to a nearby Security monitor and put in a call.

"Security alert! There's been an explosion on fourteen! Terrorists are loose in the building!" he yelled into the monitor.

In the conference room, the Security Captain twitched nervously in front of Governor Copley, Maxine Markles, and Joseph Branton. His voice was tight and strained.

"No, sir. No sign of any intruders yet. We've looked everywhere, sir."

Copley slapped his fist on the table top. "Apparently you haven't, Captain. They just destroyed Basic Service, you idiot! My God, you people couldn't find a rhinoceros if it kicked you in the ass."

"A what, sir?"

"You fool! Never mind. Search again! Use all available Security personnel. And use whatever force is necessary. Just find them before they do any more damage! Now get out of here."

The Security Captain saluted and spun on his heels. He exited stiffly.

The committee was visibly shaken by the news, especially Markles, who bordered on hysteria. She looked around the conference room as if expecting a filthy, wild-eyed VR failure to burst in and rip her throat out. Copley paced, his hands behind his back. Markles jumped up, irritated as hell, and rushed at the governor.

"I warned you!" she shrieked. "But no... you wouldn't listen! You pompous..."

Startled, Copley pulled the pearl-handled revolver from his pocket and pointed it at her. Markles looked wide-eyed at the gun. Copley smiled and lowered the weapon, flashing her a patronizing smile.

"My dear, you really must learn to relax," he said. Stunned, Markles dropped back into her seat. She could tell that his gun was not a disrupter. What was going on here? Branton kept quiet in his corner, pretending he was invisible.

Brad Jameson, trembling, scared, rode the elevator down. He had started the trip in Basic Service vision to go down to the third floor and check on the new Shangrila fragrance. He had stayed late, as had many others, to get more work done on the Shangila merchandise so they would be ready for the August roll-out. They were running a little behind and needed an extra push to finish by the deadline. Midway there, the system had crashed and he was plunged into actual reality. He was shocked at the change that had instantly come over him and his fellow passenger. The normally attractive blonde woman from Programming Support looked like a faded version of herself. Little moaning sounds escaped from her mouth as she examined the grimy elevator and her own threadbare rags. She was clearly horrified.

It only took a second for Brad to remember what Adam had tried to tell him at his home and at the "hideout." He was immediately angry with himself for not believing his best friend. He reached over and punched the button for the lobby. When the car stopped at the third floor first, he stayed inside, but as the doors opened, he could see other employees, their clothes torn and filthy, staggering up and down the hall. Some were crying; some were just cowering in fear. The doors closed and the car continued down. When it opened on the lobby level, Brad stepped off. The woman remained frozen in the car, stunned, mouth open.

There was no one at the guard desk in the lobby as Brad ran out of the building. A few other employees were so involved in their own fear that they never noticed him as he passed by. He was the only one not surprised, not afraid. And he needed to get home to be sure his wife and baby were okay.

Up on the fifteenth floor, armed Security guards raced through the hallways. VVN employees milled about like zombies, shocked and confused by their actual surroundings and each other's transformed appearance. Still constrained by Security Vision, the guards continued to ignore the virtual vision-invisible spaces, although they were now plain to see by everyone who had been in Basic Service. A female technician was curiously peering into the opening of the fifteenth floor duct when the guerrillas burst out of the hole. Adam, in the lead, accidentally knocked her down. The guerrillas headed for a stairwell door at the end of the hall. From the floor, the startled techie pointed a shaking hand.

"The intruders are over there! Look!" she called out. Two Security guards heard her yelling and followed her trembling finger to see the last guerrilla go through the door. They ran down the hall and burst through the door onto the fifteenth floor landing.

They stopped suddenly. The stairwell was empty. There was no sign of the guerrillas. Puzzled, one guard ran downstairs, while the other guard headed upstairs.

From a seemingly solid wall, Adam materialized behind the guard who had gone upstairs. He grabbed him from behind and covered his mouth with his hand.

The guard struggled, and let out a muffled yell. His partner heard the noise and ran back upstairs in time to see two people disappear into a wall.

"Oh, shit," he muttered, dropping his weapon in fear.

Adam reappeared out of nowhere. He wiggled his finger at the guard to "come here." The man approached, scared to death. Adam grabbed his arm and shoved him through the wall, effectively blinding him in the small, unprogrammed space. Jake and Diana bound the hands and feet of both guards while Adam and Max secured their mouths with gags. Then Adam plucked the badges off the guards and tossed them to Max and Jake.

"These ought to come in handy for a while," he said.

Diana noticed that Adam's mustache had slipped and now dangled crookedly off his lip.

"Adam, your mustache," she said, as she straightened the faux mustache and pressed it firmly in place.

"So far, so good," Jake said as he pinned the badge to his tunic.

"I thought my goose was cooked when that guy tackled me," Max said.

"Good thing I was there to yank you out of there or we coulda added potatoes and carrots to your goosius maximus," Jake said.

Adam interrupted before Max could retort. "Hey guys, we still have another round to go. Check your gear; check your ammo. We need to head up to twenty."

"Okay. What's the exact layout of the other modules?" Jake asked.

Adam pulled out a charcoal marker and drew on the closet wall.

"Here's Frontier Vision," he began.

The raiding party's initials identified the premium module each was to take out. Besides the five guerrillas from the alley, they knew that a couple of dozen more would be waiting to strike from the catwalks overhead. They were relying on them to give cover so that these four could maneuver safely and plant the bombs on each channel's module. After a quick run-through, they were ready. Max snapped open the backpacks and removed the bundles of explosives, giving each guerrilla their own. They tucked them under their tunics.

Adam poked his head out to be sure the stairwell was empty. Finding no one there, he nodded to his companions.

"Okay. Let's make life real."

The guerrillas left the alcove and ran up the stairs.

In singles and in pairs, dazed employees wandered aimlessly through the halls of the twentieth floor. They had never seen it like this: dirty, with flaking paint on the walls and rusted pipes running parallel to the baseboards. The ceiling was a checkerboard pattern of missing tiles and exposed wires and ducts. An old woman huddled against one wall, her gray hair matted against her lined face. She was so paralyzed with fear she couldn't even react when a big, greasy brown rat shot across her lap and hopped up on one of the rusted pipes. It scampered away down the pipe.

A pair of guards posted outside the entrance to the Control Center looked up as Adam and Jake entered the hallway from the stairs. The hallway looked normal to the guards in their Security Vision. They could see the other employees behaving very strangely, but the employees themselves still looked normal to them.

Adam and Jake, with the two guard badges pinned to their tunics, looked sharp in their illusionary bright blue uniforms. They moved briskly toward the nervous guards.

"Quite a night, huh? I've never seen anything like this!" Adam said.

The guards remained stiff and alert.

"I'm sorry, sir. I don't recognize you. Please identify yourselves," one of the guards said.

"I'm Captain Laurel and this is Lieutenant Hardy," Adam said. "And you?"

"Security Officer Hill, sir."

"Well, Officer Hill," Adam said. "You're to report downstairs to the lobby. We're here to relieve you."

Adam could feel his mustache start to slip and dangle again. He surreptitiously tried to press the plastic mustache in place, but when he pulled his hand away, the mustache came with it, leaving him suddenly clean shaven! The guards tensed up as they recognized Adam without his disguise. Officer Hill's hand reached for his disrupter.

Diana had seen Adam's mustache fall away. She knew before the guard drew his weapon that Adam and Jake were in trouble. The entire operation could be blown right here outside the doors before they even got inside. She nudged Max with her elbow and they quickly walked up behind Adam and Jake. Max reached around and shot both guards with his disrupter gun. The guards dropped. The commotion didn't seem to phase the non-Security employees in the vicinity. They had their own problems.

Outside the fortieth floor penthouse offices of the governor, two of Copley's elite Black Guard stood at attention. Their gold filigree badges transformed their black tunics into elegant, midnight black uniforms

233

accented with gold buttons, belt, and sash. Their disrupters rested in holsters that shone as brilliantly as their knee-high boots. Black officer's caps rested squarely just above the eyebrow. Copley had overseen the design of these virtual uniforms himself and was always pleased to see their imposing figures outside his door.

The ornate VVN logo was prominently carved into the oversized mahogany doors. Because of the superior materials used in construction and the quality of the original workmanship of the penthouse floor, it, like the lobby below, had not deteriorated as badly as the rest of the building.

Copley stuck his head out the door. "Look sharp!" he ordered. "Those terrorists could be on their way up here." The guards snapped to attention. Copley shot an angry look up and down the corridor and retreated to his office, slamming the heavy doors behind him.

A young secretary stumbled past, crying, as she looked at her ragged, unsightly fingernails and tattered tunic. She pulled at her stringy hair and sobbed. Henry Jones also wandered around. He had thought to drop in on the Governor with some ideas he had for the new Shangrila channel. He always had ideas, most of them quite brilliant, he thought. But before he reached the great mahogany entry, the world had changed before his very eyes. Instead of being frightened, though, he was awed by his new surroundings. Wide-eyed, he looked curiously at walls, ceilings, and furnishings, which had all turned instantly dusty and faded.

"You know, this is amazing. What do you suppose happened?" he wondered out loud. "It's quite incredible actually."

The Guards shot each other a look. They couldn't understand why people were acting so strangely; everything looked just fine to them. This was too weird.

Henry's voice trailed off as he continued down the hall toward the elevator. He was looking forward to seeing what the rest of the building, and indeed the rest of the city, would be like.

Brad had that information first hand. He ran the three quarters of a mile to his house. On the way, he saw hundreds of people milling around in the streets. Many of them had come out of their homes to congregate in groups, much like their ancestors had after an earthquake or a major power black-out. But rather than offer each other help and assistance (because, after all, what could they do?), they commiserated and speculated about what might have caused this calamity.

Brad ran up the crumbling sidewalk to his front door and yanked it open. He hurried into his living room but there was no sign of his family. However, there was a large hole in the wall where Adam had pointed. Why hadn't he believed his friend? Brad was stricken with guilt.

Then he looked around. Something wasn't quite right but he was too worried to know what it was yet. He called out to his wife.

"Suzanne? Suzanne?" He ran through the house, searching. He rushed into the baby's room. It was plain and unadorned, but surprisingly neat and clean. Some primitive attempts had been made to mend the curtains and bedding in the crib. On a table next to the crib, a small bowl of real, bright red apples stood out against the drab grays of the rest of the room. The baby cooed in his crib. Suzanne was kneeling on the floor with a rag and a crock of water, washing the floor. It startled her when her husband ran in. He had said he'd be working late and she didn't expect him for another hour. She jumped up, looking guilty, caught in the act.

His first thought was for their safety. He checked the baby in his crib and then turned to Suzanne.

"Are you okay? How's the baby?"

"We're fine. Why wouldn't we be?"

"They crashed the system. Adam was right. He..." Suddenly, the fruit on the table, and her attempts to clean, registered in his brain and it all made sense.

"Hey, wait a minute..." He glanced down at his own clothing and, instead of filthy tatters, he noticed that he wore a very old, but clean and mended, tunic. Come to think of it, the living room, even with the hole in the wall, had been neat and somewhat clean. He felt like he'd been punched in the stomach.

"My God, Suzanne. It was you, wasn't it? You told them where to find Adam."

Stunned, he grabbed her shoulders. "What the hell have you done?" He looked around at the clean room. "What's going on here, Suzanne?"

"What do you mean?"

"You have shit vision! Don't you? When? How?"

Suzanne was trembling, losing it. She had kept the secret for so long, and it had been so hard to do. The truth poured out of her now.

"About halfway through my pregnancy. Remember the headaches? It just stopped working. I thought I was going insane!"

"Dear God, why didn't you tell me?"

"I was afraid! I didn't want you to send me to Serenity Gardens! I didn't want to die there, like Trisha and her baby." She was sobbing by now.

Brad dropped his arms, his heart sinking.

"I don't understand. You don't tell me but you collaborate with Copley?"

"Someone had to watch out for our baby!" she yelled. "There you were, getting mixed up in Adam's troubles—getting us in trouble along with him! If you choose that man over your own family, I have to do something about it!"

"I've always put you first, you know that!"

"No, you don't! I was hiding in the kitchen the night Adam was here after he hit his head. I heard everything! You offered to help him. And right after that the police showed up. I was so scared, Brad."

"But I'm your husband! I wouldn't let anybody hurt you and little Bradley! I still don't understand... how on earth did you get hooked up with Copley?"

"The police sergeant left his card. I called him after you went to sleep that night. The next day while you were at work I got a call from the Governor himself."

"That snake! You can't trust him."

"That's not true," she protested. "He's been very nice to me and the baby. We have real food—see?" she said, pointing to the apples.

He didn't know what to say. She was wrong about Copley, but he could see how she would have that perception. He decided not to argue the point right now.

"Did you tell Copley you could see?"

Suzanne shook her head. "I was afraid to tell him. I just wanted to help them find Adam! For the baby! They promised to take care of my baby!" Her eyes looked wild as she grabbed his hand and squeezed. She dropped her voice and conspiratorially pointed to the apples.

"Real food!" she whispered. "He sent over a gift basket, thinking I wouldn't know the difference, but I knew. I can tell a real apple from that gray shit they feed us." She got excited and started sobbing again. "Oh, Bradley! I've been eating that gray shit for so long, I can't stand it! And now there's real food—from the Governor! For our baby, Brad! I did it for our baby!"

He stared at her, speechless. It broke his heart that she had lied to him all this time, but he understood her reasons. She had never been a very strong person. The fear had probably been overwhelming at times. He would talk to her at greater length about it later, do what they could to rebuild their bond as husband and wife. But now he had to try to repair some of the damage the guerrillas had done.

"Stay inside. Lock the doors. I'll be back as soon as I can."

She nodded and watched as he left. Then, still sobbing, she bent to finish washing the floors.

The cavernous twentieth floor control room was well-protected. They had all heard about the destruction of the Basic Service tower on fourteen, so extra security had been brought in. Four alert guards gathered on the far side of the room. Six more walked around, guns at the ready. A handful of busy technicians worked among the modules. They were disoriented by actual reality, but continued their maintenance routines, always looking nervously over their shoulders, expecting terrorists to appear out of nowhere.

The guerrillas strolled casually onto the control room floor. Adam and Diana. Jake and Max. With their guard badges as disguises, they looked like they belonged there so, for the moment, they didn't arouse the guards' suspicion. They spread out and headed for their individual targets. Max and Jake headed for the

Cartoon and UltraModern modules and were soon out of sight. Up above, other guerrillas crept silently out onto the catwalks. Sharpshooters took prone positions and prepared to provide cover fire for the guerillas below.

Suddenly, three Security guards stormed through the doors with their newly issued handguns drawn. No one else reacted except Adam and Diana, who were still in view on the near side of the room. They instinctively crouched down in a defensive posture, immediately giving away the fact that they weren't really guards at all.

The real guards picked up on it and opened fire on the two guerrillas. Adam and Diana dodged across aisles and dived for the shelter of computer hardware. Bullets ricocheted off nearby fixtures. Technicians dove for cover. The guerrillas up above started firing. The guards kept shooting but hung back near the doors, hesitant to cross the open space between them, which was now being riddled by bullets from above.

From behind a computer station, Adam and Diana took aim with disrupters.

"They're shooting real goddam bullets!" Adam had to shout over the din. "These disrupters aren't going to be worth a shit when Max blows Security Vision. You know that, don't you?"

"Tough. I'm not using a gun."

"Well, I sure as hell am."

He tossed the disrupter aside and pulled the handgun from his backpack.

A dozen guerrillas rappelled down from the catwalks. Guns and disrupters were going off everywhere. People yelled, ran, shot, kicked, and chopped. It was total chaos.

Max attached an explosive charge to the walls of the UltraModern Vision control module. He ducked and shot as he activated the ten-second delay fuse. He looked over and saw Jake scurrying away from the Cartoon Vision module. He had also set the charge on his bomb. A guard grabbed him, but he snap kicked him and the guard went down. Jake zigzagged through the modules to join Max. Gunfire kept the two of them pinned down.

Adam and Diana's targets, Frontier, Security, and Shangrila Vision, were clustered together on the far side of the large room. As they approached their objectives, a baby-faced guard spotted Adam. To the guard, Adam looked like another Security officer, except that he was suspiciously kneeling beside the Frontier module with what looked like a bomb in his hands. He motioned to the other three Guards, and the four of them moved in.

"Hey, you! Get away from there! Now!" Baby-face yelled. The guard fired on Adam, but his disrupter gun had no effect.

One of the guards knocked Adam away from the explosives before he could set it to blow, while the other three veered off and descended on Diana. Hers hadn't been set yet, either.

She drop kicked the first guy. When the second tried to grab her, she used his weight to kick out at the third, dropping him, too. Then she spun around and landed a kick to the last guy's groin, ending the fight.

Jake and Max headed for the Chapel Vision module under a hail of bullets.

Boom! Kaboom! The first two virtual vision control modules, Cartoon and UltraModern, exploded with tremendous force and heat. Shrapnel and burning plastic flew everywhere.

Twenty floors above them, in the conference room, safely behind the mahogany doors, Markles trembled with rage. She was carefully monitoring the destruction of the premium modules on her computer screen. Branton's eyes nervously flitted back and forth between Copley and Markles. Copley paced up and down not far from Markles, angrily ranting and waving the gun around.

"Don't they understand? We live in an age of unprecedented peace and prosperity! It's my duty to preserve that peace! Attacking the Network will cause nothing but panic and..." Copley's voice trailed off as UltraModern crashed into actual reality.

Markles moaned as she looked from Branton to Copley, seeing their real faces for the first time. Suddenly, they weren't nearly as handsome—and Branton was no beefcake to begin with. She could guess how hideous she herself must look by the expression on Branton's face. He couldn't help but recoil in horror from her, the bastard!

Copley momentarily lowered the gun. Puzzled, he reached up and tapped the hidden switch on the side of his head. Nothing happened.

Markles saw her chance. She flew through the air and knocked Copley to the floor. She easily wrested the gun from the old man's hand and swung it around to cover him and Branton.

"Are you happy now, you stupid old fool?" she screeched. "Look around you! Peace and prosperity, my ass!"

Copley reached out one hand toward her. "Markles, my dear," he crooned.

"Don't you 'my dear' me!"

Suddenly, she noticed that he didn't look so bad. His hair was trimmed and combed. And he wasn't nearly as thin and gaunt as she and Branton.

"Why, you son of a bitch," she said softly.

Then she saw the recess in the wall. And the rose bush. And the bowl of fruit. And a polished mirror. She was furious!

"You son of a bitch!" she screamed, pointing the gun at his head. But she hesitated, and he didn't. She was close enough for him to jump at her and try to wrest the gun away from her. They struggled, each determined to have possession of the weapon. Copley was the stronger of the two and slowly bent her wrist backward until the gun was pointed at her chest. He pulled his face close to hers and almost smiled. Suddenly a shot rang out and Maxine Markles dropped dead to the dirty floor. Branton, eyes glazed and fixed, sat frozen in shocked silence. Copley rose from the floor and calmly brushed off his clothes. He turned to Branton.

"Do you have a problem with this, Branton?"

Branton shook his head and gulped.

"N-n-no, Governor Copley," he stammered.

"Good. Call down and get reinforcements to meet us on twenty. I have business downstairs."

Copley burst through the carved doors and strode past the Guards, leaving Branton trembling in the corner. The guards fell into step behind them. As they turned the corner toward the elevators, he spotted Raven heading his way.

"You! Come with us!" he shouted.

She dutifully fell into step with them as they entered the elevator.

Kaboom! There went Chapel Vision. A wedding across town at the cathedral suddenly became a lot less resplendent.

Guards and guerrillas swarmed around, ducking, shooting, dying. More guerrillas rappelled from the catwalks. Some used their martial arts skills instead of guns.

Tucked between two modules, Adam and Diana continued their firefight with the guards. Diana still used a disrupter. They could see Max and Jake on the floor, about twenty feet from the Security Vision module. Jake had been shot. His hand was clamped onto his bleeding thigh, staunching the blood.

"Jake's hurt. I'm going to work my way over there. Hang onto this puppy and give me some cover," he told Diana. He handed her the last explosive, broke away, ducked and ran toward Max and Jake. Max saw him coming.

"Adam! Activate the detonators!" Adam veered off to the Security Vision module. He pressed the button to start the 10-second countdown on the explosive charge.

A guard spotted Adam leaving the Security Vision module, heading for the nearby Frontier Vision module. He grabbed onto Adam, yanked him around and swung a fist at him. Adam ducked and jerked free, connecting with a right to the jaw.

Boom! The Security module exploded, blowing Adam off his feet. Security Vision flickered and failed. Max and Jake took advantage of the guards' disorientation and scrambled away in the confusion, Jake limping from the bullet in his thigh.

There was a lull in the gunfire as the effects of Security Vision's failure took hold of the Security squad. Adam, burned and bleeding from the explosion, dragged himself to the Frontier Vision detonator. He winced with pain as he reached for the detonator.

"So long, Bo," he said as he flipped the switch.

A guard approached Adam from behind, furiously clicking his empty gun. He tossed the gun aside and grabbed a large piece of metal debris and raised it over his head like a club.

"Adam! Behind you!" Diana yelled.

Adam turned and looked up to see the furious guard. He rolled out of the way and struggled to his feet, knocking the guard into the module with a fist to the face. He headed back for cover, shooting randomly.

Kaboom! And Frontier Vision rode off into a smoky, twisted metal sunset.

More guards stampeded in. More guerrillas rappelled from the catwalks. Copley and Raven, guns drawn, burst in, with another dozen guards in tow. Copley immediately took cover near the door as Raven quickly reloaded her weapon.

"My God. Did the bastards leave us anything? Raven, work your way to the back and see if any of the modules are still intact. And if they are, make sure they stay that way!"

Raven nodded. As she worked her way around the perimeter, she tried to pinpoint each of the guerrillas that she knew. The time spent in that underground hell hole had paid off. She knew who to shoot at. As she crept toward the Shangrila module, she saw Diana attaching an explosive device to it. She moved fast, and as soon as she had a clear shot, she fired. Lucky for Diana, she spotted her at the last second and rolled away, but this maneuver kept her from activating the ten-second detonator.

Raven stealthily turned a corner to find Diana waiting for her, crouched, hands at the ready.

"Javier was my friend," Diana snarled.

"Tough shit," Raven said, raising her gun.

Diana was ready. She kicked the gun from Raven's hand and sent it flying. Raven was impressed but nonplussed. She crouched, too, ready for hand-to-hand.

Diana jabbed and kicked. Raven returned the favor. A snap kick. A spinning back fist.

"She's good," they both thought. They were an even match. They clambered over debris, hitting and kicking.

Raven got in a good punch and Diana went down. Raven ripped the bomb from the side of Shangrila's module and raised it to smash her foe. Diana rolled aside, grabbed a cable and whipped it around Raven's leg. She yanked and Raven went down. The bomb skidded away under a mound of wreckage.

Raven bounced back up. She grabbed a cord and flung it around Diana's neck, pulling it tight. Diana choked, struggled. She reached out, looking for anything at all. Her vision faded, it was harder to breathe. She groped, reaching, reaching, until finally her hand closed around something heavy. It was a jagged piece of metal debris.

Raven leaned into Diana's face and grinned. She twisted the cord to tighten the noose.

Diana summoned her last bit of strength and swung the piece of debris with all her might. It smashed into Raven's head and she went down hard. Blood spurted forth from the newly ripped gash.

Diana yanked the cord from her throat and gasped. She scurried behind the Shangrila module to catch her breath and calm herself. Her neck hurt and her lungs greedily sucked in the air she'd just been denied. She saw Raven's gun there and tentatively picked it up. It much was heavier in her hand than the disrupter she was used to. Her fight with Raven had left her weak. She might not be able to do it again. As much as she loathed the idea of using the gun, she couldn't leave it there. Just in case, she told herself. Then she looked around frantically for the missing explosive charge.

Diana caught a movement out of the corner of her eye. She spun around. Raven, her dark hair matted with the blood that was dripping down her face and neck, lunged toward Diana with her bone-handled knife. She was going for the kill.

Bam! Diana didn't even have time to think before shooting Raven square in the chest. Raven was stunned by more than the bullet.

"I... didn't think you had the ovaries..." she wheezed. She collapsed onto Diana, dead by the time she slid to the floor. Diana pushed her aside and scrambled out from under her. She had never killed anyone before and worse, she had done it with a gun, the weapon she had spoken out against so passionately. She took a moment, but only a moment, to reconcile herself to her reality—kill or be killed. She didn't like it, but she accepted it. Diana took a deep breath and, tucking the gun into her waistband, got back to the business at hand. She found the explosive and reattached it to the Shangrila module. She smacked the ten-second detonator button and ran like hell.

Copley's pet technician, Robert, saw her run from the Shangrila module and he rushed over to do whatever he could to stop the explosion. He didn't know how long he had. His only thought was to get that thing off his baby. He had worked too hard on Shangrila to have it go up in flames like this. He yanked the explosive off the module and ran with it. Ten feet away, it exploded in his arms. He was a goner, but the module was saved.

Adam spotted Copley still crouching near the doors and headed in his direction, keeping out of sight. He wove from one ruined module to the next, hiding behind debris. A guard jumped out at him, swinging a pipe. It connected painfully with Adam's arm. He swung it again, but Adam ducked away from it this time and landed two good punches, knocking the man out.

Copley assessed the situation and decided it was too dangerous to stay there. He picked up a dead guard's gun and ammo, turned, and ran out. Now he had two guns.

Adam barreled past a couple of guards as he followed Copley out. He had a score to settle. He arrived at the elevators just in time to see the doors closing on a car heading down.

"Shit!" he yelled as he pounded the button to call another one. He had to get down to the lobby before Copley got away. He'd never find him if he got loose in the city.

Outside the Virtual Vision Network building, pandemonium ruled the streets as the virtual vision plug was pulled and people were plunged into strange and ugly actual reality. Some screamed in terror and tried to outrun the visions; some cowered and buried their faces in their hands. A frightened crowd was beginning to congregate outside the black monolith. They didn't know what was going on, but they knew that VVN probably held the key.

Brad had run the entire distance from his house back to the tower. Exhausted, he pushed his way past the horde of dirty, smelly people gathered at the door. The stench was overwhelming to his trained nose. He stumbled into the lobby just as Copley exited the elevator. The Governor headed straight for the guard's desk. Brad was shocked to see the gun in his hand. What the hell was going on?

"Governor Copley! What's happened?" he called out as he ran up to him.

Copley rounded the desk and found the guard still tied up on the floor where Diana had left him. He shoved the old man out of the way with his foot and pounded on the computer terminal, ignoring Brad.

"Dial Serenity Gardens!" he yelled.

"Sir, please!" Brad continued, joining Copley behind the desk. He glanced down at the guard on the floor. Puzzled, he shook his head.

"What do you think happened, Jameson? Your friend Porter has put us all out of a job!"

A frazzled receptionist popped up on the computer monitor.

"Serenity Gardens. Your cares, uh..." her voice drifted off as she forgot her spiel. What a night!

"Send the van over to VVN Headquarters right away!" Copley barked at her.

"What do you mean?" Brad asked. "What does Adam have to do with this?"

"I don't think I can do that, sir. The drivers aren't... and the patients are... uh..."

Copley interrupted. "I'm the governor, you dim-wit! Send the God-damned van!"

"I'll, uh, try to get someone over there right away, sir." A rat launched itself from behind and landed on her head. She jumped up screaming and flailing her arms.

Copley turned from the computer in disgust.

"Sir. What about Adam?" Brad asked again.

At that moment, Adam sneaked up on the guard desk from behind, gun at the ready, startling both Copley and Brad.

"I tried to tell you, Brad, but you wouldn't listen. We blew up the Virtual Vision modules. We had to make sure you saw what this hell hole really looks like," Adam said.

Copley and Brad spun around to face Adam.

"We?" Brad asked. He still felt guilty over not believing and trusting his friend. "Who's *we*?"

"That's what your idiot wife was supposed to find out, you moron!" Copley spat. "I paid her handsomely and she came up with nothing!"

"What?!" Adam looked from Copley to Brad, shocked. "What's he talking about?"

Meanwhile, on the monitor, the Serenity Gardens receptionist tried in vain to regain the governor's attention. "Sir? Sir? Can you send more guards? I think we're being invaded. Sir?"

"I didn't know, Adam! I swear it!" Brad said. "Suzie just now told me. They promised her they'd take care of her and the baby."

Adam looked at Copley and leveled his gun at him.

"Drop the gun, Copley. You've ruined too many people's lives already."

"I don't think so," Copley said.

Copley grabbed Brad and held the gun to his head. He pulled his hostage away from the guard desk and walked backwards to the door.

"Like every bad vidfilm you've ever seen, right, Porter?" Copley sneered. "The villain uses the best friend as a shield for his getaway. Now why don't you put your gun down or I'll blow a hole the size of Texas in his head."

249

Adam slowly put his gun down and kicked it away as Copley dragged Brad out the door.

Even in the pale street lights, Copley could see the results of the system crashing. Except for the gleaming black VVN tower behind him, all of the downtown buildings were decayed and in disrepair. Everything was dirty and dingy.

In the street around the tower, almost a hundred people stood in groups, examining each other, comforting each other. Some were crying, some were hysterical, a few managed a brave stoicism. It was obvious that both the city and its citizens had been neglected for a very long time. Copley strained to see over their heads, looking for the van. He still held onto Brad. Suddenly, an elderly gentleman recognized him and reached out.

"Governor! What is happening to us? Please! Help us!" Others heard and gravitated toward him. The Governor! He must know! He can help! Their hands grasped and pawed at Copley. They pleaded, begged, cried. They yanked him away from Brad, away from VVN Headquarters. Seizing the opportunity to get away from Copley and the crowd, Brad ducked out of sight and crawled back toward the door, glad to be alive. He didn't know how big Texas was, but he didn't want a hole of any size in his red-headed skull.

Copley was repulsed by all of them. He recoiled from their touch. He wished like hell he was safe in his fortieth floor office. He hated these people and this city, and he especially hated the truth as it was revealed now in actual reality. It disgusted him enough to make him retch. He shrank back and looked up the street hoping to see the van. There was no sign of it yet. He had no choice; he had to get out of there. He shoved the human garbage out of his way and fled up the street.

They started to follow, arms outstretched, calling out, but they soon gave up and splintered into smaller groups again.

Adam ran out the door. He had retrieved his gun and had it ready if needed. Brad rushed up to him.

"Adam! I didn't know about Suzanne..."

But Adam wasn't listening. He scanned the crowds, searching for Copley.

"Which way?" he asked.

Brad pointed in the direction that the Governor had gone.

"Let me come with you," he implored. "Let me make it up to you."

"Don't sweat it. You better get home to Suzie and the baby."

Brad nodded unhappily as he watched Adam run off in the direction that Copley had taken.

Adam was a few blocks from the tower with no sign of his quarry when he stopped in a doorway to check his gun. He found a couple of bullets in a pocket of his tunic and slid them into the chamber. He needed more ammo though. He dug in another pocket and found nothing. Shit. He checked the gun one last time and moved out into the street.

Pow! He took one in the leg. It skimmed the muscle on the side of his thigh and passed right through, knocking him on his ass. And then he saw Copley half a block up the street, running away.

He struggled to his feet and, dragging his injured leg, he tried to run after Copley. He kept to the shadows near the buildings now. It was slower going, but safer.

Back at VVN, the Serenity Gardens van finally barreled around the corner, scattering the people in the streets. It slowed near the tower. Someone pointed up the street that Copley and Adam had taken and the van accelerated in that direction. As it came near, Adam hobbled out from the shadows and waved it down. The driver stopped. It was Carl. He had seen an opportunity to get away from the madhouse that Serenity Gardens had become and had jumped behind the wheel of the ambulance himself. He didn't recognize Adam, covered in dirt and blood.

"Hey, what the hell? Who are you? I'm supposed to pick up the Governor."

Adam yanked the door open, grabbed the man and tossed him out onto the pavement. He hoisted himself and his gimpy leg up into the driver's seat.

"I'll take it from here. How do I make this thing go?" he asked, pointing his gun at Carl's head. And suddenly, he recognized the cruel orderly who had taken him into Serenity Gardens that day. He shoved the gun into Carl's cheek, hard.

Carl leaned in, really scared. He pointed to each of the pedals.

"This one to go, this one to stop, and steer with your hands on the wheel." With that, he jumped back and cringed, expecting to be shot and killed.

Adam slammed the door shut and stomped his foot on the gas pedal. The van took off like a shot, scaring the shit out of him, and leaving Carl trembling in the street. He swerved a couple times, easing off on the gas, before he got going a little straighter and headed down the street toward his quarry.

Copley heard the van about a block behind him and turned toward the sound. But instead of the Serenity Gardens driver, he could see Porter behind the wheel. His eyes narrowed. He stood in the middle of the street, raised his gun with both hands, and aimed it right at Adam.

"I've had just about enough of you," Copley said.

252

He took careful aim and squeezed the trigger. Adam ducked as the bullet shattered the windshield. He slammed on the brakes too hard and nearly flew over the steering wheel.

Copley shot again. Adam ducked, but the bullet grazed his shoulder. He was really pissed now. He pushed the gas pedal to the floor.

The next one missed. Copley shot again. Another miss. The van kept coming. Two more shots also missed the target.

Copley jumped out of the way as the van careened past. He ran up onto the sidewalk and up the crumbling stone steps of the old, run-down cathedral. He disappeared inside, pulling the doors closed behind him.

Adam's hands danced around the steering wheel. He was panicky, trying to keep control, but he was losing it. He felt like a vidreel cowboy trying to tame a bucking bronco.

Gas, brake, gas, brake! The van's tires screeched as it swerved and zigzagged all over the street. Suddenly a train whistle blew. The tracks ran parallel to the street at the cathedral and right now a train full of frightened people was chugging past. They never even saw the van. They were busy staring at each other and at the run-down railroad car they were riding in.

Still struggling for control, Adam barely registered the approach of the train. He wrenched the steering wheel hard to the right to avoid hitting a frightened pedestrian.

The van flew over the curb and across the tracks, right in front of the train! He let out a yell as the train clipped the tail end of the van, sending it spinning. It finally came to a stop as the last of the train passed by.

Adam was panting, his eyes wide as saucers. He calmed a bit and looked across the way at the cathedral. He had seen Copley go in there. With grim determination, he pointed the van straight at the church and floored it.

The van shot back across the tracks and across the street. It charged up the cathedral steps and crashed through the doors, smashing them to splinters.

The smoking hot van wedged itself into the last rows of busted up pews. Its aging batteries and dried wiring, some of which was actually exposed in the rear section of the van, threw out sparks which easily ignited the tinder-dry contents of the ambulance. The small fire quickly spread to the old sheets and blankets in the back of the van and in seconds the old mattress also burst into flames. Adam's head was swimming, but he held onto his gun as he staggered out of the van and tried to stumble away.

A bullet smacked the van near Adam's head. He ducked, suddenly alert. It had come from the choir loft behind him. He crouched down and limped toward the stairs in the back corner.

From his hiding place above the fiery van, Copley watched Adam below him moving toward the side aisle. He raised the gun and aimed.

A bullet smashed into a pew near Adam. Adam ducked, swung around, aimed quickly toward the choir loft, and fired.

The bullet grazed Copley's arm. He ducked out of sight.

Adam limped to the stairwell and headed up to the loft. Fire spread around the van and licked the underside of the choir loft. The crackling echoed in the big empty building, lighting the place with a flickering orange glow. It was a far cry from the beautiful cathedral it had been in Chapel Vision.

Copley hid in the loft, checking his guns. He had exhausted the ammo in one of them. Tossing that aside, he pulled out the second pistol. It had a full cylinder.

He clawed the torn cloth away from his wounded arm; it wasn't a serious injury. He looked around for a place to hide and squatted behind an overturned chair, watching the top of the stairs, waiting for Porter to show.

Adam slowed and took the last few steps into the loft cautiously. He knew Copley had the advantage here. Adam couldn't see into the loft yet, but Copley could see the entry where Adam would come in. And he did.

A bullet slammed into the wall near Adam's head! Then another one! *Different sound, different gun,* he thought as he shot back in the direction it came from.

"Give it up, Copley! It's all over!" he called out. There was no response. "Come on, Copley! Your phony paradise is falling down around your ears!"

Copley sent two more bullets toward his adversary. Adam ducked out of sight as best he could.

"And what gives you the right to destroy paradise?" Copley's voice thundered out from the resonant choir space.

Flames from the van below crackled and licked higher on the loft. Copley's advantage was lessened by the lack of light and the rising smoke which interfered with visibility. He shot twice more in Adam's general direction.

Adam ducked and scrambled to one side. He took a deep breath. He was so tired. His whole body was leaden and, except for his injuries, an odd kind of numb. He'd had enough. He had counted six bullets.

He stood, painfully, bleeding and sore, and grimly faced Copley.

"It wasn't paradise," Adam said. "It was hell. And you knew it."

Copley stood, too. The choir loft blazed behind him. He turned his gun on Adam.

"I knew I had to protect them."

Adam shook his head. "No. You condemned them, you greedy bastard."

"No!" Copley shrieked. Click. His gun was empty. Click, click. He tossed it aside and grabbed a large flaming hunk of wood and charged, swinging the huge torch at Adam's head.

Adam ducked. His injured leg gave way and as he fell to the floor, the back of his hand hit hard on a broken chair and his gun was jarred out of his aching fingers. He heard it clatter to the floor but he couldn't see where.

He struggled, pulling himself up on his hands and knees, searching for the weapon and knowing that this was a bad position to be in. He couldn't see Copley, but he knew that Copley hovered over him, ready to deal a fatal blow.

Copley smashed the torch against Adam's back. Weakened, Adam collapsed again.

Copley, triumphant, raised the hunk of fiery wood above his head. He stepped back to lend more force to the final blow and found himself surrounded by the rapidly spreading fire. He felt the searing flames licking their way up his legs!

He looked down at his inescapable fate and went berserk. Screaming, he charged forward, swinging the heavy wood down on his nemesis!

Adam twisted away from the fiery blow. His hand found his missing gun and, in a split second, he raised it and fired once.

Copley stopped, a small black hole between his wide-open eyes. A tiny drop of blood dripped out.

He tumbled backward over the railing and crashed spread-eagled on the roof of the van, completely engulfed in flames.

Adam pulled his aching body up, barely able to stand, and looked over the railing. He called down to the body. "Your ride is here, Governor."

He dropped the gun and turned just in time to see Diana, Jake, and Max barreling up the stairs toward him. He sat down hard. His legs didn't want to hold him another second.

Diana rushed to his side, checking his injuries. She couldn't help herself; she gave him a hug.

"Are you alright, Adam?"

He nodded. He was actually really glad to see her— to see all of them. Max looked over the railing at Copley's body as Jake had a look around the loft.

"Thought you might need some help," Jake said, suddenly grinning.

"Time to go, people," Max said. "This place isn't safe. That fire will be all over this loft in about three minutes."

Diana and Max grabbed Adam under the arms and dragged him down the stairs and out into the night air. Jake limped behind them.

The cathedral walls were stone so the blaze would not spread to the rest of the city. For now, the orange flames eerily illuminated what was left of the stained glass windows that had once made this church so beautiful. The four battered guerrillas staggered away, leaning on one another for support. They headed back toward the rendezvous point in the alley to meet up with their squad. They soon spotted Flo rushing up the street toward them with her medical bag.

"Where's the rest of the team?" Max called out to her. "Everybody get out okay?"

"Our team is fine. I don't know about the others yet. What about you? Jake? Adam?"

Jake grinned, limping along beside the others.

"Twins. Both with holes in our legs. Ain't we cute?"

Flo shook her head. She had to smile. "I thought I told you to take care of yourself, Jakie."

TUESDAY

It was still dark. The morning sun would linger another hour before showing itself in the eastern sky. A small, shadowy group pushed a wheeled cart through a break in the fencing that surrounded the city's southern boundary. Max and his brother, George, pushed the cart as Diana walked beside it, her hand resting gently on her friend Javier's shrouded body. Adam and Jake both limped behind them, leaning on hand-made canes.

Two men with shovels awaited them in the small cemetery. Outside the city since the creation of the virtual vision grids, it was the only place where members of the Underground could safely bury their dead. It had been a cemetery in days long past. A half dozen trees struggled to shade the few headstones that survived. Most of the grass was brown and dry, although it looked as though the groundskeepers had tried to maintain its color with what little water they could put on it by hand.

The mourners approached the shallow grave and the two brothers slowly and carefully lifted their comrade into his final resting place. Diana stepped forward and opened a small book that she had borrowed from Savannah. She read out loud, her voice shaking with emotion.

A search for meaning
In a meaningless landscape
Emptiness remains

She paused, filled with grief, and, her hands shaking, turned to another page.

Loyalty, laughter
True friends bring great joyousness
My heart swells with love

"Farewell, dear friend," she said, wiping a tear from the corner of her eye. She closed the book and tucked it into her pocket as she turned away from the gravesite. Max and Jake said silent good-byes and then followed her toward the city. Adam and George took up the rear as the two grave diggers, members of the Underground's southernmost satellite, hurried to cover the hole with dirt, trying to return the area to its previous condition as much as possible, just in case someone from the city happened to be able to see it. Their cemetery was off the grid, but it was always safer to take precautions like these. Once finished, they would follow the others back into the city and to the nearby satellite area that they called home.

As the sky lightened to dawn, the city came back on line as one grid after another transformed from actual reality to the magical land of Shangrila. What had begun as an ordinary sunrise grew increasingly magnificent as the little town of Appleton found itself suddenly perched in a high mountain valley amidst snow-capped mountain peaks that rose up to pierce a dazzling pink and silver sky. Every person in every glittering home took on the characteristics of the fairy tale Far East setting. No longer clothed in filthy rags, subscribers were suddenly resplendent in harem pants and silk saris, even if the fabric did feel more like burlap to the touch.

All over the city, citizens sat glued to their gold-encrusted vidvision monitors, waiting for word on what had happened. They were comforted at the sight of the familiar VVN logo which dissolved into an outlandishly costumed reporter.

"And so, this night of mayhem is at an end. From what we have been able to gather, terrorists destroyed several Virtual Vision Network transmitters yesterday and began broadcasting their own, demented virtual vision channel. They also succeeded in destroying the downlink to Off Line and that's why you're not able to turn it off... One moment please..."

The reporter touched his ear as a message came through his earphone. "I'm told that Governor Branton, the new head of Virtual Vision Network, is standing by with an important announcement."

The camera cut to a close-up of Governor Joseph Branton. He was dressed like a fairy-tale sultan, with an ostentatious jeweled turban on his head.

"My fellow citizens," Branton officiously intoned. "You are all to be commended for the courage you displayed during last night's cruel ordeal. We here at VVN want you to forget the horrors forced upon you as a result of this despicable act of terrorism. To that happy end, until the downlink to Off Line is repaired, it will be our pleasure to supply, free of charge, VVN's newest premium channel, Shangrila, which we have programmed to override the terrorist channel. We haven't got all the bugs quite worked out yet, so there may be a few problems here and there, but in the meantime, please... enjoy."

"Enjoy! What a crock! All that work and now everyone's stuck in Shangrila!" Jake burst out. The Underground had gathered in the common hall for breakfast and debriefing. They hooted and hollered angrily in response to Branton's lies. Unlike the dazzling sultan the subscribers saw, their vidvision monitor showed Branton's bare-headed, hawk-nosed face as gaunt and ugly as ever.

Flo sat next to Jake, nodding her head in agreement. She was tired. It had been a busy night for her and her medical team. They had patched up Bobby's bruises and wrapped his leg. He'd be on crutches for a few weeks, but he'd be okay. They had treated a lot of scrapes and burns, and Victor had taken a bullet out of Jake's thigh. Lu Yi stitched up Adam's leg wound and sent him off with a cane, then quickly turned to another guerrilla whose left hand had two broken fingers. Most of the guerrillas had come back injured and needed stitching.

Unfortunately, eight of their members had not come back at all. Flo hated to even think it, but she hoped they were dead and not being interrogated and tortured by the new regime. Until Jason found out for sure, it meant being extra vigilant and extremely careful in their comings and goings. If GovCorp found out where the Underground was headquartered...

But there was good news, too. She had removed three implants from their newest members: Brad, Suzanne, and little Bradley. And she had assured a very frightened Suzanne that all three of them would always have enough fresh fruits and vegetables to eat, and a safe place to raise their child.

Victor and Lu Yi had also removed implants from Max's brother, George, and his wife, Casi, and their son, George, Jr. It was good to have two new young families join their community and share their lives.

It had been a difficult night for Jason, too. He had sent his only daughter out on the most dangerous mission of her life. He hadn't tried to talk her out of it—

she would have been insulted—but he had worried himself sick all night. He had never felt more helpless and frustrated as he waited for everyone to return. George had carried Bobby in first, but he had no news of the rest of the guerrillas, only that Adam and Diana had continued recon from there.

Jason had known exactly when Basic Service had been destroyed by the reactions of the people on the street, but other than that he knew nothing. He pieced the story together as the guerrillas trickled back, but none of them could tell him what had become of his daughter or the three men who had been charged with the most important aspect of the mission.

It wasn't until after midnight that Diana, Adam, Jake, and Max had dragged themselves back to the safety of the Underground. That's when he learned the heartbreaking news that Raven had been a traitor and a spy and had murdered his friend Javier. Jason mentally chastised himself for allowing his trust in Javier to blind him to what otherwise would have been his usual suspicion of anyone new, especially Raven, a member of the Black Guard. It was no small consolation to learn that Raven had been killed, although he felt Diana's inner distress over the fact that she had been the one to pull the trigger. They had talked long into the night about it before she had left him to join the funeral procession for Javier.

Adam and Brad had also talked—about Suzanne and the baby; about friendship and trust; and about their future without implants and virtual worlds to work and play in. When Adam returned from the burial, they resumed their talk in earnest. By morning, they had renewed their bond and had joined the others in the mess hall for millet porridge with almonds and fresh berries.

Jason joined them at their table. He still had questions about the mission. He wondered why Adam had agreed to lead the guerrillas in Javier's place.

"What made you change your mind?" Jason asked Adam that morning over breakfast.

Adam set his cane aside and reached for a couple of strawberries from a bowl in the center of the table.

"I really like these strawberries," he said as he popped one in his mouth. "I thought other people might like them, too."

Jason knew there had to be more to it, but he wasn't going to press the matter.

Diana walked in with Boomer on her shoulder and sat down next to Adam. As their shoulders touched, not entirely accidentally, Boomer jumped from her shoulder to Adam and ran down his arm to nestle in his open hand and nibble on a berry.

"Good morning," Diana said. "Did I miss anything?"

Max pointed to the monitor where the reporter reiterated for the forty-third time that Branton was now the Governor.

"We still have work to do," Max said. "They brought up Shangrila."

"Hell yeah," Jake yelled. "Every good story has a sequel, don't it?"

They laughed at his outburst. He had always been among the most determined of their group. Adam smiled. He was glad to be a part of their group, too.

He handed Boomer back to Diana and stood, leaning heavily on the wooden cane that Lu Yi had given him. After excusing himself, he hobbled out of the dining hall and found his way back to the hydroponics room. Caryn greeted him, dragging a heavy hose behind her.

"Well, aren't you the eager one," she said. "Go take a few days to rest and heal up. Then we'll see where to plant you."

"Thanks," Adam said. "Actually, I'm wondering if you have a flower garden. And if you do, am I permitted a small bouquet?"

She smiled and pointed to the far corner. A bouquet meant gossip and she'd be eager to speculate who the recipient would be. *Probably Diana Ames,* she thought.

He made his way to the area she indicated and found a few rose bushes, gerbera daisies, and various other colorful blooms. With a pair of snips, he carefully cut each stem on an angle until he was satisfied with the beauty of the bouquet. He found a small vase and a spigot nearby and arranged the flowers as best he could. Then, nodding to Caryn, he limped out of the room and headed down the corridor.

His first stop was at his room. He slipped inside and limped over to the dresser. Trisha's photo looked out at him, the sapphire brooch still leaning against the frame.

"It's time for me to move on, Trish." He pulled one small flower from the bouquet and placed it next to the brooch.

"But you knew that, didn't you? And you would have been pissed off at me for being a jerk these past three years, wouldn't you?" He shook his head. This was his life now. He had to get on with the business of living it. He took a last look at the photo and left the room.

He made his way down a familiar corridor. The door was open. She was alone. He entered and placed the flowers on the table next to her, then carefully sat on a pillow at her feet, putting his cane aside. She took both his hands, her eyes sparkling in the candlelight.

"Tell me your dream," she said.

"I dream of a real tomorrow. For me. For everyone."

She smiled warmly and squeezed his hands in hers.

"And what of yesterday?"

"I guess we all have to accept the hand we've been dealt, no matter how painful it might be at times. Yesterday's behind me now, but that's okay."

"The memories will live forever in your heart. That is as it should be. Now tell me of the child."

He looked up at her, surprised. How could she know? He hadn't told anyone.

"I didn't understand what you meant by 'surrender' until I came across a little girl crying over her dead mother in an alley. The poor kid didn't even know her mom was gone. I can't even begin to describe the feelings. I just knew I couldn't let it happen again; they all have to see life as it is if there's any hope of cleaning up this mess—to see it, know it, and then change it.

"Then go, child, and make it happen."

He nodded and left her, feeling for the first time at peace and at home. He knew there would be more raids, and he hoped he would be a part of them. Until then he wanted to work with the plants and the flowers. Gossip or not, it was his world now and he wanted to soak up every bit of it. By the time he had rejoined Diana in the mess hall, he was smiling broadly. He sat next to her and, for a brief moment, made sure their shoulders touched, not entirely accidentally.

www.ingramcontent.com/pod-product-compliance
Lightning Source LLC
Chambersburg PA
CBHW020614260626
47157CB00003B/1008